MW00878600

Of Winds And Rage

Of
Winds
And Rage

A Novel By
F. Mark Granato

F. Mark Granato
fmgranato@aol.com
Fmarkgranato.com
www.facebook.com at Author F. Mark Granato

Published in the United States of America 2011

Of Winds And Rage

A Novel by

F. Mark Granato

Also by F. Mark Granato

Titanic: The Final Voyage

Beneath His Wings:
The Plot to Murder Lindbergh

Finding David

The Barn Find

Out of Reach:
The Day Hartford Hospital Burned

UNLEASHED

This Boy

Stars In Our Window

This book is dedicated to my wife,
a loving lady whose favorite place in the world
is Paris in the spring.

Enough said.

One

~~~ ∽ ~~~

September 9, 1938
Matam, Senegal

Anxious voices rose suddenly above the howling desert sandstorm, interrupting the lone Frenchman working in a tattered canvas tent pitched on the banks of the sweet water Sénégal River near Matam. Irritated by the disruption, he pushed stone weights to the corners of the yellowed geographical charts he had been poring over to keep them from blowing off a badly weather-beaten rectangular table. A surplus military issue revolver, fully loaded and strapped into a worn hand-tooled Moroccan leather holster, hung from a rusty nail in a table leg. The desert dwellers, who lived by plunder, would not be welcomed here. The Frenchman had met many of these nomadic bandits
~~~

in his years of travel across the parched terrain of Sénégal and the small nations of northwest Africa. He still lived to tell of them because of just such precautions.

The battered table was one of only two of his meager possessions that still tied him to his native France. Closer inspection would reveal that it was actually an ornately inlaid mahogany desk with fluted legs and gold leaf trim; a small masterpiece handcrafted for the court of Louis XVI some seventy years prior. The Frenchman had discovered it quite by accident in a Dakar street market, paying but a fraction of its actual value. But its worth was well hidden now. The man who owned it was tall, almost gaunt and slightly stooped, but the long robes of the desert dweller mostly hid his frail physique. He had carted the desk with him, strapped to a camel's back, as he chased the weather across the Sahara over the next decade. Now bleached and sandblasted by years of exposure to the cruel sun and harsh winds of the desert, only the Frenchman knew of its prized history. The other possession was a mother-of-pearl inlaid straight razor, which he hadn't used in months.

Pushing his long, graying blond hair back off his eyes, Jean-Pierre Chandon wound a muslin cheche scarf, baked to the color of lightly toasted white bread, around his forehead and mouth and threw a loose afghan over his shoulders. His skin, leathered and bronzed by the cruelly unforgiving desert sun, had the color and texture of a pair of well tanned riding boots. Until he opened his mouth to speak, the question of his origin was a mystery. Certainly, he no longer resembled the man of esteem and privilege he had been as a student many years before.

Chandon was by education and training a meteorologist, a graduate of the Sorbonne and the Institut Pierre Simon Laplace in Paris, where he received his doctorate. Nearly fifty years old, he was now employed by the Institut to monitor and track weather conditions on the northwestern desert territories of Africa. He had not returned to Europe in more than fifteen years. His life and identity had been absorbed by the Wolof people indigenous to Senegal, Gambia, and Mauritania.

He knew little of his family's well being or the state of affairs in France, and cared less for the politics of the German named "Hitler" who seemed to be stirring up things on the continent. He followed the news only on his infrequent visits to the port city of Dakar, more than five hundred kilometers to the west. Endlessly roaming the northwestern edges of the Sahara, Chandon was a man of science, albeit a young science, who had gradually become completely engrossed in the pursuit of the unpredictable nature of the African desert climate and its effect on world weather patterns. Although he was deeply lonely, his overwhelming wanderlust prohibited any opportunity to find companionship. He had willingly become almost completely inured to the rest of the world.

Before the disturbance, the meteorologist had been charting a massive sandstorm that had enveloped his small party of hired guides and laborers for the last two days, overtaking them just after they had ridden out of the spectacular *Gorges de Talary* on the Sénégal River in Mali. They had been fortunate to travel a scant ten kilometers since, and his men were exhausted. The Frenchman had recognized at once that the winds of this storm were different, unusually blowing to the west and toward the Atlantic Ocean, instead of the normal southeast path.

Chandon could not conceive an explanation for the extremely odd behavior of the wind. It unnerved him and added to his growing frustration with the inadequate tools of his discipline. Although the twentieth century was nearly four decades old, the science of meteorology still relied on measurement devices conceived hundreds of years before - the primitive 16th-century thermometer, the mercurial barometer of the 17th century, and the weather vane dating back to medieval times.

He stepped outside the tent to investigate the commotion, instinctively shielding his eyes from the sand-laced wind which he guessed was gusting above fifty kilometers per hour. Squinting, he saw the source of the excitement. A small Wolof caravan on camels was approaching from the south, just visible in the blowing sand. Chandon was alert, but not alarmed. He sensed the strangers posed no danger. The Frenchman watched as the visitors finally made it to his campsite by the river, a small patch with plentiful acacia thorns and other desert weeds where the camels could feed and water.

The meteorologist picked out the first camel driver, assuming correctly that he was the caravan's leader by the quality of his desert scarf, a light blue silk wrapped tightly about his head and across his mouth.

"Salaamaalekum!" Chandon called out in greeting, as always experiencing a fleeting confusion over why the Wolof widely used the Arabic greeting instead of their own tribal tongue, a non-tonal language of the Niger-Congo family. It was another of the inexplicable mysteries of Africa that he silently accepted even if he did not entirely understand.

"Maalekum salaam!" the Wolof leader responded without hesitation. The slightly built nomad dismounted athletically from his camel and took three long strides to reach Chandon, who extended his hand in welcome. The two men shook hands warmly and the Frenchman invited the visitor to his tent. He signaled to his servants to offer food and drink to the members of the Wolof caravan and to tend to their camels. Then he motioned to a black skinned boy who was perhaps in his early teens. The boy nodded knowingly and followed them into the tent.

Chandon spread open the doorway with a sweeping gesture and bid the tribesman to enter. He invited the stranger to sit at one end of the large, well-worn Chiadma rug placed in the center of the pitched hut. The rug had once been a hand-woven masterpiece of horizontal stripes and repeating geometric hooks, squares, and triangles in soft earthen tones. But it too had been robbed of its grandeur by a lifetime of exposure to the desert elements.

Still, the rug offered a welcomed respite for the Wolof after long hours in the saddle. He smiled in thanks, wordlessly took his seat and unwound his scarf, revealing the face of a young man whom Chandon thought to be in his late twenties. The nomad's glistening black skin exaggerated the white of his eyes, which were a deep brown. He had no facial hair to speak of, and Chandon wondered if a razor had ever touched the Wolof's face. The Frenchman sat down at the other end, crossing his legs into a lotus position, as had his guest, and also removed his scarf. Both men were silent as the young servant prepared Chinese tea with green mint over a brazier. It was a favorite Senegalese refreshment.

"Ada heydi?" Chandon inquired if his guest was hungry. The black man raised his hand and shook his head, "No".

The nomad again smiled his appreciation as they were served the tea.

"Ah, Ataya!" he said, recognizing the hot liquid and nodded to his host. "Jërëjëf," he said, graciously thanking the servant and waiting for his host's cup to be filled before drinking from his own. Chandon raised his clay cup in a sort of mock toast.

"Naka nga tudda?" Chandon asked in Wolof, inquiring of his guests' name, but not sure he had asked correctly. Despite his years in the desert and his great affinity for its people, the Frenchman still struggled with the language and its exceedingly complex nuances to the Western ear.

The nomad grinned, showing remarkably white and well-preserved teeth for a desert dweller. "I am called Seipati Anta Gueye," he announced proudly, in perfect English, but with a decidedly British note. Chandon threw up his hands in relief. English he could handle.

"But most people just call me 'Sam', my Sahib," he added, showing respect for the elder Frenchman.

"Sam?" Chandon asked in genuine surprise, chuckling somewhat. "And how is it that a Sénégalese Wolof comes to master perfect English?"

The young man smiled again. He had faced the question many times before. "I left Dakar when I was seventeen and was privileged to attend the London International School, followed by four years at Oxford," he answered without a hint of braggadocio.

Chandon raised his eyes, intrigued. "My father happened to be Ambassador to England at the time," the nomad continued, lowering his head in humility. "I have been very fortunate. My father is a great man. Now I work for him. He is involved in the export of African art to Europe and the Americas."

Chandon's interest was piqued. "An admirable pursuit, my friend. I have long been seduced by the art of the African culture, especially the primitive work I have experienced in the sub-Sahara basin and the Sudan. A pity the world knows so little of it."

"Exactly, Sahib," Gueye replied, delighted at the genuine interest of his host. He instinctively liked this man. "My job is to seek out the works of desert artists and craftsman. It causes me to spend my days and nights roaming the Sahara, but it is an occupation that suits me well."

"Sam, I do not often have the honor of talking to a Wolof of such education or business sophistication," the Frenchman said genuinely. "My name is Jean-Pierre Chandon. I was born in France and educated in Paris, where I completed my doctorate. I am a meteorologist employed by the Institut Simon Pierce Laplace."

"Yes, I know. That is why I have come."

Chandon was puzzled by the response. "I do not understand."

Gueye took a long drink from his tea before responding.

"I have just left Matam, where I contacted friends in London who got your name from the Institut," the Wolof said. "I was not aware that a meteorologist of your acclaim was on assignment in Sénégal, but was delighted to learn so. It is perfect that we meet."

Chandon shook his head in confusion, slightly distraught that his visitor had caught him so off guard. "Sam, I am confused. Here I was thinking you were a nomad probably looking to trade palm dates. What on earth could you possibly want of a meteorologist?"

Gueye appeared startled, thinking he had insulted his host. "Forgive me, Sahib, I did not mean to offend you in any way..."

"Oh dear," Chandon muttered, now even more off balance. "I am afraid this conversation is turning quite awkward, my young friend. Please, I am not offended, just confused. Perhaps we should begin again."

The smile returned to the Wolof's concerned face. "Thank you, Sahib. Allow me to explain why it is that I have sought you out in the middle of the desert."

"I am all ears, Sam," Chandon replied, making sure to grin as he said it. The wind outside seemed to have picked up, and the howling storm required him to raise his voice.

"Upepo unavuma," Gueye said, lapsing into his native tongue while shaking his head and wringing his hands unconsciously. "The wind is crying. Sahib, I am quite concerned by this storm." He paused. "I would like to hear your thoughts of it."

Chandon did not hesitate. "It will pass, as it always does. No need for concern."

"It is not the ferocity of the winds that distresses me, it is the direction in which they blow," Sam replied. He hesitated for a moment. "Would you have a map of the coastline, Sahib?"

Chandon rose and retrieved one of the topographical charts he had been working with. "Will this suffice?" he asked, handing it to the

Wolof. Gueye spread it out on the rug and examined it quickly. "Yes, perfectly."

He did not speak again for long moments. Then, "Forgive me Sahib, but I assume you have noted that the winds off the Sahara in Northern Africa nearly always blow to the southeast. Am I correct?" he asked, looking into Chandon's eyes.

"Quite correct, Sam. I have noted the odd course of these winds. But I hardly think it a concern."

"Please pardon my fears, Sahib," the Wolof replied humbly. "It is true, I have seen many storms in my life, some far more dangerous than this. We can be sure that the winds will cause some discomfort in Dakar - perhaps by sometime late tomorrow night I would guess?"

Chandon nodded his agreement.

Gueye's eyes narrowed as he looked into Chandon's face. He was genuinely worried, the Frenchman thought. "What concerns me is what will happen when these winds finally find the ocean," the nomad continued. "Is it not possible that they will spawn dangerous conditions off shore - perhaps even as far as the North Atlantic? I do recall from my days of study in London that..."

Chandon interrupted him, finishing his thought. "That such wind may cause low tropical depressions over the open ocean water? Yes, Sam, you are quite correct." He expected to see a look of satisfaction on the young nomad's face. Instead, he saw the look of worry over his brow intensify.

"We know that such winds emanating from the Cape Verde islands can cause great storms that we call 'hurricanes'," Chandon continued. "These hurricanes are usually fearsome in size and power, but seldom make landfall. However, at least one such Cape Verde hurricane is believed to have made land at Galveston, Texas in America in 1900. More than eight thousand people were drowned."

The Wolof jerked his head back as Chandon finished his sentence, startled. The whites of his eyes grew larger and showed fear. The Frenchman was puzzled by the reaction. "I do not understand the reasons for your concern, Sam."

Gueye averted his eyes from Chandon's gaze. "I am embarrassed, Sahib," he said, almost in a whisper.

"Sam, forgive me, but I do not understand," he said, impatiently. "I am a man of science and events such as these are nature's way. There is little reason for worry. What will be, will be. You are an educated man, yet you surprise me with..."

"That is precisely the point, Sahib," he said, humiliated by the difficulty he was having in expressing his concerns." I am educated, I know there is more to the world than the desert, and I have studied the white man's books and heard his teachings. So I should know better. But books and teachings do not account for all things."

"Preposterous, my friend," Chandon shot back. "There is nothing in the world that cannot be accounted for. There is reason for everything and anything."

The Wolof drew silent, his eyes lowered.

"It has come to me in a dream, from the same spirits that have guided my father throughout his life," he said, finally lifting his head to face Chandon and locking on to the Frenchman's eyes. "The spirits who have visited me may not have their foundation in fact or in books, Sahib, but in my world, they are to be reckoned with."

Chandon was startled by the intensity of his words. "I meant you no disrespect, Sam. All men confront spirits and demons in their lives at one time or another, some real, some contrived. Some men live by the whispers in their dreams, while others, like me, seek more ordained and disciplined understandings of things that are not easily understood.

"But what is it that the spirits have confided in you, Sam? Can you tell me?" Chandon was suddenly uneasy; he felt a slight chill despite the damp heat.

The nomad hesitated for several long minutes.

"The spirits - perhaps they are demons -- have shared with me the nature of these winds, Sahib." The young man's eyes grew wide again and his hands trembled.

"They have ordered the winds of Cape Verde to move out to sea in a great wave that will travel faster than man has ever known. And they told me that the great wave will be hungry. It will overwhelm the waters and suck them up into a whirling heavenly storm so powerful that no God will dare to stand in its way."

Chandon watched intensely as the young man closed his eyes, appearing to relive the nightmare that had been visited upon him.

"When the storm has tired of the sea, it will seek nourishment from the lands and grow into a monstrous beast, devouring all in its path. Nothing will survive in its wake. Whole cities will fall beneath its torrents. Whole families will disappear under its relentless waves. No man, woman or child will be safe from its insatiable hunger."

Chandon stood, suddenly terrified of the stranger and the words coming from his mouth.

"Your books will not help those in its path, Sahib," the desert dweller continued, his hands shaking as he raised them slowly toward the heavens. "Days from now the innocents will turn to their God for deliverance from the sea and the wind. But not even the power of the almighty will be able to save them from the devil's furious breath."

"And as you said, Sahib: 'what will be, will be'."

Friday
September 16, 1938

Two

~~~ ~~~

Napatree Point
Watch Hill, Rhode Island

"I hate school," Katherine Lapkin announced for the third time to no one in particular. The seven year old sat sullenly at the breakfast table, her chin resting lazily in the palm of her hand. With the other she traced figure eights with a spoon in the bowl of hot oatmeal and cream her mother had just ladled. The early morning sun was already pouring into the kitchen of the rambling beach house on Fort Road on Napatree Point as Kate and her siblings readied for school.

Geoff Lapkin failed to look up from his newspaper, feigning complete disinterest in his daughter and continued to peruse the morning's *Westerly Sun*. He was an old veteran of this game,
~~~

as was his wife, who likewise didn't bother to respond. Emily busied herself instead with fetching freshly baked scones from the oven. The girl's three older brothers –James, fourteen, Brian, two years younger, and Geoffrey, nine – didn't look up either, typically ignoring her obnoxious behavior.

The Lapkin family had become almost immune to whatever came out of the precocious Katherine's mouth, and with good reason. The child was nearly eloquent for someone so young and was already reading at a level far ahead of her second-grade classmates. But the entertainment quality of Kate's gifted persona could be wearying, and at times her parents had difficulty distinguishing their daughter's manners between "cute" or just ill behaved.

So Kate, already an expert at the game of being ignored, simply said what was on her mind again, and would continue to do so until one of her parents responded or her brothers threatened to tape her mouth shut.

"I hate school," she said again, finally eliciting a rustle of the newspaper as well as a sharp rebuke from her big brother, who had heard enough.

"Katie, will you shut up? No one cares if you hate school," James scowled at his sister as he finished the last of his oatmeal. She scowled back and stuck out her tongue at him, a small drip of cream curling down her chin. "I can't wait to go back to school just so I don't have to listen to you," the eldest of the brothers continued. In another two weeks, James would be starting his second year at the Choate School in Wallingford, Connecticut, a college preparatory school that fit well his aggressive and highly competitive personality.

"That will be enough, James," Emily scolded her son. "But my word, Katie, do be quiet," Emily Lapkin interrupted. "It's a beautiful day for a change, and there's absolutely no reason for you to be carrying on. For heaven's sake, it's only the second week of school! Haven't you had enough of summer? All it did was rain..."

The young girl dropped a spoon into her cereal bowl and angrily pushed back in her chair. "That's the problem, mommy," she said defiantly. "As soon as the sun comes out I have to go back to school. Well, I hate it and I'm going to tell Mrs. Crandall that I'm simply not going to be interested in what she says all school year. So, there."

When there was no immediate response, she turned and caught her father ominously staring at her over the top of his newspaper, his reading glasses pushed down to the end of his nose. She had pushed her luck too far.

"My darling Katherine," he said calmly, pronouncing the syllables of each word slowly and precisely as he was prone to do when irritated. He folded the newspaper and laid it gently on the breakfast table. "That will be quite enough."

He paused for a moment, ensuring that he had ended her tantrum.

"We all know that you didn't have enough sunny days in which to play at the beach this summer, Katie, but that can't be helped," her father said, surprisingly composed despite his daughter's behavior. "Life goes on, young lady."

Katie said nothing as she picked up her cereal bowl and spoon and silently carried them to the sink. She knew when to stop. Emily leaned down and gave the little girl a big hug, brushing her brown hair back off her forehead, and whispered into her ear. "Go and give your father a big kiss, it will make you feel good all day." Katie turned and hesitantly approached her father. As she put her arms around his neck, he suddenly reached out and grabbed her under the arms, mercilessly tickling her. Katie squealed with surprise and delight. "Get out of here you little brat, you'll be late for school," he said, smiling the smile that always made her laugh. She skipped off to get her book bag, the confrontation already forgotten.

"She has a right to be frustrated, Emily," Geoff said in genuine empathy as he heard the screen door bang a moment later. "What an awful summer it was. When it wasn't raining, it was gray. I'm surprised the kids didn't drive you crazy all cooped up the way they were." His wife of fifteen years didn't respond but smiled at him, the ends of her lips curling slightly upwards into an almost mischievous grin, a beguiling look that had captivated him from the moment he'd first set eyes on her as a girl of seventeen. He still reveled in her beauty and was continually mystified by her ability to escape the aging process even after bearing four children. She looked at least ten years younger than him, he thought, but wasn't jealous. It gave him a sense of security that she would be with him all the days of his life.

"Oh, now darling, you know what good children they are, so well behaved, even stuck here in the house so much of the summer," she replied, brushing aside a stray lock of hair that had fallen in her eyes. The sun rays, reaching through the oversized bay window that framed their breakfast table, gave a warm radiance to Emily's long, light-brown hair which was usually bleached almost blond by this time of year from long hours out in the sun with the children. Geoff still loved to watch his wife even when she was doing little, inconsequential things, like she was now, tidying the kitchen. "Honestly," she continued, "It wasn't the children that nearly drove me mad - it was the sound of the rain on the front porch, day after day. I thought it would never stop. I swear, even my window box flowers seem a little droopy."

Geoff chuckled to himself at the word "droopy". It was probably the harshest word he had ever heard her use.

Indeed, all along the New England coast, the summer of 1938 had been filled with cloudy, gray days and what seemed like continuous rain and unusually cool temperatures from late spring right through Labor Day. While Emily was normally enchanted with Watch Hill and especially their summer home on Napatree Point, on several occasions the weather had actually made her long for her own childhood neighborhood in the city of Providence, some sixty miles northeast. At least in the city there was always something to do, no matter the weather, and it always felt at least ten degrees warmer.

Napatree Point was a long, finger-like sandy spit that had slowly formed over thousands of years by ocean drifting off the Rhode Island coast. It now extended a mile and a half into Little Narragansett Bay (an estuary of the Pawtucket River that separated Connecticut and Rhode Island), and then curved northward another mile or so in a thin branch known as Sandy Point. The resulting hook-shaped peninsula was an extension of the small protected harbor village of Watch Hill, which in itself was a community within the small town of Westerly.

Over the last century, Napatree Point had been haphazardly developed by wealthy residents of Westerly who desired summer homes directly abutting its white, sandy beaches and the ocean. More than a hundred years before, the peninsula was actually heavily wooded and uninhabited, but that all changed when the Great September Gale of 1815 had blown the sandy spit clean, leaving nothing but pristine beaches. There had not been another major storm or hurricane since. By the 1930's there was virtually no community memory of severe weather in Westerly and most property owners had become disciples of the belief that their coastline was "hurricane proof", safely tucked inside Long Island Sound.

The wealthy wanted their summer homes on the water with no constraints or concerns and that's what they built along the length of Napatree Point to the very end of the peninsula, known as Sandy Point. Thirty-nine mansions were built on the land jutting from Watch Hill. Nearly all were extravagantly large, two- or three-story wooden structures characterized by broad, open porches. Most were built on piers literally yards from the ocean surf. On the Atlantic side of the peninsula there were concrete walls, three- to four-feet high, which protected the mansions from high surf or storm surges when the Atlantic kicked up its heals. On the Bay side, it wouldn't take more than a couple of minutes for the average "cottage" owner to walk out his front door and stick his feet in the water or to launch a small boat from his private dock.

It wasn't unusual to see children swimming between the docks, back and forth from neighbor to neighbor. About the only distraction in this private paradise were the constant cries of the native sandpipers, racing the tides and flocking to the sand bars at low tide.

The four Lapkin children and the dozens more who summered on Napatree Point had known the tranquil beaches of Little Narragansett Bay their entire lives. They took for granted, after stifling winter months in school, the seemingly endless days of bright, warm sun and a salt air breeze that had traveled thousands of miles across the Atlantic Ocean, bringing with it a revitalizing bouquet. The children spent their days building sandcastles at low tide, racing through the dunes in imaginary games and swimming for hours in the mild surf. Their parents also succumbed to the slower pace that was life south of Westerly from well before the summer solstice until the autumnal equinox signaled the end of the season. It was about as close to heaven as one could get in New England.

Some of them weren't born to the paradise. On weekends as a child, to escape the sweltering heat of their third-floor tenement flat, Emily and her parents made the long drive from North Providence to Misquamicut, public beaches adjacent to Westerly. The McBride's camped out on the shore which ironically was just a few miles east of Napatree Point.

Her father, William J. McBride, had worked in a textile factory for nearly twenty years before she was born, almost from the day the young man had arrived in Providence after a grueling trip from County Cork in Ireland to Ellis Island. A cousin, who had come over before him, took in the younger McBride, gave him a mattress in his cramped apartment and even scrounged up a job for him at the textile factory where he worked. William never made enough money to buy a home in the blue collar suburbs surrounding Providence let alone a summer cottage at the shore. Yet it was the family's weekend trips to Misquamicut that instilled in his daughter a lifelong love of the ocean, and especially, the feeling of warm sand between her toes and a salty breeze in her hair during the summer months.

Many years later, while living in Westerly, Geoff, a rising executive with the George C. Moore Company proposed that Emily come along for a drive out to Napatree Point on the pretext of checking out a spot for his company's summer barbecue. Actually, he had something quite a bit more romantic in mind.

So on an early April morning in 1934, in one of life's truly cherished moments, Geoff Lapkin drove the length of the Napatree Point peninsula and parked his new Cadillac convertible a few feet from the surf at the end of Sandy Point. There he invited the woman he adored to step out barefoot onto the beach that would be the front yard of the mansion he planned to build for her on the occasion of their tenth wedding anniversary.

The spot the couple chose to build their English-influenced "summer cottage" provided them full views of both the Atlantic and the Bay. At night, reflections from the lights of Watch Hill rippled in the light surf that lapped within yards of their front porch. The house was completed just before Labor Day and the Lapkin's held a party for their new neighbors with a fireworks display that could be seen all over Little Narragansett Bay.

The Lapkin mansion was not like the estates found on Ocean Drive in nearby Newport, where the Astor's, Vanderbilt's and other millionaires had established breathtaking summer palaces years before. Geoffrey and Emily designed their beachfront property to be the kind of place that would not only be a respite for family and friends during the summer months, but one that would be endearing for its charms and warmth. It was to be the kind of home that their children -- and *their* children -- would never dream of parting with.

Rising just yards from the ocean surf at high tide, the Lapkin's house was three floors in the style of an English Tudor cottage with a steeply pitched, cross-gabled roof. It had nine bedrooms, eleven full baths, two dining rooms (one for formal affairs, another for daily use), a billiards room, library, sun porch and quarters for a housekeeper. Just inside the front door, at the base of a grand, natural oak staircase, was an enormous "sitting" room. The children always laughed when Emily referred to the room by its formal name. In actuality, there was little "sitting" done there by the family. Geoff and the children liked to call it the "playpen", because that's where they would all gather and jump on their father's back the minute he walked in the door after work, knocking him to the floor and smothering him with hugs. Emily had long ago given up any notion that the "sitting" room was for reading or other intellectual pursuits, but recognized it instead as perhaps the happiest spot in the entire house.

The mansion also had an oversized kitchen with huge, double hung, multi-paned windows facing both the Atlantic and Bay shores so as to ensure a steady stream of sunlight and ocean breeze. It was adjacent to a cozy breakfast nook that was meant just for the family. Although the Lapkin's could well afford to employ a full time cook, Emily insisted on preparing breakfast for the family each morning. She couldn't bear the thought of the family not being together at the start of each day.

Shelly Whetstone, their housekeeper, did the honors for dinner, a task the portly British immigrant reveled in. Grand gourmet cuisine was her particular passion, rivaled only by her love of the Lapkin family. When Emily had organized a party for Shelly's sixtieth birthday the summer before, the children presented her with a framed parchment document declaring her official adoption by the family, addressing it to "Shelly Whetstone Lapkin".

The mansion was built within a cedar shake structure with twelve- foot-high ceilings, abundant windows and shuttered dormers, natural wood floors and as few interior doors as possible so as not to impede the flow of traffic through the house, which was usually considerable. With walls and ceilings painted in soft pastels, the effect was light and airy; and combined with Emily's love of French country furnishings and a generous dash of wicker and rattan, fresh cut flowers and windows thrown wide open, the house radiated style but with a warmth and informality that made it more than a decorators' showcase. It was a home.

Like most of the homes on Napatree Point, the Lapkin house was not intended for all-season occupancy. Instead, the huge house was built on more than two hundred piers that were exposed underneath, which allowed water to actually flow beneath the structure in the event of an unexpectedly high tide or storm surge. Although all of the other thirty-eight homes built on Napatree Point utilized the same pier design, none was as grand as the Lapkin house.

For Geoff Lapkin, the summer mansion was just one of the luxuries he reaped from his labors, but even he was surprised at how quickly wealth had come to him. In 1923 he was a member of the first graduating class of Providence College, estabalished by the Dominican Fathers four years before in the heart of the city. He'd joined the George C. Moore Company upon graduation. Specializing in elastics and rubberized fabrics, Moore had opened the firm in 1909 and built his factory in Westerly. At first, the company was modestly successful with its line of elastics; but when war began in Europe a half decade later, it brought with it monstrous new weapons that created an insatiable demand for Moore's products. One of the most horrible of the weapons was poison gas. Consequently, the need for military issue gas masks soared as did demand for the Moore Company's elastics as a sealing device for the masks. Many an American "Doughboy" and British "Tommy" owed his lungs and his life to the Moore elastic that provided an impervious seal between the gas mask and his face. By war's end, George Moore was a very wealthy man and his company had earned a solid reputation with the US government.

Moore had taken a real shine to the young Lapkin when the college graduate showed up at his office door in the summer of 1923 with a degree in accounting in his back pocket. He had hired the handsome, athletically built lad on the spot on a hunch that there was a fire burning in the young man's belly. George Moore was seldom wrong about such things, and his instincts for Geoff Lapkin were no exception. Promotions came quickly, and Moore began doling out more and more responsibility to his protégé, who seemed to relish the challenge. By the time Moore celebrated his 70th birthday, he was comfortable in handing the keys to the castle to Lapkin, who by this time had become indispensable to his boss. At just thirty-five, after ten years of tutelage under the strong hand of company Founder and President, George C. Moore himself, Lapkin had been appointed the firms' chief operating officer and a member of its Board.

Life was good for the Lapkin family, and although there had been other grand parties at the summer mansion, none quite equaled the 1938 gathering on the Fourth of July. As luck would have it, the Fourth fell on one of the few good weather days that the Rhode Island shore community had enjoyed that entire summer. Privately, Geoff and Emily had celebrated a lot more that night than the nation's birthday with their two hundred guests. Indeed, with their love for each other stronger than ever, four happy and healthy children and wealth and success, life simply couldn't get much better.

A soft breeze blew off the ocean that night while they lie awake in each other's arms in the great summer house on Napatree Point. Emily silently wondered to herself if it would always be that way.

The night air suddenly seemed to cool and she pushed herself closer to Geoff and pulled a light blanket up around her chin.

But the chill she abruptly felt on the back of her neck would not go away.

Three

~~~ ~~~

Wethersfield, Connecticut

The afternoon sun began to settle behind enormous White Elm trees that lined the upper banks of the Wethersfield Cove, a small, oval-shaped natural inlet of the Connecticut River near Hartford. Three centuries earlier, the Cove had served as an important maritime port for the first settlers of the community for which it was named. Today, only a solitary sailboat, slowly tacking its way toward the mouth of the river, disturbed the lazy waters that shimmered with reflections of the softly luminous, September sun. Two young lovers, huddled together in the cockpit of the sleek keelboat, delighted as they rode beneath the sloop's bleached canvas mainsail and jib. The sails had filled with a brisk early evening breeze, all but
~~~

ensuring that they would make port downriver in Essex, some twenty miles away, before nightfall.

The Elm trees were at least several hundred years old and had been part of an enormous grove that had once surrounded the pond-like Cove, creating a sort of natural amphitheater. It was the same stage from which the Puritan immigrants, who had first come to Wethersfield in the early seventeenth century, conducted a thriving trade with the West Indies.

The Cove trade flourished and the Wethersfield settlement grew rapidly - too quickly for the Puritan elders of the village who reacted with harsh measures to maintain control. As a result, even by the 1930's the small New England town was still a bastion of conservative ethos and ethics which visitors would find abundantly evident, especially in the more ancient section of town. This area, bordering the Cove and the great riverside meadows, was appropriately referred to as, "Old Wethersfield".

Life in the village was simple and quiet. When its days as an international trade port came to a close near 1830, Wethersfield intuitively turned to farming and industry for its economic mainstays. It became a quaint, close knit New England community, founded and fostered by characteristic ingenuity and spirit, just like hundreds of others between the cities of Boston and New York.

So it was that the State's decision to establish the Connecticut State Prison at Wethersfield in 1827, with the transfer of eighty-one felons from the

Newgate copper mine prison in nearby Granby, was not happily received. Citizens disagreed with the state government's decision, arguing that it was completely incompatible with the nature of the small town. They quarreled that the new State Prison, built on a spot overlooking the Wethersfield Cove, would serve as a most bizarre landmark for the town that would hurt rather than help its prospects for economic and commercial growth. The townsfolk largely grumbled at their lack of voice in the decision, as well as their fate. Ultimately, they agreed that if nothing else, the prison might bring jobs to the town, and accepted the new three-level, red-brick prison complex as an eyesore and little more.

Even as the penitentiary's guest list grew more than ten-fold over the next century with a number of them occupying five-foot by eight-foot cells on "Death Row", there was little consternation or worry among Wethersfield residents. Indeed, when the occasional alarm was sounded that a prisoner had escaped, the townsfolk took the news in stride and unceremoniously pulled their fresh laundry off backyard drying lines lest they unintentionally assist the escapee with a change of clothes from his prison-issue, blue-denim uniforms.

Luckily, escape attempts were few; but occasionally they were successful -- a fact that must have been far from the minds of three armed prison guards who waved a black, mud splattered Ford Model A stake bed truck through the Wethersfield

State Prison exit gate just before dinner call on this blustery afternoon.

There was no reason for the guards to give the truck more than a cursory glance, recognizing the driver as one of their own. The four large wooden crates the truck was hauling were not inspected either. Street lights were just coming on as the truck pulled out of the prison grounds and took a left toward Main Street, its cargo jostling slightly in back.

The truck was headed for a railroad freight spur several blocks away off Church Street, where its crates of freshly stitched denim shirts, handmade by convicts in the prison sewing workshop, would be loaded onto a waiting box car. In the morning, the freight car carrying a dozen or more large crates of the shirts would be picked up by a New Haven Railroad train that would hug the Connecticut coastline in route to New York and then on to Ohio, Michigan, Indiana and Illinois. Here the prisoner-made garments would be sold to farmers and men who labored at whatever jobs they could find in the last days of the depression that had gripped the country for nearly ten years.

The Wethersfield Prison actually made money off the mandatory labors of its captive workforce, while keeping the hardened thieves, armed robbers, rapists and murderers busy during the long years of their confinement. It was presumed that the labor in and of itself was rehabilitating and all convicts were required to work; the only exceptions were those men awaiting execution. Those guilty of the most heinous of crimes spent the remaining days of their wretched lives on Death Row reading, writing, praying or pacing in their claustrophobic cells.

For the other inmates, work in the sewing shop, the kitchen or laundry went on seven days a week. The labor was as stupefying as it was endless, but that was exactly the intention. The correctional system assumed that after several years of confinement, solitude and mindless drudgery, a man would be cured of whatever devil had landed him in prison in the first place.

This supposed cure began at nearly the moment a prisoner arrived at the facility in a heavily guarded bus, shackled tighter than a mad dog on a leash. Few other than repeat offenders were cognizant of the profoundness of the next moment of their lives - the time it took to step off the bus and walk a few yards into the prison. In those fleeting seconds, a man turned his back on the world he had known without so much as a goodbye, and was instantly absorbed into a hell of bricks and mortar. From that moment on, for as long as his sentence remanded him to confinement, the prisoner was deprived of any interaction with the world outside. It was the purest form of oblivion.

From there, the prisoner was given a cursory medical examination and his head was shaved down to a fuzzy nub. He was issued prison garments and then marched to a tiny jail cell, where he found a sink, a toilet and an iron bunk hanging from angled chains covered with a thin mattress.

Next, the prisoner was dragged into a mind numbing routine. At daybreak, a loud bell rang and the doors of all cells opened. Forming a line, the convicts marched to the outside yard where they washed, no matter the season or climate. They then marched to a large dining hall for breakfast. From there, the convicts would go directly to their workshops where they would toil all day, stopping only for a twenty-minute dinner break. The food was filling but plain and rarely changed. At sunset, the convicts were led back to their cells and the iron doors and bars were locked again. Precisely at eight o'clock, all lights were extinguished and each prisoner would spend the night alone with his thoughts in complete darkness, until, at daybreak, the bell rang and the cell door swung open again.

Some work assignments were considered better than others. Working in the prison's sewing workshop was considered a lucky break. The work detail was an innocuous means to pass the daylight hours, requiring little skill, not much physical effort and the least amount of interaction with the guards. Still, the work was deadly boring, especially if you were assigned to the human-powered treadmills which provided power to the sewing machines and compressors.

There were other benefits as well. If a man kept his nose clean in performing one of the half dozen or so tasks meted out in the sewing workshop, the guards were not apt to roust him. Prolonged good behavior might even find the guards occasionally looking the other way, allowing a man a quick cigarette or the chance to pass a forbidden note to another inmate.

Stooped over a table set in a far back corner of the rectangular workshop, a large brooding man silently and continuously fed cloth patterns into a sewing machine he operated. The inmate worked slowly but methodically, seemingly oblivious to the bustle of the room where as many as one hundred prisoners worked at any one time. He sat alone at the machine. Fellow inmates gave him a wide berth and the guards all but ignored him. The lone convict's solitude was not the consequence of his silence or systematic work, but rather the respect other men instinctively paid to someone nearly twice their size. Actually, they were terrified of the somber giant whose six-foot-eight and nearly four-hundred pound frame dwarfed the industrial tool he operated.

Charles Dewey stopped only occasionally to wipe the sweat from his face with a soiled, denim remnant that he pulled from his own shirt pocket. The material was stiff and scratchy; but he hardly noticed, as his dark growth of beard was the texture of eighty-grit sandpaper. A mop of long, black and greasy hair hung down well over his collar and into his eyes. His brow was a thick, fleshy ledge which was covered with an unbroken line of wild, course hair. The heavy protuberance so shaded the sockets of his dark eyes that they seemed abnormally sunken into his skull. This exaggerated his large jagged nose, the crooked shape of which suggested that it had been broken violently, and probably more than once.

The convict had thick, almost fur-like black hair growing on his arms, and tufts sprouting out the top of his collared shirt which suggested that his chest and back were covered as well. The guards thought he looked a bit like an ape; but between their sheer terror of the man and his own oddly quiet behavior, they kept it to themselves.

Charles Dewey's dark appearance made even his most hardened fellow inmates uncomfortable, if not afraid. There was something else about him that frightened people when they first encountered him. His unusually calm outward expression appeared incongruous to his dark features and huge size. Some thought he was a victim of mental retardation, but others feared he was hiding something much more sinister inside. Few people had the courage to look past his ominous appearance and into his black eyes; but those who did quickly looked away, so petrifying was his gaze. For while Charles Dewey may have appeared ape-like, the resemblance to that easily enraged primate did not stop there, and there was an aura of violence about him that one could almost smell.

Intellectually though, Dewey was no ape. In fact, his brain was of a caliber that he might have been a university professor, if not a felon. He was smart and cunning and unusually literate for one remanded to incarceration, although these were facts he kept well hidden. What the prison guards also didn't know was that he was a student - not in an academic sense - but as one who never tired of looking for another man's weakness or the tiniest edge of opportunity in any given situation.

It was not a newly acquired skill for the thirty-two-year-old convict who was in the third of a twelve-year sentence he had earned for armed robbery. Dewey had learned even as a young child, the seventh son in a family of eleven children reared by two dirt poor farmers in rural Durham, North Carolina, that his large and somewhat deformed appearance preordained the assessment of his intellectual capacity by others.

By nature a quiet boy rather satisfied to be left alone, he gradually came to understand that if trouble brewed anywhere near him, the blame would typically be laid on his shoulders just because he looked like trouble. Consequently, he gradually became the angry, violent hulk that others imagined him to be, capable of almost anything dishonest, violent or both. Amazingly, he never got caught. His sharp mind and eye for an advantage served to save him from jail time and again despite a youth filled with all manner of crimes including rape, armed robbery, burglary, mayhem, assault and any number of vicious acts. Most of these were fastidiously planned and carefully executed so as to guarantee he would escape punishment. He had even gotten away with murder - several times.

Dewey's corrupt lifestyle finally came to an abrupt halt when he pulled a gun on the wrong man at a service station just outside Americus, Georgia, one rainy night in April, 1935. He had staked out a filling station for several days, noting the comings and goings of its owner, even tailing him to the bank one morning when he made a deposit of the previous day's receipts. Dewey knew there were only two other employees and the station shut its gas pumps down at ten o'clock each night, leaving the cash register full of bills until the following morning. He also assumed that the station was unoccupied after closing. He was wrong.

On the third night of observation, Dewey finally broke into the building just before midnight brandishing a .38 caliber hand gun. Unfortunately, one of the pump jockeys who happened to be between rents and was sleeping in the office heard him and greeted the felon with a twelve gauge. The employee put a load of buckshot into Dewey's right arm and thigh, dropping him like a rock. After a few days in the county hospital, a judge remanded him to twelve years of Federal incarceration. After six months in the brutally overcrowded Georgia State Penitentiary, he was transferred to the Wethersfield Prison to serve out the remainder of his term.

Over the next thirty months, Dewey worked hard at blending into the background of the workshop in spite of his enormous profile. He was assigned to the sewing detail, but also the treadmill, where he would begin his labors each morning by taking his place on the rubber belt and walking for the next three hours without a break. He would also complete his day on the treadmill, walking the last hour before sunset. The task was exhausting, but it kept his body lean and muscular, just what a runner needed. And true to form, Charles Dewey did indeed intend to run as soon as he saw his opportunity.

He thought the right moment might come towards the end of a work day. After months of carefully scrutinizing the guards' behavior - specifically when the inmates re-gathered for the day's last hour of work following their dinner break, he saw his chance for escape at the loading dock.

Two large shipping crates, each big enough to hide a man, lay open about twenty feet in front of him as he took his place on the treadmill and the belt started up. The crates were about half full of shirts that would be brought to the train station that night and shipped in the morning. By sunset, the two crates would be full of denim shirts and each would be closed with a wooden panel that was nailed in place.

Dewey walked the rubber at a brisk pace, careful not to do anything to attract undue attention. The three guards assigned to the workshop had gathered for a cigarette and were busy talking baseball. He watched as several convicts began carrying bundles of folded shirts to the crates, placing them inside. Then, almost seamlessly, Dewey stepped off the belt, walked a few steps toward a pile of waiting shirts and gathered up a huge bundle in his arms. He carried it high on his chest, so that the clothes hid his face.

Cautiously, he waited behind a convict who was depositing his load. Then, as the man turned to walk away, Dewey stepped forward behind him, dropped his bundle inside; and in a single motion, gripped the uppermost edge of the crate and swung his body up and over the lip, falling noiselessly into the huge pile of denim inside. Instantly, he tore into the pile, pulling shirts up and over his body, burying himself in the clothes.

The convict held his breath for what seemed like hours, waiting for a cry or a whistle or the sound of a guard cursing. Nothing happened. Neither inmate nor guard had seen him fall into the crate.

As happened each night, the crates were filled to the brim with the day's production, then topped off with a wooden closing panel that was nailed in place at each corner. As Dewey lay motionless inside, he eventually felt it being lifted and moved, and listened as several of the inmates cursed as they struggled to carry the overweight crate to the loading dock. Luckily, none complained to the guards about its unusual heaviness. The men weren't stupid, and correctly surmised that one of their own had somehow entered the crate without being noticed. A couple of them winked at each other. Charles Dewey's secret was safe for the moment.

The next thing the huge man felt was a jolt as the crate was dropped unceremoniously into the stake bed of the black prison truck. A few minutes passed and then he heard and felt the truck start up and slip into gear. He could feel the vibration of the truck's rear differential whirring beneath him as it lurched forward about thirty yards, then slowed as it passed through the prison gate. There was a heavy bump as the Ford dropped down off the curb and turned left onto newly paved State Street. It slowly picked up speed as it rolled down the elm-lined road, past well cared for houses and men coming home from work carrying their lunch pails. A bus pulled away from the curb as the prison truck passed, and the two drivers waved as they did at this exact hour each day of the week.

The black truck merged onto Main Street, passing the Chas. Hart Seed Company and the First Congregational Church before turning right again onto Church Street. The prison driver had to slow for a group of children playing an early evening baseball game in the street, and smiled as they jeered him while he passed. In the back, Charles Dewey listened intensely trying to get a bearing on his proximity to the prison, but could not. A mile up the road, the truck pulled to the right and into the small freight yard of the New Haven Railroad spur in Wethersfield.

The prison guard backed the truck up to a waiting box car, killed the engine, and got out of the truck. He lit a cigarette while waiting for help in loading the crates onto the freight train. He took the last drag of his butt and flicked it to the ground just as four muscular men in overalls approached the truck.

"Hey there, Rufus," the eldest of the freight yard men called to the driver. "Hot enough for ya?" The driver nodded and shrugged his shoulders without speaking. They played the same game every time the prison driver pulled into the yard.

"Yah, I guess. Time for a goddamned beer, hey boys?" he replied.

"No question 'bout that, boss," the lead roustabout yelled back. "You buyin'?" They all had a good laugh at that.

Without further conversation, the four men unloaded the two crates from the truck and lifted them onto the freight car. The whole operation took less than five minutes. Then, tipping the brim of his prison issue hat to them, the driver got back in his truck.

"Hell, boss, that last crate damn near broke my back," one of the men called out. "What the hell you make them shirts out of, lead?" he joked, drawing a muffled laugh from the others.

"Nah, you boys are just gettin' old, maybe a touch of arthritis settin' in. Go on home now and have that beer," the driver said with a laugh as he drove off. "See ya tomorrow."

Even as the guard pulled the truck back into the prison yard a few minutes later and called it a day, Charles Dewey was literally putting his back into freeing himself from the crate. Sensing that he was alone, he cleared away all the shirts beneath his boots until he touched the bottom, then, kneeling and doubled over, slowly raised his head and shoulders until the back of his neck hit the crate's closing panel. He maneuvered himself into one corner, then raised his legs beneath him and used his head and shoulders to press against the wooden lid. The top raised up several inches as his brute strength forced the six-penny nail holding it to loosen from the wood. Then with his right hand, he reached up and bent the two-inch nail out of the way. He repeated the effort on the other three corners, and in minutes he was out of the crate.

It wasn't until bed check, just before the lights were extinguished, that inmate Charles Dewey was discovered missing. A search party found the open crate near midnight, but by that time, the prisoner was long gone. All night, prison guards along with the Wethersfield Police and the town's Volunteer Firemen searched for the escaped prisoner, but to no avail. Just before dawn the next morning, the Connecticut State Police issued an all points bulletin alerting state, local and adjoining state law enforcement that Charles Dewey, a convicted armed robber, was on the run and was considered extremely dangerous. The bulletin described him in detail, and the photograph accompanying it did little to hide his fearsome physical features.

What the bulletin failed to include was a warning about the prisoner's mental state – primarily because the system that had incarcerated him as it would an animal had failed to recognize his extreme psychosis. It did not include the fact that Charles Dewey was suffering from a grave personality disorder that left him incapable of normal social functioning. His prison experience, steeped in forced isolation, drudgery and humiliation, had adeptly erased any remaining normalcy in his thinking, and consequently, his behavior. While he still resembled a man, the ape-like tendencies that had slowly been overwhelming his consciousness and behavior over the last decade, had once and for all gained control.

What the bulletin should have warned was that Charles Dewey was now a full blown psychopath capable of the most unimaginable depravity.

And he was as free as the wind.

Four

~~~ ~~~

The Atlantic Ocean

Although he dutifully reported the unstable winds brewing in the Sahara by shortwave to weather stations along the Caribbean Sea shipping lanes, only the French meteorologist and his young Sénégalese visitor suspected their ominous potential. Within the next twenty-four hours the volatile winds collected on the coast and moved slowly westward toward the Cape Verde Islands. There, they collided head on with the trade winds causing further tumult. Combined with abundant moisture from the equatorial heat, the winds became a small tropical storm, first taking the form of clusters of thunderclouds and gradually becoming a wave of energy that moved westerly from the Islands. The tropical depression that
~~~

formed at the center of the wave grew stronger as it moved west, its telltale spinning clouds now whirling toward the Caribbean at roughly twelve to fifteen miles per hour.

There was nothing particularly remarkable about this development. Tropical depressions occurred at least several times a year off Cape Verde, typically causing the formation of such tropical storms. In fact, the few ships that encountered the disturbance in the eastern Atlantic Ocean noted heavier seas building, and the nuisance of aggressive wind and driving rains. None found the weather particularly alarming.

The growing storm continued its trek across the vast open waters of the Atlantic over the next six days however, fueled by humidity and warm waters. The winds of the Sahara gradually became more violent, forming a huge, whirling maelstrom of frightening proportions. By the night of the fifteenth of September, the storm had pushed some sixteen hundred miles into the Caribbean and had become a dangerous hurricane. Few ships had crossed its path since the warnings by the French meteorologist had been posted, so land-based weather stations along its route knew little of the storm's fury.

That was to change quickly. When the dark of night enveloped the *SS Alegrete*, a tramp freighter flying the Brazilian flag under the command of Captain Flavio Mattos, the ship had just cleared the Leeward Islands. The ship was bound for its home port of Belém, a small city on the Amazon River estuary in the northern part of the country, when, without warning, it encountered the hurricane.

Mattos, in the wheelhouse of the aging steamer, had been nervously studying the horizon after watching with alarm as the sky above it had darkened and taken on an eerie, yellowish pall. Being a superstitious man, the color reminded him of the Habanero peppers that he often carried as freight on voyages to Miami. The Habenero, reputed to be the hottest pepper in existence, was native to Brazil, Venezuela and Peru and turned a sickly yellow if left to grow on the vine long enough. Legend had it that the small fruits of the Capsicum Chinense species had claimed the life of more than one unsuspecting connoisseur. Mattos had no way of knowing that the skies following the yellow horizon were potentially just as deadly.

As the ship sailed on, the modest chop and easterly breeze that had marked smooth sailing for most of the *Alegrete*'s journey was quickly replaced by heaving seas and a howling noise - the same howling that had haunted Jean-Pierre Chandon in the desert. In another ten minutes, the waters began pounding the twenty-two thousand ton freighter with thirty-foot waves breaking across her bow. The howling noise grew to an almost unimaginable roar, prompting crewmen below to break out their rosary beads.

Too late, Captain Mattos realized that he had sailed right into the mouth of the devil - a hurricane with winds blowing at least seventy-five miles per hour. That made it a Force Twelve storm on the

"Beaufort Scale", a hurricane measuring definition created in 1806 by Sir Francis Beaufort, a noted British military seaman and hydrographic expert. The scale of sixteen classes measured the effects of wind conditions on the sails of a "British Man of War" - then the primary fighting ship of the British Admiralty. At zero, the warship's sails would be fully deployed. At Force Eight, half to three quarters of the ships sails would be stowed by the crew before they were torn away. At Force Sixteen, the small fragments that were left of the entire boat would be scattered over miles of ocean.

Suddenly, the *Alegrete*'s decks were inundated by torrential rains and pounded by monstrous waves that were breaking almost at the top of the ship's bridge. Mattos barked orders to the quartermaster manning the ships wheel, screaming at the young man to point the ship into the waves, lest they be broadsided by a wall of water and capsized in a matter of seconds.

For more than five hours, the helpless Mattos and his crew rode out the storm, precariously hanging onto their will to stay alive, as the previously unreported hurricane battered the ship. All Mattos could do was radio a warning to the US Weather Bureau in Jacksonville, Florida. The Brazilian reported the storm's position at about three hundred fifty miles northeast of Puerto Rico and estimated wind speed at anywhere from eighty to one hundred miles per hour. He ordered a deckhand to take a barometer reading, and found that the air pressure was an ominous 28.31 inches and falling. The winds hammered the straining ship as it rode down into the sea's cavernous troughs and then somehow, miraculously, climbed back up again, barely cresting the mountainous waves. Indeed, the crew of the *SS Alegrete* was in dire straights but had no recourse except to ride out the storm and pray that the ship would not founder.

After a long, grueling night in the grip of the powerful hurricane, the *Alegrete* finally broke free of its vengeful grasp just after nightfall the next day. Several crewmen were badly injured from falls on the ship's heaving steel decks, and the drive shaft of its port side propeller was bent and rendered useless. The *Alegrete*'s pumps were still working however; and remarkably, the ship had not sustained damage to its hull. The tired tramp would eventually make home port, limping along on one engine, wearier but wiser.

In Jacksonville, the US Weather Service had been shocked by the *Alegrete*'s report, and was frantic for more news of the storm which had surprised even the most veteran of the forecasters stationed there.

It was steaming hot across Florida in the early morning of Friday, September sixteenth, a scalding one hundred and two degrees in Jacksonville. It was even hotter inside the US Weather Bureau's Hurricane Center, an operation only several years old and managed by Grady Norton, an usually unflappable twenty-year veteran of the service.

Norton had just finished his early morning public radio weather report. He was a familiar voice to Floridians who were accustomed to his somewhat slow going, Alabama-farmboy inflection, which most folks found comforting when the weather was something to worry about. This morning was no different as he announced, "A tropical disturbance of potentially dangerous proportions has been reported." Although he could provide few details of the approaching storm, he felt uncomfortable in raising the possibility of more urgent news. But he was far from satisfied with the performance of his small staff.

"Goddamn it to hell, Gordon, y'all got to get me some more information on this 'sum bitch, will ya for Chris' sake? I mean, just what the fuck is the holdup anyway?" Norton hollered uncharacteristically at his assistant, Gordon Dunn. In disgust the beleaguered station chief pushed his chair away from his beat up desk and stood up behind it. A cigarette hung loosely from his lips, the first smoke he had taken from the third pack he'd opened in the last twenty-four hours. "Goddamn it, come on y'all, we need to get a fix on this 'sum bitch -- now!"

The two dozen or so people milling around the office with ties undone, sleeves rolled up and perspiration stains soaking their shirts, looked up in frustration. Things had to be real bad for Grady Norton to speak to them in that tone of voice. The normally reserved station chief was admired by just about everyone who worked with or for him, and none of them liked letting him down. They all knew what was eating the old man.

Norton, Dunn and every man on the staff had been up all night trying to pinpoint the location of the hurricane reported by the *Alegrete* and somehow get a bead on its projected track. Gordon Dunn, the assistant chief forecaster and Norton's oldest and closest friend listened to his boss' rant without responding. He knew Grady too well to take offense at his impatience. Besides, the profane tirade coming off the lips of a guy with slicked back, thinning hair, coke-bottle-thick spectacles and a frame that a strong gust might blow over seemed almost comical. But no one laughed.

"We gotta get movin' here, Gordon," Norton went on with his friend. "Shit, that tramp skipper was probably a hundred miles from the eye of that 'sum bitch, and the barometer was already below twenty-eight and a half. I'm worried. Y'all got a monster brewing out there boy, and no telling where it's headed!"

Gordon was by training and intellect far more predisposed to approach a problem analytically while Norton was more empirical in his thinking – meaning he usually just shook his head and went with his gut based on observation. The two different styles made for some interesting debates, and often, sparks between them.

"Hell, Grady, that's just a guess..." Dunn challenged his friend.

"A guess?" Norton slammed his open hand down on the wooden desk, scattering meteorological charts. "A guess? You're goddamned right it's a goddamned guess, 'cuz you ain't getting me any goddamned information, Gordon! Y'all ain't listenin' to me -- get going, boy - I need information yesterday for Chris' sakes." His face was red and a large vein stood out on his neck. Dunn was caught short by his boss' intensity but responded calmly.

"I'm on it, Grady. We've sent out an advisory to all ships in the area asking for more information and also issued advisories for the Key's, Miami, and from the Atlantic coast to North Carolina," Dunn said. "One way or another we ought to hear something back from some boats in the area within the next twenty-four hours, and we've set the wheels in motion for an evacuation of the Florida coast from Miami to Jacksonville if we need it. Christ, Grady… relax."

Norton sat back down at his desk but his eyes never shifted from those of his friend.

"Relax? Hell, the last time you and I relaxed over a call on a storm this big, it ate us alive, remember?" Norton finally said, his voice trailing off.

"Yah," Dunn responded, looking away.

"Yah," Norton mimicked his friend. "We relaxed and four hundred thirty-eight people were drowned by a killer storm just like this one - because we let 'em know about it too goddamned late." Dunn winced at the memory. In the background, someone's chair squeaked. It sounded like thunder in the room.

On Labor Day 1935, a Force Sixteen hurricane had come roaring across the Florida Keys, a killing machine that caught everyone by surprise. Most of the dead were penniless US military veterans who had survived the war in Europe, only to come home to find no jobs, bread lines and a government that was more interested in celebrating its victory than in taking care of the men responsible for it. Even when Washington finally recognized the problem, not much happened. It wasn't until Franklin Delano Roosevelt launched the New Deal in 1932 that the vets found jobs in the Works Progress Administration.

On Labor Day 1935, more than four hundred veterans were working on the WPA construction of Florida's section of US Highway 1 in the Keys when the hurricane pounced on them with no more warning than a barn owl would give a mouse. Most were killed when Florida Overseas Railroad's ten car evacuation train sent to rescue them arrived too late - at the height of the storm. Then, fully loaded as it tried to flee northwest and to safety, the entire train was washed off its tracks and out to sea. Grady Norton and Gordon Dunn had seen the hurricane coming and sent out advisories warning of the approaching storm, but they had vastly underestimated how powerful the hurricane was. The two men were racked by guilt and vowed that it would never happen again.

A scant three years later, they were looking at almost precisely the same scenario. Later that afternoon, Norton and his colleagues sat transfixed around the station's shortwave radio as it intercepted SOS messages urgently being broadcast by the *SS Athena,* a nineteen thousand pound freighter flying the Greek flag.

The ship had run head on into the storm, now positioned several hundred miles northeast of the Leeward Islands. The *Athena*'s crew had seen the same eerie, sickly yellow sky just minutes before encountering huge seas and winds that they estimated at more than one hundred forty miles per hour. The ship was taking on water as there had been no time to batten all its hatches, and was in imminent danger of capsizing. The *Athena* was desperate for help, but no help would - or could - come to its aid.

Norton tried several times to query the *Athena* on the atmospheric conditions, almost desperate for a barometer reading, but was unable to get the radio operator's attention. The Greek seaman was completely focused on broadcasting his ship's position and desperate plight.

On *Athena*'s bridge, Captain Demetrius Andréa Papandreou braced himself against the wheelhouse in a vain attempt to hang on as he desperately tried to steer into the mountainous waves that were overwhelming his ship. If the *Athena* were to pitch too far to port or starboard, she would capsize in seconds. But Papandreou, a grizzled, gray haired seaman who had been sailing the oceans of the world since he was thirteen, now nearly half a century, was far more terrified of another possibility. Alarmed, he began counting the seconds between waves aloud.

Over and over he counted, beginning with the moment his ship would breach the crest of a monster wave, and then fall like a stone down the wall of water into a trough sixty to seventy feet below. He would stop counting when the five hundred ten foot long *Athena* rose up again to the top of another great wave, then wait until the next set and start counting again. He repeated the process over and over for nearly ten minutes.

Finally, just as his crew on the bridge thought the old man had lost his mind amidst the watery nightmare, he yelled out.

"Goddamn it… I thought so… the bastard's are coming faster… we'll not be able to hold her…" he screamed above the howling that filled the brightly lit wheelhouse. Just as the words fell from his lips, straight ahead, a wave of even more monstrous proportions rose up in front of them to an unimaginable height. In abject resignation, the Captain's hands fell from the wheel that he had wrestled so bravely and he instinctively clasped them in prayer. "Our Father, who art in heaven, hallowed be…" he prayed aloud as his ship began climbing the juggernaut wave, higher and higher and higher…

Just as it seemed the battered ship might reach the top, the *Athena*'s bow pitched up and the white froth at the very tip of the rogue wave blasted into the ship's exposed underbelly, pushing it backwards. As the massive vessel careened over upside down, an explosive crack shuddered from its bow to stern. The ship's backbone, its forged steel keel, shattered at the center of its length, breaking the ship almost precisely in two at its expansion joint. The now liberated sections of the mutilated boat fell into the next trough and submerged just below the water. Before either the bow or stern could bob to the surface again, perhaps allowing the crew to abandon ship, the next wave struck, driving both ends deep below the ocean. It was all over before the crew could even think of escape.

Commercial vessels within a hundred miles of the wreck, perhaps two dozen or more, listened in frustration and awe to the wave of urgent but helpless messages being sent by the *Athena*. Then suddenly, there was nothing. For hours after, they attempted to raise the ship, but the night was filled with quiet and emptiness.

The same silence that now filled the airwaves was perhaps the loudest in Jacksonville, Florida, as Grady Norton and his small cadre of tired meteorologists and forecasters slowly absorbed the horror of what they had heard. And then, to a man, they silently and spontaneously not only clasped their hands and hung their heads in respect to those who had been lost, but also in prayer.

For now they understood the temperament and the terror of the beast that was coming.

Five

~~~ ~~~

Middletown, Connecticut

Charles Dewey was soaking wet and freezing.

He shivered through drenched cotton overalls that he had stolen to hide his denim prison uniform, the heavy fabric clinging to his body as cold rain fell on him without letup. He thought he could feel each drop as it landed on his back, every one an icy needle pricking his raw skin. The escaped convict could not have been more miserable, despite his sudden new freedom. His mood was black and dangerous.

The weather had turned about two hours after he had escaped from the Wethersfield Prison, blanketing northeastern Connecticut in unseasonably cold temperatures and a steady downpour. He should have been thankful for the
~~~

rain, which undoubtedly was complicating the search efforts to find him. But the soaking was also taking its toll on his already frayed nerves. Dewey badly needed a change of clothes, a hot meal and some time to think. But it wasn't as if he could just check into a motel.

Hunkered down low in a row of large evergreens that served as a hedge between two houses on a dimly lit street in Middletown, Connecticut, he watched what appeared to be a couple of young men bent over the hood of a car in front of a large, shingled house that was blazing with lights. The house had some kind of a sign over the front door spelling out words he didn't understand. He mouthed them to himself, awkwardly sounding out "Theta Nu Epsilon". Dewey had no idea what the phrase meant but the words somehow intimidated him, nonetheless.

He turned his attention back to the boys, one of whom was holding an umbrella and a flashlight while the other was bent over inside the engine bay. He decided to watch for awhile, taking advantage of a moments rest.

The escaped convict had been running since the moment he had pried himself out of the wooden crate in the railroad box car. He had considered swimming out to one of the many small pleasure boats anchored in the Cove, but he was not a strong swimmer and besides, there was no way he wouldn't be spotted. Instead, he turned back across the railroad tracks and headed north, coming to Route 9, a two lane gravel road that had been named after America's first Ambassador to France, Silas Deane. The Silas Deane Highway had been built in 1930 and now was a ten-mile stretch that was the major thoroughfare between the City of Hartford and towns south of the state's capital. To Dewey, it looked like a ticket to freedom.

There were a few businesses and markets on the highway, but all were closed now; and there was nearly no traffic. The convict stayed off the road until darkness fell completely, hiding his enormous frame in some tall dried brush about thirty yards off the road, and he watched as house lights came on one by one in the adjacent neighborhoods. He lingered another thirty minutes until the only light on the highway was the reflection of red votive candles coming through the stained glass windows of the empty "Corpus Christi" Catholic church just south of where he was hiding.

Finally, he got to his feet, slowly and carefully looking all around him before he moved again. Then, satisfied that he had not been spotted, he walked quietly to the edge of the highway and stopped. Across the street was a shabby hot dog stand painted a fading bright blue. Dewey had watched its owner lock up and drive away about twenty minutes before.

There were no street lights and not a car to be seen, so bending low, his long arms hanging, he lumbered across the highway with surprising speed and hid behind the shack, stopping again to make sure he hadn't been seen. He moved quickly for such a giant of a man, but he was not athletic and his gait was awkward, as if his fine motor skills had never caught up with his huge size. He wrenched open a back door, pulling it off its hinges without much effort, and snuck inside. It was a blessing he hadn't been spied. His huge, morbid outward appearance, coupled with such powerful but ungainly physical coordination almost justified the unkind opinion of the prison guards from whom he had escaped: Charles Dewey appeared and acted like a primate, a virtual picture of Darwinian evolution theory, one step removed from the human species.

With temporary shelter he at least had a moment to think. His mind, far more evolved than his ape-like body, was racing, trying to focus on what to do next. The convict knew he had to keep moving. He was certain the local police would soon begin a door-to-door search for him, probably with bloodhounds. He knew from experience that once the damned dogs caught a scent, they were relentless. The window blinds were shut, so he carefully pried open two slats and peered out, trying to get a bearing. Up ahead, Dewey could just make out a highway sign to the north that said "Hartford" and knew he did not want to head into the city. The police would be everywhere.

Just ahead of the sign he saw what looked to be a large lumber yard, about three hundred yards away, dark and obviously closed. It was fenced in, but he was sure if he could make it inside he would probably be able to find a truck or some kind of vehicle that could get him out of town. He decided to go for it.

Dewey scanned the highway up and down, then seeing no one, bolted out the front door, sprinting back across the highway and back into the brush. From there he made his way north to the lumber yard, off the highway and fairly hidden. It took him fifteen minutes to get to the fence; but sure enough, the first thing he spotted was a pickup truck parked near what looked like the yard's front office and locked up for the night. Just as he went to scale the fence, a loud, shrill siren broke above the evening silence, filling the air with a warning from the prison. His escape had finally been discovered. He had no more time to waste.

Panicking, he lunged at the chain link fence and hoisted himself over, falling heavily to the ground on the other side. The ruckus instantly alerted a guard dog, a Doberman pinscher that was left to roam the premises at night. Oblivious to the animal, Dewey was picking his way through piles of stacked lumber towards the pickup when he caught sight of the dog out of the corner of his eye. In the second or two he had before the beast lunged to tear out his throat, the convict turned to face the dog head on and crouched as to duck the animal's charge. His furrowed brow cast an even darker shadow over his face, exaggerating the whites of his sunken eyes. It was a look so evil, it might have stopped a sane man dead in his tracks but the dog attacked on instinct, without hesitation or fear. Dewey tensed as the black beast leapt at him, its hideously sharp incisors glistening, and crouched even lower. Just as it seemed the dog would sail over his head, the giant reached up and caught it in mid air - his burly hands grabbing the sinewy attacker by the throat, just below his bared teeth, his jaws wide open in a salivating snarl.

The dog never had a chance. Dewey caught his balance, then stood straight up, his hands still wrapped around the animal's throat. He looked into the dog's eyes for a moment, even as the brutal giant tightened his grip to squeeze closed its windpipe. Whimpering in sudden fear, the large dog hung over his captors head in the noose of his giant hands, its back legs desperately clawing at the convicts chest, trying to tear free of the man's mighty grip. The enormous victor could easily have released his choke hold on the terrified dog, its spirit broken and desperate for a run to safety. Charles Dewey never considered the option, finding greater delight in what he did next.

Pulling the dog's seventy-pound body under his right arm and trapping it, he reached over with his left hand and grabbed the animal's muzzle. With a fiendish roar of laughter, he twisted the animal's head forcing it almost completely around -- until he heard a loud snap, the sound of its spine shattering. Instantly, the struggle was over and the dog went completely limp, its long tongue hanging obscenely from its mouth.

Finally satiated, Dewey threw the carcass down at his feet in disgust, his heavy breathing the only sign of the assault. The dog twitched several times, prompting the convict to laugh out loud again, a chilling grin coming to his face.

It took him only a few minutes to hot wire the pickup. Dewey slammed the truck into gear and floored it, the rear wheels kicking up a spray of dust and gravel. Intentionally, as if to desecrate his enemy, he ran over the dog's body and laughed again at the resounding "thump" as he passed over it. Then he nosed the pickup into a locked chain link gate which blew apart, the doors exploding open. He turned the car south down the Silas Deane Highway, having no idea where he was or where he was headed. What he did know was that he had to get away from the area fast before the police could set up roadblocks.

God help the innocent who strayed into his path.

He drove south for perhaps an hour, completely unsure of where he was or where he was headed. He stayed on Route 9, crossing through the small towns of Rocky Hill and then Cromwell without incident, and finally into Middletown. Nervously, he pulled the truck off the road in a small clearing by the Connecticut River under the Arrigoni Bridge and parked, killing his headlights.

He was disoriented and badly needed a plan. Dewey got out of the truck and studied the bridge, which he thought looked new. In fact, it had been completed only months before, linking the City of Middletown with neighboring Portland by two spectacular six hundred foot steel arches. Dewey sighed, surprised again by a melancholy which sometimes came on him out of nowhere. He wondered how it was that he had been born to no future, a virtual outcast all of his life, and why it was that some men could design and build bridges, others became doctors and lawyers. These were men who enjoyed the sunlight. All he was good at was robbing, hurting and killing - skills that condemned him to lurk forever in the shadows. He shook his head in self pity, then let the moment pass. Quickly, he got back in the truck and headed for the lights of Middletown.

After a couple of miles, he found himself on Main Street where a smattering of businesses were still open. Driving slowly, he went past a bar, its door open, seeming to welcome him. Inside he could see men drinking, smoking and talking loudly. He would give anything for a drink, he thought, but going in was out of the question, especially dressed as he was in his prison uniform. The urge was stupid, he knew, but overwhelming and he had an idea. He drove on, slinking down behind the wheel when he encountered a city police car going in the opposite direction. The cop never even glanced in his direction.

Dewey finally found what he was looking for and turned right down the next side street. He went up about a block, then turned into a driveway and parked the truck in a lot behind a three-story tenement. Lights were on in all three floors, so he quickly killed the motor. He figured it was time to ditch the truck. It might already have been reported stolen from the lumberyard near the Wethersfield

Prison. No sense in pressing his luck, the little he had.

He turned the collar down on his shirt and walked quietly through the lot, making his way back to Main Street, where he took a left and found the liquor store he had spotted. He crossed the street and sat on a bench, wishing he had a cigarette. For the next fifteen minutes, Dewey studied the store front, watching as several people entered, bought what they came for, and left. He looked up the street and noticed a clock on the steeple of what looked to be the town hall. It was just a few minutes before nine o'clock. He guessed correctly that the owner would be closing up shop when the hour struck, and casually made his way back across the street. Just as he got to the door, the owner had his hand on the dead bolt to lock up, then saw Dewey and let him in, cheerfully.

"Hell, never too late for one more customer. Help yourself, friend," the slight, bespectacled man said warmly, letting the convict pass. Dewey walked to the counter and watched as the gray-haired owner, who he made out to be in his late 60's or so, came over and stood behind the cash register.

"Now what can I get you?" the owner said, kindly, but suddenly wishing he had taken a closer look at the man before letting him in. He was just now seeing how enormous the customer was and how bizarre he looked. And what was up with the clothes, he wondered. Then it hit him.

"Gimme a quart of Seagram's and a carton of Camels," Dewey said, without looking, sliding his right hand into his pocket as if searching for his money. "You got any matches?"

"Oh, sure, sure... can't smoke 'em without fire, now, can ya, eh?" the owner replied. "They're right under the counter here, now let me see..." He ducked below the counter as if to find the matches, then came up quickly with a sawed-off, twelve-gauge shotgun that he pointed directly at Dewey's head. The convict, who had been about to pounce on the elderly man, stepped back, surprised by the slight man's action.

"Now wait a minute," the escaped prisoner stammered... "I haven't done anything to you... what the hell..."

The old man was feisty. "Not yet you haven't. I know who you are. The police were here not an hour ago to tell me there's been an escape. I'm pretty sure you wanted more than whiskey and cigarettes coming in here... well, too darned bad pal, the joke's on you."

Dewey glared at the man, biding his time, waiting for him to make a mistake. "Now you just stay right there while I call the cops, you hear? I'm not afraid to use this..." he said, warning the convict. His voice was suddenly a bit shaky as he realized the size of the intruder in front of him. "Damn, you are a big fella... just stay where you are and I won't hurt you," he said, hopefully, but suddenly not at all sure about what he had started. He reached for the telephone.

"I'm going to call the police, now..." the owner said, awkwardly trying to keep the gun pointed at

Dewey as he struggled with a trembling finger to dial the number on the black rotary Bell telephone. "Damn," he swore again, after dialing an incorrect digit. The owner looked down at the phone for a split second, which was all the time the convict needed to step forward and knock the gun out of the much smaller man's hands. The shotgun fell heavily to the floor a few feet away from the counter. The owner went for it, but Dewey stepped forward and launched his size eighteen leather boot directly into the smaller man's exposed ribs, kicking him with all his might. He heard a sharp crack as the man fell to the floor, unable to breath, totally incapacitated. The convict stood over him, watching the elderly man struggle for air.

"You son of a bitch - you were gonna shoot me, huh?" he said through clenched teeth, his fists coiled up into blocks the size of a sledge hammer. "You don't know nothin' about me but you thought you had the balls to kill me, is that right, you old fuck?" In disgust, he loudly coughed up a load of phlegm and spat it into the prone man's face, even as he still struggled to breath.

Dewey suddenly remembered how easy it was to see into the store and ran to kill the lights. He locked the door and closed the large window shades, then returned to the owner, who was breathing only a little easier, but was still on his back in agony. The convict thought for a moment, then reached down and grabbed the man by the neck of his shirt, hoisting him into a chair behind the counter.

"Listen old man, you got any clothes here - something that will fit me?" he hollered into his face. The elderly man lifted a finger and pointed to a door that led to his warehouse. "Coveralls," he said, bloody spittle now leaking from his mouth. Dewey quickly found them and pulled the brown cotton uniform on over his denims. The work clothes didn't fit very well, but he had no options. As he left, he picked up a four-foot length of cast iron pipe propped up in a corner.

"These will do fine," Dewey said to the man, then uncapped the bottle of Seagrams and took a long pull. "Goddamm, it's been awhile," he said. He walked back to the man. "You want some, old man?" The owner shook his head, refusing.

"Too bad." Without another word, Dewey picked up the pipe and swung at the elderly man's head as if it was a baseball. A sickening thud was followed by a grotesque spray of blood, fragments of bone and bits of gelatinous brain matter that stained the wall behind the counter a ghastly shade of runny crimson. The liquor store owner's body fell heavily to the floor, his skull shattered. Blood poured from a gaping head wound.

"Fuck you," Dewey said, lighting a cigarette and inhaling deeply. He sat in the old man's chair for a few minutes, taking swigs from the bottle and smoking another cigarette. Then he rifled the cash register, pocketing maybe a hundred dollars, loaded his coverall pockets with cigarettes and a couple of pint bottles of whiskey, and carefully hid the gun inside the uniform. He let himself out the back door of the liquor store and headed north on foot. It was still pouring rain.

After a couple of blocks, he found himself in a heavily treed section of the city, its streets lined with large two- and three-family tenements. As he walked, he gradually became aware that he was in some kind of organized neighborhood with clusters of brick buildings strewn in with the houses. Eventually he caught sight of a sign on a building that read, "Wesleyan University". He walked some more, keeping to the shadows cast by large, stately elm trees. Heavy raindrops from the trees made walking even more miserable. He turned the collar of his overalls up; then abruptly spotted some activity ahead and dropped behind some bushes in the front yard of one of the houses. That's when he saw the two boys.

After watching for about ten minutes, and not seeing anyone else around, the hulking man left the cover of the bushes and slowly approached the car.

"What's the problem?" he said, trying to sound like a concerned neighbor. The two students turned and jumped at the sight of the huge man. The smaller of the two turned the flashlight on him, illuminating his face from below, making his already sunken eyes look like black holes bored into his skull. The boy nearly dropped the torch at the sight.

"Jesus fucking Christ, you scared me, man! Where the hell did you come from?" the taller of the two boys yelled.

Dewey didn't answer, but pushed his wet black hair off his eyes and smiled. "What's the problem?" he asked again, not quite so neighborly this time, and grabbed the flashlight from the kid who was still holding it on his face.

"Aw, this piece of shit won't turn over," the bigger boy stammered, trying to recover from his initial fright. He wore glasses and the convict thought he looked like a chipmunk.

"Let me see," Dewey said leaning into the engine bay without an invitation. Working from the glare of a streetlight, he reached in and pulled a couple of spark plug wires, reversing them. "That should do it. Someone been messing with the engine?"

The taller boy jumped behind the drivers' seat and turned the ignition. The engine started at once. "Yah, guy next door put some new sparkplug wires in for me. It's been coughing and spitting and running like shit ever since. Whatja do, man?"

"Wires were fucked up."

The three stood in awkward silence. "Well, thanks, big fella, thanks for the help. We gotta go." The smaller one suddenly looked nervous.

"Where you headed?" Dewey asked innocently.

"Uh, Newport. My girl goes to college there," the tall one said, glad to be rid of the weird looking guy.

"Sounds good." Dewey said.

"What do you mean?" The little guy was about to shit a brick.

"I mean get in the fucking car and drive, midget," he said coolly, staring into the young man's face. Terror struck the youth.

"No, I don't think so…" the taller one started to say, then stopped when he saw the gun Dewey had pulled out of his coveralls. The three climbed into the car, the two boys in the front and the convict in the back with the shotgun on his knees. He uncapped a pint of whiskey and took a long pull, then offered it to the boys. They declined. "Suit yourself. Now drive."

The older boy turned around to say something, but instead watched as Dewey lit a cigarette. The convict blew a mouthful of smoke at him making him cough. The boy stared into his face and suddenly felt fear: deep, primal fear. He turned around again, his face ashen white and started the engine as he had been told.

As they pulled away, Dewey broke the silence.

"Now, tell me about your girlfriend and this place called 'Newport'," he said from the back seat, almost whimsically, the orange ember glow from his cigarette reflecting in his black eyes as the son of Satan amused himself.

Saturday
September 17, 1938

Six

~~~ ◆ ~~~

Little Narragansett Bay

The sleek white wooden sailboat knifed through an afternoon chop on Little Narragansett Bay, its sails full in the warm breeze of yet another post Labor Day weather renaissance. The Watch Hill Yacht Club's fifteen-foot *Josephine,* the pride and joy of the Westerly, Rhode Island sailing set, was under the command of Geoff Lapkin, whose relaxed grip on the tiller and studious fix on its bursting spinnaker gave evidence that he knew his way around boats. In fact, he had been racing since he was a boy of just seven; and there was little he didn't know about sailboats, Little Narragansett Bay or the whole Rhode Island coastline for that matter.

But today, the fit and tanned husband and father of four wasn't concerned about a race or
~~~

finding a school of dolphins to play with. All he wanted on this glorious afternoon, while his factory was humming away in Westerly and his children were off at school, was a few hours alone with his girl. Not the girl named *Josephine*, but the woman named Emily. She was the first love of his life, and he knew there could never be another who would so totally captivate his every waking moment. And there weren't nearly enough of those, he thought. He simply could never find enough time to satisfy his desire to be with her. The George C. Moore Company was his livelihood, but Emily was his life. He felt genuinely blessed to have reached that conclusion even before the birth of James, their oldest son. Now, three kids later, he still couldn't take his eyes off her.

Especially today. Emily sat just a few feet away in the small boat's cockpit, a light blue sweater tied loosely around her shoulders. She too was tanned, though hardly as deep as other summers when the sun had been far more welcoming during the summer season. The wind blowing in from the Atlantic across the Bay tossed her long light brown hair, just a shade away from blond, back from her strikingly beautiful face which accentuated the elegance of her neck line. Geoff was simply mesmerized by her loveliness, just as he had been the moment he laid eyes on her as a boy of seventeen.

"Geoff!" she suddenly turned and yelled back at her husband. "I thought we weren't going to go too far out… look where we are!" She pointed to the coastline just above Watch Hill Harbor, which now was three-quarters of a mile farther away than it had been fifteen minutes earlier. He'd let the boat drift as he watched her, transfixed.

"Sorry, darlin', let my mind wander a bit," he laughed, shaking his head. "It's not everyday I get to spend alone with the girl of my dreams..."

"Oh, you..." she said, a slight smile coming to her delicate lips and waving him off with a slender hand. Emily was always somewhat embarrassed by the way he looked at her, although secretly she cherished the fact that he adored her and wouldn't have it any other way. She always hoped he knew just how much she loved him. It was Geoff's relentless pursuit of her that had finally won Emily over. They had met one night at the Yacht Club the summer after graduating from high school. He was a local boy from a wealthy family, she came from a family with blue collar roots in Providence that had never tasted the finer side of life. Emily had taken a job as a waitress at the Club, not as much for the pay as for the opportunity to spend the entire summer on Watch Hill.

They might never have gotten together if not for the drunken guest of a club member who had helped himself to a generous squeeze of her bottom one night. She was serving the customer a drink when she jumped back, startled at his unwelcomed touch. The drink fell to the floor and the glass smashed, drawing the attention of the dozens of patrons being served. The guest laughed and grabbed her hand, pulling the young girl to him.

Geoff had been dining with his father a few tables away and saw her situation. Quickly pushing back from his chair, the six-foot-three, two hundred pound teen dropped his napkin on the table, buttoned his jacket and walked over to the buffoon.

"Let her go," he said, quietly but with intensity only a blind drunk couldn't recognize.

The man shakily got up from the table, swaying as he got to his feet. The older man was about the same height as Geoff, but considerably heavier, a large belly extending from his rumpled, light blue poplin suit jacket. His face was red and his collar undone, his tie askew. There was a bit of food on his chin. The drunken man looked every bit the part of a boorish clown, and now he was acting like one as well. The Yacht Club member who had invited him grabbed his arm in embarrassment and in a vain attempt to get him to sit down. The drunk brushed him off.

"Hell, what have we here is a hero in boys clothes, I guess," the clown spat out, mocking the young boy's determined stare. He released his grip on Emily and pushed her away, as if to discard her. The jugular vein on the side of Geoff's throat grew large, and his stare hardened. The inebriated man ignored the glaring warning signs in front of him. The elder Lapkin still sat at the table, shocked at his son's quick reaction. Only his concern dampened the tingle of pride he was feeling in his chest.

"Now who's gonna make me, kid? You think you can, huh, big shot?" the stranger said and then pushed Geoff backwards with both hands on the boy's chest. The teenager stood his ground. Still the drunk didn't get the message.

"I'll teach you to mind your own fucking business, you rich brat…" The drunk took one step forward and launched a wild haymaker aimed at crushing the right side of Geoff's face. The boy sidestepped the sucker punch easily and the fat man staggered to one side, landing heavily on the table. The sound of falling silverware, braking crystal and china filled the room. Enraged, the man got back to his feet and charged the teen like a wild bull, seeking to wrap Geoff in a bear hug.

The boy sidestepped him again, and when the man drew back his fist for another swing at him, Geoff reared back and with all his might, threw a punch of his own, hitting the heavier man squarely at the base of his sternum in the solar plexus. The drunk doubled over in agony, his knees buckling. Without hesitation, the seventeen year old nailed the loudmouth with an uppercut that snapped his head back. The man's eyes rolled into his head as it lolled backwards, but his enormous belly pulled him forward again, and the drunkard fell to the floor face first. There was a thud and it was over.

Silence followed. Geoff stood back, his fists at the ready, waiting for the man to get up and come at him again. He was hardly breathing heavy, only the redness of his face evidence of the adrenalin coursing through his veins. Slowly, he dropped his hands as it was obvious the man wouldn't be getting up any time soon. He turned and looked somewhat sheepishly at his Dad, who still sat at their table, his mouth agape.

Emily, the unwitting prize of the sudden confrontation, stood a few feet away, her hands covering her mouth in shock, her eyes wide. She couldn't believe what she had seen. Suddenly, someone in the dining room clapped. Then another… and still another. Geoff's father got up from his table and joined in. In anther moment, every diner in the room was clapping for the teen and his chivalrous display. Such gallantry was not often seen, and there was a touch of romance in their approval. Handsome young knight saves beautiful damsel in distress. The moment could not have been scripted more violently, yet more elegantly.

Geoff, now embarrassed, turned to Emily and took her hand, escorting her from the room to the stares and applause of its patrons. Out of the spotlight with the young waitress, he turned to face her. "I'm so sorry, I didn't mean to embarrass you, that guy just…" he began to apologize. He caught himself, feeling as if a bolt of lightening had hit him in the head. My God, she's beautiful, he thought, his tongue tied.

Emily stared into his eyes, not at all sure of how to react to the young man who had come to her rescue. He was handsome, she thought, in a rugged sort of way. His nose was a little crooked, like an athlete's and his tousled brown hair looked as if it always needed to be combed. He had very high cheekbones that gave him a chiseled appearance and steel blue eyes that were as clear as any she had ever seen. But what really startled her was the look in them. His eyes were full of kindness.

She didn't know what to say other than, "Thank you, I don't..."

Geoff stopped her. "It's okay, I've got a sister, would hate to see anyone treat her like that."

Emily smiled at him. "I wouldn't mind being your sister..."

"I would," Geoff shot back, finding his wits. "Because then I couldn't ask you out." He just said it, later wondering where the words had come from. He was not usually so forward with girls, being almost pathetically shy.

Too shocked to respond, Emily leaned forward and gave him a quick kiss on the cheek, her hands gently brushing his chest.

"I have to get back to work... uh,..."

"Geoffrey, I mean Geoff. Geoff Lapkin," he said. "I live here."

"In the Yacht Club?" she asked, confused.

"No, no, I mean, here... here in Watch Hill. On Napatree Point. On Fort Road," he stammered awkwardly.

"Oh, right, Napatree Point." She smiled again. "You're lucky...Geoff. Thanks again. I have to go..." She turned and almost ran away from him, very unsure of her feelings. He watched her go back into the dining room to help clean up the mess, her face pink with embarrassment. That night, he waited for her to get off work, and walked her back to the small cottage she and three other girls were sharing for the summer, just below the Harbor with a wonderful view of the Bay. He bravely tried to hold her hand, but she resisted, unsure of the boy and a little afraid of him, remembering what he had done to the drunk. Geoff waited for her every night after and then finally got up the nerve to ask her out. On the third try Emily said yes and held hands with him as they walked. He brought her flowers. Then he kissed her. And that was that.

Now, Emily Lapkin was as loving and caring a wife as she was a mother, and she would have been even if life had not been so kind to her. But the wealth Geoff had carved out for them with his tireless dedication to his work and career gave her opportunities she knew few other women her age could imagine.

She wasn't much for the country club set, and really didn't care for kibitzing with the local ladies, even those her own age. Instead, Emily doted over her children and relished her time alone with them. Her only vice was golf - a sport she had recently been drawn to after following the exploits of "Babe" Didrickson, a young, professional golfer who hailed from Texas. In recent years, "Babe" had set the women's golfing world ablaze with her amazing play and signaled the end of the "for men only" reputation of the sport. Emily became a serious student of the game.

"Why shouldn't a woman be able to play with the men?" she had argued to her husband one wintry night over dinner.

"Of course women should be able to play with men," Geoff responded, desperately trying to look interested in the conversation and to sound sincere.

"Why, you don't agree?" Emily shot back, ready for an intellectual debate.

Geoff just smiled and shook his head, saying nothing, knowing never to challenge Emily when she felt passionate about something. Not that he thought she was wrong - he just knew that whatever he said from here on, it probably wouldn't come out as he intended and he'd just end up sleeping on the couch.

"You look lovely tonight..." he said, smiling at her, desperate to change the topic of conversation. It didn't work.

Actually, Geoff encouraged her to compete and to broaden her life however she wanted. He hated the idea of her waiting for him to come home from work, and his job demanded long hours. It gave him comfort and satisfaction knowing she had a life of her own. So with Geoff away in the factory Monday through Friday and often on the weekends, and Emily tending to the children and sneaking in as much playing time as she could on the golf course, their time together, especially in the summer months, became precious.

Geoff had literally swept his wife off her feet this morning by starting the day with breakfast in bed, then, after informing the children that Shelly would be minding them for the afternoon, he led her to the car without explanation and drove directly to the Yacht Club. They cast off from the dock less than twenty minutes later, just after Emily discovered the long stem roses and champagne he had hidden on board.

"Whatcha think, darlin' – does it get any better than this?" he asked his wife as they turned out of the Harbor and towards their home on Sandy Point, at the very tip of the peninsula. When she didn't respond immediately, he pushed his sun glasses down to the end of his nose and glared at her. Sixty seconds went by without a response. Patience gone, he let go of the tiller and launched himself at her, using his substantial weight advantage to push her down on the cockpit bench. Then, straddling her, he began to mercilessly tickle his bride. Emily squealed in absolute delight trying to catch his hands. She loved being the center of his life.

"Say it, say it!" Geoff demanded as she struggled to get away from him.

"Yes, yes, you're right… stop it, you're driving me crazy... no more please…" she couldn't stop laughing as he tickled her. Suddenly he stopped, then slowly brought his hands to her face, cupping her flawless skin. He looked into her deep, sapphire blue eyes and turned completely serious.

"Mrs. Geoff Lapkin," he demanded. "Do you know how utterly in love I am with you?"

Her heart filled with love for him too, but she only smiled, not knowing what to say. Then she reached up and put her arms around his neck, pulling herself closer to his face. He met her halfway, their lips coming together in a long, soft kiss. She suddenly felt one of his hands move to her breast.

"Why Mr. Lapkin," she said firmly, feigning outrage at his behavior and pushed her husband off her with surprising strength. "Don't you dare - out here in the middle of the ocean... what are you thinking of?" she cried, forcing him to move. "Don't you know there are whales out here - or that we could hit an iceberg or something..."

He smiled and jumped back to grab the wayward tiller.

"Aye, aye, Captain," he said, grinning like a young boy caught with his hand in the cookie jar. "My wish is your command," he teased her. He had never felt so whole or satisfied in his life.

Long minutes went by, just the two of them relishing each other's company, not needing to say anything. The sun was getting lower in the water and he turned the boat back toward the Watch Hill Harbor.

"Hey lady," he finally said, breaking their happy silence. "How's about I buy you a steak at the Ocean House?" The Ocean House Inn was romantically set atop the ocean bluffs overlooking the Harbor, and it was Emily's favorite restaurant.

"What about the kids?" she asked, remembering they'd be expecting their parents for dinner.

"Well, hell, they eat steak too, don't they? We'll stop by the house and pick 'em up, okay?" A devilish grin broke out on her face. This time it was her turn to jump on him.

"What about the icebergs?" he hollered in mock terror as she pinned him to the cockpit bench.

"Forget the icebergs," she said. "Okay, Mr. Lapkin. The Ocean House it is. But tonight, after we get the kids to bed, I've got a mind to end the perfect afternoon in the perfect way."

He smirked at her. "And what would that entail?" he asked, playing the game.

"I'm thinking candlelight, an ocean breeze, a nice bottle of wine…"

His smile got bigger as his love for his wife grew by the second. "Sounds like a plan," he said, rather officially. "But I was wondering…"

"What?" she said, curious that he would have a caveat to her proposition.

The twinkle in his eye gave him away.

"Maybe we should just skip dinner…"

They needn't have worried about the children, who had not wasted a single minute of the glorious sun that had eluded them for most of the summer, particularly James. In a week, he'd be returning to the grueling schedule of the Choate School, and weather permitting, he intended to spend as many of his remaining hours on Sandy Point in the water, surfing.

James was the most serious of the children, and Emily often fretted about him, worried that he was taking life too seriously at such a young age. But today, thoughts of school were far from his mind as he paddled out from the shore, catching every wave he could. The blond haired boy was lugging his heavy, ten-foot long, wood surf board up onto the beach for a much needed breather when his precocious sister Kate met him at the waters' edge.

"Mommy said that you were to teach me how to surf before you go back to school," she barked in her typically abrasive style. James ignored her, dropped his board onto the sand and stretched his nearly six-foot frame over it to bake in the sun for awhile. Of course, Kate pursued him. This time she screamed with a voice so shrill it caused a flock of seagulls scavenging on the beach to take flight. Even the gulls' piercing shrieks and cries couldn't drown out the sound of her voice.

"James, do what Mommy said!" she demanded again.

He sat upright and stared at her, using his most serious face and causing the girl to take a step back. "Katie, if you don't leave me alone, I'll tie you to my surf board and let the current take you away! Now bug off..." There were times, he thought, that you just had to treat her tantrums with one of your own.

Young Geoffrey Jr., a wiry, spunky little fireplug of a boy who was naturally as mischievous as his namesake father, watched the confrontation from atop the porch railing of the Lapkin cottage. He'd about had it with Kate's behavior as well after being cooped up with her for most of the summer. They were only two years apart in age, but years more in terms of social graces. For every ounce of Kate's precociousness, he weighed in with pounds of impetuously rogue-like behavior. He bore an uncanny resemblance to his matinee idol, George "Spanky" McFarlane of "Little Rascals" fame, and was as quick to find himself caught in an act of tomfoolery as his silver screen hero. His father often laughed that Geoffrey was born for the business world. "Monkey business, that is," he'd add, chuckling. Emily would always chide the senior Geoff not to encourage the boy's penchant for naughtiness or his streak of recklessness.

Now, grinning devilishly and biding his time until Kate was positioned just right, in an instant he sprang off the railing and on to the hot sands. With a running start and a wicked yell he ran the several yards between them and tackled his unwary sister, sending her sprawling across the beach. She immediately began to cry, and when it seemed no one had noticed, she set to screaming again, which quickly attracted their housekeeper's attention.

"What in tarnation..." Shelly said, abruptly dropping her knitting needles and yarn into her lap and stood up to peer over the porch rail for the source of the commotion. Without knowing, she expected Kate would be involved somehow, instigator that she was. But she was wearing her reading spectacles and couldn't be sure. Brian, who had watched the whole thing from inside a large hole he had dug out of the sand, was roaring with laughter, which made Geoffrey Jr. all the more proud.

"You deserve it, Katie," Brian hollered from his sitting position in the damp sand. He often dug huge, gaping holes in the beach outside the family cottage. Just "why", he never could say. Sometimes he would wait, sitting in his hole, so deep that not even the top of his head showed, and wait for the tide to come in and begin spilling over the lip. He'd sit there as the water slowly filled the hole, sometimes until it was almost up to his neck, then scramble to safety before it rose over his head. One night Geoff and Emily decided to go for a moonlight walk along a sandbar that appeared at low tide, and in the darkness, the two of them failed to see one of Brian's excavations and promptly fell in.

"What in the hell?" Geoff said to his wife, who just smiled. The two of them laughed out loud, then realized the romantic opportunity they had literally stumbled into and made slow, but very passionate love beneath the moon's subtle light. Neither bothered to scold Brian the next morning when he came to the breakfast table, sharing a muffled snicker between them instead. "What's so funny?" Brian asked, oblivious.

Shelly was not feeling as patient. She walked over to the railing, shading her eyes against the sun and hollered. "Listen you kids - just because your mom and dad aren't around doesn't mean you can take advantage of me!" she yelled, more irritated at the interruption to her knitting than angry at their behavior. "Now settle down or we're all going inside, you hear me?"

Kate, the source of all the trouble as usual, got up from the sand, brushing it off her pink bathing suit. She wiped at her eyes, as if she had shed real tears and looked around for someone to take her side. Finding no sympathy, she sat down on the beach and pouted. James, suddenly feeling like a big brother, took pity on his little sister.

"All you had to do was ask nice, you little brat," he said to her. Kate looked up at him, surprised by the gentle tone of his voice and gave him her most fetching smile - an art she had crafted while staring in the mirror in the bathroom.

"You mean you'll teach me?" she said, bubbling as only a seven year old can, her big wide eyes giving away her surprise.

James laughed, knowing he had her in the palm of his hand.

"Yah, follow me, 'Munchkin'," he said to her, referring to the little characters she most liked in her favorite book, *The Wizard of Oz*. Despite its age, the little girl hung on every word of the story each night as either her mother or father read to her from the book's brittle and yellowed pages.

As the two children paddled out in the mild surf, Brian joined Geoffrey in his damp pit and grabbed a shovel. "Girls," he said, muttering under his breath as he helped his older brother dig. "More bother than they're worth." Brian did not respond, of late having other, rather confusing thoughts of the opposite sex. After a couple of minutes, he absentmindedly said, "I guess," to which both boys chortled loudly.

As they laughed together, their parents were also sharing a last delicious moment on the Bay with the day's last breeze at their backs, completely and mercifully oblivious to the winds and rage building behind them.

Seven

~~~ ❧ ~~~

U.S. Weather Bureau
Jacksonville, Florida

It was only seven o'clock in the morning, but Grady Norton had already sweat through his first shirt of the day and knocked off a half pack of Camels. The air was thick with smoke at the U.S. Weather Bureau Hurricane Center in Jacksonville, as most of the staff had either been working all night or had arrived in the early morning after a few hours sleep at home. Norton, the station chief, hadn't been off his feet in nearly thirty-six hours. His anxiety level was so high he couldn't have slept if he had too.

At eight o'clock, the station's forecasters and weather analysts gathered in the sweltering building to lay out what they knew and turn that
~~~

into a plan of sorts. They were determined to stay ahead of this hurricane. Major tempests had nailed Florida twice in the last decade, and both times the Weather Bureau had blown the call. They had been wrong on the direction once and wrong about the magnitude the second time. Either way, the storms amounted to disasters for Florida that took hundreds of lives. The Bureau was far from proud of its track record. At the same time, they had to be sure before they issued a warning that could send the entire state into a panic.

This much they new from ship reports monitored through the long, humid night. Just before midnight the storm had been situated slightly north of Puerto Rico and east of the Bahamas. It was packing sustained winds of well over one hundred twenty miles an hour, and commercial vessels were frantically trying to avoid the killer storm.

One that couldn't was the British tramp freighter *SS Corales* that had been caught in the raging storm even as it tried to flee out of its path. The *Corales* reported the same sickly yellow sky followed by monstrous winds and huge seas. But more alarming was the air pressure reading the ship reported. Even though the *Corales* was at least one hundred fifty miles from the eye of the storm, the barometric pressure had dropped to 27.90 inches *and was still falling*. The Jacksonville station asked the ship's captain to repeat the reading three times. The lowest barometric reading ever recorded - 26.35 inches - had been produced in the eye of the nightmarish Labor Day hurricane, just three years earlier. They were aghast as the forecasters and analysts realized that closer to the center of the hurricane, pressure may have dropped even lower.

As the clock ticked past midnight, reports from ships at sea pegged the storm at just east of the Bahamas, but now packing winds of more than one hundred sixty miles per hour. At two in the morning, the Bureau upgraded the hurricane to a Force Sixteen, the most powerful storm on the Beaufort Wind Force Scale. By sunrise, Grady Norton finally admitted to himself that what he was dealing with was a killer storm - a monster capable of winds in excess of 200 miles per hour. And it was bearing down on the City of Miami with frightening speed.

While Norton fretted over the dwindling supply of messages from ships at sea as they scurried to avoid the storm, Gordon Dunn had been up all night mapping the storm. By 8:30 a.m., he had placed the hurricane at six hundred fifty miles east-southeast of Florida and determined that it was moving at more than twenty miles per hour. If the colossal depression continued on its current course and speed, Miami residents would be staring straight into the jaws of the monster by daybreak Tuesday morning. Dunn was resolute that Norton must send up the flag warning Miami of the impending storm.

"Gordon - y'all sure?" Grady Norton probed his assistant, knowing the answer before he got it. Dunn never made a decision based on guesswork.

Norton could have faith that the conclusions his friend had come to were based on the best and most recent analytical data he could scrounge up. He demanded the action. There was no other option.

At 10:30 a.m. Norton took to the airwaves again, broadcasting the first of many progress reports of the impending storm that he would issue over the next two days to listeners all over Florida. This time, the normally folksy, reassuring voice of the state's highest ranked meteorologist had an edge to it that many listeners picked up with alarm.

"This is Grady Norton, United States Weather Bureau, reporting from Jacksonville," the meteorologist began, his voice steady but with a more serious intonation than his listeners were accustomed to. It was abundantly clear that what the voice of Florida weather had to say needed to be listened to. There was dead silence in the station house, as all eyes were on the perspiring Norton, a handkerchief in one hand, the microphone in the other. Gordon Dunn lit a cigarette for him and passed it over.

"As reported, the severe hurricane now closing in on the Bahamas is located about one hundred twenty miles east of Watling Island or six hundred miles east-southeast of Miami. The entire Florida coast, from Melbourne to Key Largo should take preliminary precautions to prepare for this dangerous hurricane, which, on its present course should reach the Florida mainland in about seventy two hours. Further advisories will be issued as new information on this storm becomes available."

The silence in the room lasted another thirty seconds or so, as each man and woman took in the gravity of the situation, knowing full well what the reaction to Norton's warning would be throughout Florida. Many residents of the state, particularly those living in Miami, had been nervously following news of the storm since the first news on Friday. The Weather Bureau report would now set in motion a host of different reactions by residents long accustomed to the threat of violent storms. Some would prepare to evacuate entirely, heading north to Jacksonville and inland safety. Others would begin to hunker down, deciding to ride out the storm no matter how severe, and begin closing storm shutters or nailing up plywood sheets over the windows of their houses.

All over Florida, there would be a run on dry good stores as those who would decide to brave it out stocked up on flashlights and batteries, candles, kerosene lamps and canned goods. At home they filled every available receptacle - from bottles to bathtubs - with fresh water. In fact, there were few Floridians who hadn't experienced nature at its worst and most knew how to prepare. That same experience was also a serious danger. Some folks had lived through so many storms, they found it hard to get excited about the next one and wondered how much worse it could get. Somehow though, Grady Norton's tone this time had an edge that frayed everyone's nerves.

That was by design. Norton knew all too well the danger of taking one of these storms too lightly.

The 1935 storm still filled his restless nights. He'd blown the call on how severe the hurricane would be, but often wondered if it would have made any difference. People in these parts figured they had pretty much seen it all. He was hoping that attitude had shifted after the disaster three years before.

"Well, that's that, Gordon. We've got the wheels turnin' and God help us, I hope folks listen this time," Norton said, staring out the window in his office. It was a clear day, not a cloud to be seen. The sun beat down on the small station office, making for stifling conditions inside. "Now all we can hope for is a recurve."

Dunn shook his head, then sat down heavily at his desk. He was exhausted, only adrenalin keeping him on his feet. "I dunno, Grady. Suppose we would have seen signs of that already, don't you think?"

The two men were referring to a phenomenon common to hurricanes that were generated off the Cape Verde Islands. It was not unusual for these African coast bred storms to come blazing across the Caribbean, curve around Bermuda, then suddenly turn north into the Atlantic Ocean where they would eventually die in the shipping lanes. Meteorologists referred to it as the process of "recurving".

"Yah, y'all probably right, Gordon," Norton replied. "It would have slowed down some by now – that's always the clue the 'sum bitch is gonna turn northeast."

He looked out the window again, watching the flag in the front courtyard ripple with the light breeze. Norton suddenly felt a wave of fatigue but shrugged it off quickly. There was no time for rest now. He reached into his shirt pocket and pulled out his Camel's, offering the pack to Gordon. He already had one lit.

He took a long drag from the freshly lit cigarette and exhaled into the cloud of smoke that now hung over the room. Every man in the office was practically living on cigarettes and coffee, the tension robbing them all of any appetite.

"I dunno, Gordon," Norton said again, as he sat down heavily in his desk chair, slumping low. "I got me a bad feelin' in my bones 'bout this storm. Ain't felt this way before." He took another long drag.

"This bastard's pickin' up speed while we sit here with our thumbs up our ass," he said in frustration. "Lord Almighty help us… I tell you this 'sum bitch is a mean one, I can feel it."

He turned back to the window, squinting while his eyes adjusted to the brightness of the raging sun, his mind churning with worry about his own family.

"Yep, I tell you we got a goddamned sea devil comin' right at us."

Eight

~~~ ~~~

Stonington, Connecticut

Charles Dewey knew nothing about the state of Rhode Island and less about the City of Newport other than what the two kids in the front seats had told him, but he liked the ring of the name coming off his tongue. From the way the two college kids had described it, Newport sounded like a rich man's playground. It was tempting, but the convict was also smart enough to know that where there were rich people, there were plenty of police to keep them safe and happy. Newport was out.

Dewey and his two teenaged hostages had been driving along the Connecticut shore for hours, driving through towns and villages he'd never heard of. The boys explained that the only way they knew to get to Newport was to follow Route 1
~~~

to Jamestown and that it was at least a three hour trip, maybe longer. Since the escapee had no other plans, he sat back and enjoyed the ride, forcing them to stop only once on the roadside in a small coastal village called Cornfield Point to relieve himself.

He was relatively calm with the young men, trying not to be too threatening so they wouldn't get flustered and attract attention. The boys answered his many questions as they drove, the gun in Dewey's lap being quite a motivator. The huge man looked almost comical in the back seat of the Model A, his head rubbing against the car's headliner. It was a Tudor sedan, so Dewey had to lean back in the seat to avoid being seen through the oversized rear windows. There were few streetlights, and for the most part he could relax in the shadows in the back seat.

"The Rhode Island border is only a few miles up the road," said the driver, who seemed to be the older of the boys. The convict hadn't asked their names. He didn't care and it would make it easier in the long run. "We're just past Stonington… I think it's the last town in Connecticut along this route."

"Get off the main road," Dewey growled in response. "Right here, take a right," he ordered. The boy turned the car down North Waters Avenue and almost immediately they came upon a residential section. They drove in silence, passing slowly by large, well kept houses. Most were dark as it was well after midnight. Dewey told the boy to turn again when he saw a sign that read "Elm Street". It was a dirt road, and the convict's hunch was right that it would lead to the water. They passed by a harbor that was full of what looked like pleasure boats and Dewey nudged the driver to kill his headlights. The boy started to argue, but quickly felt the barrel of the shotgun on the back of his neck. At Island Road they turned again.

"Pull over there, behind those trees," he said, as they reached what appeared to be the end of the road. Dewey could hear the sound of waves breaking ahead, although he suddenly remembered that he had never even seen the ocean. "Get out of the car and leave the keys," he ordered the boys as the Ford came to a stop behind a large tree that blocked out the moonlight. It was almost pitch black.

"Walk toward the water, no funny shit, got it?" he said quietly, leveling the gun at their backs as the three walked in the darkness and on to the beach. Ahead, they could see streaks of phosphorous eerily moving toward them as the mild surf broke on what appeared to be a badly deteriorated wooden jetty that was ahead to the right. Weathered wooden pilings ran from the water up the beach, and Dewey could see that they were bleached almost to the color of ash by the constant exposure to the sun and salt water. The columns gradually got taller the farther they were from the water. He quickly turned his head in all directions to make sure they were alone. The place seemed pretty desolate. This would do, he thought.

"Mister, you can just leave us, ya know..." the younger boy stammered ahead, suddenly turning around to face his captor. He was terrified, his voice cracking. "We won't tell anyone, I promise... and you can keep the car," he pleaded. His friend, afraid to turn around, yelled into to the darkness ahead. "We've both got some money you can have, too," he begged. Dewey did not respond. He was always amazed how people sensed they were about to die and how they would beg for mercy even though they knew there was none to be had.

"You prayin' boys?" he asked quietly, looking over his shoulder again and squinting into the black night.

The older one answered. "I go to church sometimes, with my mother. She's alone, my father died," he said shakily, trying to appeal to the man. "She's sick, old," he added.

Dewey thought about it for a minute. They weren't bad kids, they just had shit luck. There was no possible way he could let them live.

"Sorry about your mother. You got thirty seconds to pray if you want," he said, wryly. The younger boy moaned aloud and peed in his pants, then started to wail. Dewey took three steps closer to the boy who was sagging to his knees and put a shell into his chest, killing him instantly. A bright red mist blew from his back and was carried by the breeze coming off the ocean. Some of it hit the older boy in the face, mixing with the tears streaming down his cheeks.

"Oh, God no, please, please mister, don't kill m..." In less time than it takes for a heart to beat, the boy's life ended as Dewey emptied the shotgun's second barrel into his face. Without a second of remorse, the huge man turned and began walking away even before the boy's body fell to the sand. As he walked back to the car, he suddenly realized he was out of shells, having forgotten to take some from the old man at the liquor store. "We'll just have to find some," he said aloud.

The dark figure cast a terrifying shadow as he walked back to the car with the moon at his back. He lit a cigarette and rested for a few minutes and contemplated a nap in the car. But he thought better of it. Dewey had no problem with killing, but he couldn't stand being around death. He started the car and turned out of the tree stand, making his way slowly back to Elm Street with the lights off, sneaking along the dark roads. A mile and a half farther, he flicked his headlights back on and merged back onto Route 1, continuing east toward Rhode Island.

As he drove, Dewey noticed a cluster of rock houses overlooking the ocean at Wequetoquock Cove. The lights were on in the small cottages and he could smell the smoke from roaring fireplaces. For a moment he let himself imagine how warm and dry it was inside. But before he could finish his thought, the car's headlights suddenly illuminated what appeared to be a huge cemetery draped over a vast rolling hillside. As far as he could see, the moonlit burial ground was strewn with gravestones and small white crosses marking the dead.

The tombstones loomed even larger as he drove by. Abruptly, long finger-like shadows from a stand of wild crabapple trees along the roadside crept out of the night, casting a confusing and intricate web of shadows on the cars' windshield, almost as if the glass were shattered. He felt a pang of fear and swallowed hard.

Fed by a slow breeze coming off the ocean, the trees swayed in the moonlight and caused the shadows to waver. As he drove by, Dewey had a chilling thought that the flickering shadows were beckoning to him, as if there was someone or something waiting for him on the hills inside the sacred and gated grounds. The convict gripped the wheel of the Ford with his huge, hairy hands, trying to push down the gnawing fears that were rising in his throat.

He forced himself to look away from the sea of grave stones; but as he shifted his gaze ahead, he suddenly saw a young boy standing next to a street light marking the entrance to the cemetery not a hundred yards away. Immediately he felt a tug of reality pulling and was immensely relieved to realize he was not alone. But as he drove closer, he saw that the boy was actually a young man who was waving to him, calling him to come closer still. Dewey was drawn to him, suddenly wanting to hear his voice, or even to touch the sleeve of his coat – anything to ground his mind against the irrational fear that was making his flesh crawl. He pulled the car up next to the boy who inexplicably had turned his face into the shadows. Dewey opened the door, cautiously, and called to the boy. The figure did not respond.

The convict took a deep breath, then got out and walked to the boy. Without warning, the young man turned his face towards the giant advancing figure, his features fully lit by the overhead streetlight. The huge man clutched his heart from the ripping pains that shot across his chest, the shock of what he saw almost knocking him down.

It was the mutilated face of the boy, the older of two who had begged him for mercy before he was murdered.

Terrified, Dewey turned to run but fell hard to the ground, scratching the dirt with his hands to regain his footing. He raced to the car and threw himself behind the steering wheel, simultaneously stabbing with his foot at the accelerator pedal. The black Ford lurched forward, its rear wheels spinning on the slick road. The motor's straining insides roared at the sudden and relentless demand for power, but the noise was almost drowned out by the guttural scream coming from the mouth of the driver. The two sounds grew in parallel until they merged into one blood curdling howl, followed quickly by a burst of steam coming from underneath the hood as the engine overheated. Dewey lost consciousness, the air in his lungs finally exhausted from his screams. The car slowed, veering off the road and through a tall, natural hedge of wild junipers before coming to rest thirty yards away in a stand of thick pines. It came to rest not ten feet from the shore of a sprawling pond.

As his massive body slumped unconscious over the steering wheel, the last remnants of sanity that had somehow clung to Charles Dewey's rotting soul, drifted into the rainy night.

Sunday
September 18, 1938

Nine

~~~ ꩜ ~~~

Westerly, Rhode Island

By Sunday morning, the rain had returned to the Rhode Island coast, the brief reprieve of sun and warmth already a memory. The slight drizzle was an irritant but not enough to stop Geoff Lapkin from surprising his wife again by taking the children for the morning and letting her sleep in. Besides, he thought, later today he was going to give instructions to the young college boy he'd hired to help close up the cottage for the season. The kids hated the first signs of shuttering up the place. He might as well give them one last chance to whoop it up.

Leaving Emily still sound asleep in their bedroom, Geoff awoke his children, shushing them so as not to disturb their mother; and as a reward,
~~~

promised them fried egg sandwiches at their favorite hot dog stand in Westerly, just a few minutes away. It just so happened to be next door to the *Flying Horse Carousel,* an amusement ride that had been abandoned by a bankrupt carnival company in the late 1800's and promptly adopted by the town as their own. It was a sort of landmark now for Westerly, attracting scads of tourists during the summer months, and was indisputably Katie's most cherished place "in the whole world".

Miraculously, they left the house without awakening Emily and climbed aboard the blue Cadillac to drive the few miles to Bay Street, almost adjacent to the entrance to Napatree Point. The children were quiet as they traveled the length of Fort Road. It became obvious to them that some of the summer mansions were already closed up for the season. Most of the rest were in various states of being shuttered, and here and there they saw hired college boys busily putting away outdoor furniture, taking down awnings and boarding up windows. The Lapkin kids were silent as they took in the activity. The last day of their summer holiday on Sandy Point was akin to the day after Christmas: a giant let down.

"Let's take a ride through Westerly first, okay guys?" Geoff said -- a suggestion that was met with a chorus of loud protests. The kids knew they were taking the detour only so their father could drive by his factory. Overruled, they drove to Westerly, where traffic was light as most of the tourists had gone for the season. There were church services all over town, which were well attended by the locals; and if you listened closely, you could hear the sounds of parishioners and choirs singing, lilting pipe organs and the harmonious ringing of bells hung high in their steeples.

Geoff swung the car down Elm Street; and as they passed by Christ Episcopal Church, the choir was in its full glory. None of them paid much notice. The family did not attend services, although Katie and Geoff Jr. attended catechism once a week after school.

Neither of their parents was religious, adhering instead to a philosophy that their spiritual lives centered on family, which in itself became their higher power. It wasn't something they discussed much with outsiders, though neither Emily nor Geoff was reluctant to do so. It was just their private choice. They had decided shortly after their marriage that they would not judge others for their religious beliefs, and in return, expected only the same consideration. Unfortunately, there were small-minded individuals who couldn't see the logic in that, and whom busied themselves with gossip about "wealthy atheists". Rather than wasting time defending them, Emily and Geoff simply wrote off those who would sit in judgment of them. It wasn't particularly difficult to ignore people you didn't want in your life anyway.

Slowly winding their way through Westerly, the Cadillac finally turned onto Beach Street where they drove extra slowly by the gates of the George C. Moore Company factory. "Okay, Dad, it's still here. Now can we go to the Carousel?" James asked knowingly. Geoff went to reply, then thought better of it. He knew when he'd been caught and turned back to Watch Hill.

A few minutes later Katie let out a squeal of delight as the Carousel came into view, operating at the end of Bay Street in spite of the light rain. The boys were much more interested in the adjacent hot dog stand named after its owner, a retired factory machinist named "Louie". Geoff parked the car and the three boys sprinted for "Louie's Dogs & Things", actually a converted 1915 Lamsteed Kampkar, a "house on wheels" truck. It had huge wooden wheels and a glaringly bright, circus-like, Kelly green with gold-leaf paint job that Louie himself had managed with a house painters brush. Anheuser-Busch of St. Louis, Missouri had built the specially outfitted rig. When Louie stumbled over it for sale at a garage in Pawtucket a half dozen years earlier, it had just been driven east by a family from Oklahoma who had become disenchanted by the dust bowl life of Midwestern farming. Louie bought it on the spot, tuned it, made some much-needed repairs to the brakes and added the flashy paint job. He then outfit it with "Prest-O-Lite" acetylene tanks that provided him a grill, stove and working lights. Finally he added an oversized icebox and an ice cream maker and the result was a rolling kitchen. He was in business and shortly thereafter retired from the Moore factory in Westerly where he had been one of Geoff's most trusted foremen and a voice of experience that the younger man had come to rely on. In no time flat, Louie's Dogs & Things became as much a fixture on Bay Street as the Flying Horse Carousel. Some local folks thought that Louie's attracted more tourists than the Carousel.

Geoff Lapkin gave a wave and a grin to Louie, who was already sweating profusely in the hot mobile kitchen, as he chased after Katie who had eyes only for a sparkling brown and white palomino on the Carousel. He pointed to his three boys who had already queued up underneath the ordering counter and Louie caught the message. "What'll it be, boys?" he hollered to them while wiping the sweat off his face with a greasy apron.

Katie had already talked an attendant into boosting her up into the leather saddle of her favorite horse as Geoff caught up to her. "You hang on, Katie," he called, "be careful and forget about the brass ring." She beamed and leaned down to clutch the real horsehair mane of her solid wooden steed and rubbed its agate eyes. The attendant stepped back and started up the ride, which quickly picked up speed. The carousel got its "Flying Horse" name from the fact that its horses were not attached to the floor, but were suspended overhead by steel chains. There was no wooden floor, so as the ride picked up its speed, the horses literally "flew" out wide over its dirt floor. Riders were encouraged to grab for a brass ring that was mounted just out of normal reach as the horses flew by. Catch a brass ring, win a free ride.

The seven-year-old Katie had been an enthusiastic rider almost before she could walk. Her first gallop came on her very first birthday, as Emily clutched her to her chest. Baby Katie had laughed out loud in delight, and her three brothers had almost wet themselves laughing. Geoff chuckled to himself as he watched her now; she was still laughing out loud. The little girl reached way out for the brass ring on her next pass, completely ignoring her father's caution. That's no surprise, Geoff thought to himself, wondering how it was that such a little girl could be such a handful.

"Got it!" she shrieked, holding the brass ring jubilantly over her head. Her father simply shook his head. Geoff turned back to Louie's to check on the boys and settle up the bill, but couldn't spot them. He thought they might have walked over to the Harbor to check on the fishing boats coming in and wasn't particularly concerned. He knew that James was very responsible when caring for his younger brothers. Lapkin turned his attention back to his daughter who was still wide-eyed and laughing aloud as the Carousel horse went round and round.

Later, Geoff would recall his lack of concern for his three sons, and regret it. But he could not have known that the boys would meet an intriguing stranger who asked them a lot of questions about Watch Hill on this drizzling Sunday morning, when all but the locals took shelter. They told their father all about their experience on the drive home after he had finally found them wandering on the docks.

The boys were full of wild descriptions of the man Brian described as “a huge, hairy giant”.

They all laughed when Geoff Jr. said he thought the man looked more like an ape.

Ten

~~~ ~~~

U.S. Weather Bureau Headquarters Washington, D.C.

Charlie Pierce ripped a report off the teletype and read it while standing at the machine. The twenty-eight year old junior forecaster from Springfield, Massachusetts was quickly becoming intrigued with the hurricane brewing near the Caribbean, although tracking the monster storm was not his responsibility. He would only become involved if the storm were to slam into southeast Florida, as the US Weather Bureau's Jacksonville station chief, Grady Norton, had forecast, or if it bypassed Florida all together and headed out into the Atlantic Ocean. Only then would responsibility for tracking the storm and issuing further advisories transfer to the Washington, D.C. office. A part of
~~~

him hoped that the killer storm would turn north before hitting Florida, just so he could get a crack at this huge beast. If that happened, he would be in charge of monitoring the ship-to-shore reports from vessels in the storm area - virtually the only "vision" the meteorologists had of the hurricane.

Pierce was low man in the Washington station. His only other job had been as a weather forecaster for Trans World Airlines, and he'd only worked there for a couple of years before signing up with the US Weather Bureau in early 1937. Still, he had an excellent education in the science of meteorology, having studied at Clark University in Worcester and Boston University.

His atypical "blue blood" rearing and education made him a sort of outsider within the Washington station, and consequently his colleagues formed an almost immediate general opinion that he was overly confidant in his abilities. To make matters worse, he was naturally a shy, soft-spoken young man who largely kept to himself - personality traits which unfortunately labeled him as arrogant, as well. But Pierce was oblivious to the whispers about him, focusing instead on his work at the Bureau, which truly invigorated him. It was not unusual for him to be the first one in the office in the morning and the last one to leave the cramped offices at the busy corner of 24th and M Streets at night.

When he read the latest reports from Norton and Dunn late Sunday afternoon, Pierce also noticed that the approaching storm had not yet shown any signs of "recurving" to the open waters north of Florida, as Cape Verde Island hurricanes were prone to do. He found it hard to believe that a storm of the magnitude being reported would make landfall in such a powerful condition. The consequences would be enormous, no matter how much warning time Florida residents were given by the Bureau's forecasters. He didn't envy the heavy burden of responsibility that Norton and Dunn were shouldering and imagined the tension in the Jacksonville station. Pierce knew the two veteran forecasters mostly by their significant reputations, but had instinctive respect for the two. They served in one of the most volatile weather environments among all the Weather Bureau's locations, and the weight of the decisions the two men routinely had to make in the face of such killer hurricanes would bring many a man to his knees.

At any rate, it would be some time yet before his colleagues in Jacksonville were going to be able to make the final call on this storm - it was still at least four hundred miles away from Key Largo and a lot could happen over the next forty-eight hours. Even with his limited experience, Charlie Pierce had learned that there was no more fickle lady in creation than the weather. She could love you and kill you in the same day, and there might only be a few hours of romance in between.

No sooner had he finished reading the teletype than the machine began spitting out another report, this one from a commercial freighter located well south of Cuba on the fringe of the storm which shed some light on its barometric pressure, speed of winds and travel, and the size of the "eye".

Pierce's own eyes widened as he read with alarm that the recorded pressure was 28.73 and falling and that the storm had picked up a bit of speed, now tracking northwest at twenty-two miles per hour. Based on analysis performed by Norton and Dunn, the estimated size of the eye - the very center of the storm where air pressure was at its lowest -- was staggering. The two veteran forecasters believed it was more than fifty miles across and packing sustained winds in excess of one hundred eighty-five miles per hour.

This was no beast, Pierce thought. This was a monster storm that was going to raise unchecked hell no matter where it landed. A direct hit on Florida was almost unthinkable. Even if the winds died considerably, the tidal surge driven by such low barometric pressure would be cataclysmic. And if God had mercy on them and the storm eventually did recurve, he guessed that it would raise havoc along the northeastern seaboard - even if it skirted by fifty or more miles offshore.

He had a fleeting thought about the possibility of the hurricane somehow reinvigorating itself after a near miss on Florida. It could pick up some steam as it absorbed warmer waters and then… but no, he thought, Cape Verde storms always veered to the north and eventually committed suicide in the cold northern waters.

Then the young forecaster felt an unnerving chill creeping up the back of his neck as the next logical question came to mind.

But what if it didn't?

Eleven

~~~ ~~~

Wequetoquock Pond, Stonington

Charles Dewey was also up early on Sunday morning.

It was still raining at dawn when he awoke in the front seat of the stolen car, cold and groggy. The convict painfully pushed his oversized body off the steering wheel he'd been draped over for several hours. It took a few minutes for feeling to return to his arms, numbed as they were from being caught under the dead weight of his heavy upper torso the entire time. As his head cleared, he anxiously looked around, not sure where he was.

Nor was Dewey aware of what had happened to him. The frenzied anxiety attack he had experienced hours earlier had sent a surge of
~~~

adrenalin through his body, increasing his heart rate and breathing to the point where it had nearly cut off the flow of blood to his brain and causing him to black out. Now he was fully cognizant again, but he was jittery and his throat was parched. He instinctively reached into his coveralls and was relieved to find the bottle of whiskey still there. The giant of a man drank down nearly half the pint in one swig, then lit a cigarette. He sat for a few minutes more, letting the alcohol and nicotine do the job of dulling his nerves.

Kicking open the car door, he stepped out and for the first time realized how close he had come to going into the large pond just a few feet away. Dewey didn't think he was far off the road, but the good news was that the car was well hidden in the grove of pines and he could afford a few minutes more to rest. He had no idea where he was, trying to remember the name of the town one of the boys from last night had mentioned. "Stone" something, he thought. He sensed that he hadn't driven very far from there.

For a split second he recalled the beach and murdering the two boys. He grinned as he remembered the older of the two begging him for mercy. He liked it when they did that. But then something bothered him - it felt like an itch on his brain and he couldn't scratch it. He hit the side of his head a couple of times with the palm of his hand as if to knock water out of his ears after a swim. The itch was still there.

He pulled out the bottle again, and the drink seemed to make it go away. Lighting another cigarette he thought about what he should do next, but after a few minutes decided to get back in the car and continue east and see where it took him. The only thing that worried him was the police and he figured they wouldn't be looking for him this far away from the prison. Besides, what did he have to lose?

Dewey got back in the car and pulled slowly away from the pond, carefully accelerating so as not to dig the rear wheels into the soft, damp earth near the shoreline. He had to maneuver the car back through some heavy brush; but as he did, the road became visible.

Just as the convict pulled back onto Route 1 near the Rhode Island border, he remembered he needed shells for the shotgun lying across the front seat. "Shit," he swore under his breath. His furrowed his thick, heavy brow as he considered the problem.

As the car picked up speed, he rolled down the window to let some of the light rain blow into his face. The cool dampness triggered some raw sense that reminded him that he was a free man again, his lonely months and years in prison just a long, bad memory. Instinctively, he let out a whoop of celebration, snarling like a circus big cat who'd escaped the cage and its tormentors.

And just like the animal, he now had an insatiable appetite for killing, just for the sheer and thrilling pleasure of revenge.

Twelve

~~~ ঌ ~~~

Stonington Beach

Middletown Police Detective Sergeant Irv Nicklas and his partner pulled up to the crime scene at Stonington Beach a few minutes after 11 a.m. on Sunday morning. The drive had taken them two hours even with the unmarked car's lights on and siren blaring. Nicklas was pissed and in no mood to take shit from anyone. Melvin Hills, a gentle old man who never had a bad word to say about anyone or anything, was an old friend of his. Late Saturday morning, the veteran detective had been called to the murder scene in the Middletown Liquor store that Melvin had owned for more than three decades. Nicklas spent the rest of the day looking for evidence by sifting through the gore left from the savage blow to Hills' skull.
~~~

Whoever had killed the old timer had nearly decapitated him with the blood drenched length of pipe Nicklas had found lying on the floor next to Hills' body. The bastard hadn't even bothered to wipe his fingerprints from the cast iron pipe, which was either plain stupid or an extraordinary show of arrogance or indifference. The cash register had been emptied, which implied that robbery had been the motive for the killing. But Nicklas wasn't convinced. The horrific way that Hills' skull was smashed suggested whoever murdered him might have done it just for fun. The detective had been a cop for nearly twenty-five years and had seen more than his share of bloody accidents and killings. But looking down over the remains of Melvin Hill's head, he thought he'd never seen anything quite so savage.

The report on the fingerprints that Nicklas' pathology guys had taken off the pipe had been phoned in from the FBI lab in Washington, D.C. late Saturday night, and the results didn't really surprise him. The guy they were looking for had escaped earlier in the day from the Wethersfield Prison, no more than ten miles away from downtown Middletown. His name was Charles Dewey, a real loser doing twelve years the hard way for armed robbery. The thirty-two year old prisoner had an arrest record the thickness of a cheap paperback and it was clear there wasn't much he wasn't capable of. The Prison had supplied a photograph of the man, which caused Nicklas to catch his breath when he saw it.

"This fuckin' guy looks like he stopped a friggin' truck with his face," the detective said to his partner, Sam Cawley. "Holy shit, you can almost understand why the guy's so pissed. "Christ, fuckin' Frankenstein would look like a goddamned Hollywood gigolo next to this asshole."

Cawley chuckled. "Hell, tell me how you really feel about him, Irv." The two men had been partners for eleven years and read each other like a book. "Let me see that." Nicklas passed him the photograph.

Cawley whistled at the sight. "Goddamn. That boy could scare the freckles off a redhead," he swore.

"Prison records say he's six foot eight and weighs more than four hundred pounds," Nicklas continued. "And he's supposedly real anti-social, although you gotta wonder about anyone who'd wanna get close enough to him to make friends."

"You think this is our guy?"

"Well aside from the fingerprints on the murder weapon, you moron, just look at that face," Nicklas chided his partner. "I'd book the son of a bitch just based on the look on his puss. There's already an APB out on this bastard, but let's fire it out again with new details. Murder one," he added, referring to the felony charge for murder in the first degree which alleges the act was premeditated.

"Yah. This freak just earned himself a date in the electric chair," Cawley said. "But if you're right about him amusing himself with the pipe and old man Hills' head, chances are he won't hesitate to do it again. "In fact, the son of a bitch might want to do it again. We need to find Mr. Dewey pronto."

The phone call from the Stonington Police came early Sunday morning. Nicklas asked the investigating officer not to remove the bodies of the two teens until he got there.

"There's one other thing, Irv," reported Nicklas' counterpart in Stonington, a Detective David Meir.

"We found identification on these two young fella's that says they are students at Wesleyan. Ain't that up your way?" Meir asked.

Nicklas swallowed hard. "Hell, yes, Dave. Try to keep the press out of this until I can get word to the school, okay?" the detective responded. "No telling where the kids are from, Wesleyan's a pretty fine college and they come from all over the states. I'm sure it will take some time to notify the next of kin. I know the Dean of Affairs and I'll call him right away. See you in about an hour."

The two bodies were covered but still lay in the positions they had been found when Nicklas and Cawley rolled into Stonington. Detective Meir took them through the few facts they had been able to pull together.

"Coroner says time of death was sometime after midnight, probably closer to one in the morning," Meir reported. "Both kids have money in their wallets, still wearing pretty good watches. Think we can rule out robbery. One took it in the chest, the other point blank in the face. Looks like the work of a twelve gauge - shit there's pieces of these two boys spread all over the beach. Goddamn seagulls were pickin' at em' when we got here around eight o'clock this morning."

"Who found them?" Nicklas asked.

"Couple of older folks; I know them. Out walking the dog. Don't think the missus will ever recover," Meir said. "They're over on the other side of the jetty if you want to talk to them."

"Anything else?" Cawley asked.

"Yah, just one thing. We found a fresh set of tire tracks about sixty yards off the beach," Meir told him. "Looks like a Goodyear tread, something like you'd find on a car, maybe a Chevy or a Model A."

"Well, that certainly narrows things down," Cawley said sarcastically. "Mind if we take a look at the bodies?"

"Suit yourself. Hope you didn't have breakfast."

The two Middletown detectives gently pulled the drape off each of the victims, and the veteran cops took their time to assess the wounds and any other injuries or pertinent facts. They also tried to assess the facial expressions of each at the time of death. That was only possible with the younger of the two college students, the other no longer had a face.

"Poor bastard, never had a chance," Cawley said. "I'd guess the bigger one knew it was coming, might have seen his friend shot. A hard face to forget."

"Yah," Nicklas responded. "But at least one mother will be able to take a final look at her son,

son of a bitch…" The hardened detective felt bile building up in his throat. He fought the urge to puke. The two detectives regrouped with Meir.

"Don't think we're gonna get any prints out of this, Irv," the Stonington detective said. "So far, all we've come up with are a couple of cold cigarette buts over by those trees. 'Camel's for sure, but that ain't worth shit. We also found some footprints around the tire tracks, three sets. We're going to try to make some casts. Two sizes - a couple that are probably eleven, maybe twelve. The other ones must have come from a fucking gorilla. They gotta be size fifteen or better. Maybe closer to twenty. I've never seen anything like it. Only the big ones return to the car. The light rain helped to preserve them, otherwise they probably would have drifted over with the wind.

"It would seem we're looking for a pretty big man, you think?" Meir asked Nicklas.

"Seems like a safe bet. I think we're looking for the same guy, Dave," Nicklas responded. "All the pieces fit. Kids are from Middletown where my guy ended up dead, and we got the footprints of a fucking cave dweller. That sure as hell fits the physical profile of one Charles Dewey, the con that escaped from the Wethersfield Prison sometime late Friday afternoon."

"He's got the kids car - where do you think he's headed?"

"Well, he's been traveling southeast… I'd bet the son of a bitch is still headed that way. He's poor southern trash, can't imagine he knows anything about New England. Let's see now, he's got at least a ten hour jump on us, maybe as much as twelve," Nicklas said, glancing at his watch. "Hell, he could be as far as friggin' Maine by now."

There was silence as the three men absorbed what they knew.

"I dunno, Irv," said Cawley. "Dewey's been running since he scooted his jail cell. I got a feeling he's holed up in one of the towns within twenty miles of here. Someplace on the Rhode Island coast."

Nicklas considered his partner's thought. Cawley had great instincts which he rarely challenged. No sense in starting now.

"You might be right, Sam. Dave, can I impose upon you to update the APB and make sure it's gotten into Rhode Island?" Nicklas said. "I think Sam and I are going to mosey on up the coast a bit, see what we might find."

"Sure, Irv. Police Chief in Westerly is a good friend of mine; I'll let him know you're going to be in his neighborhood. Good luck, guys," Meir responded. "Do me a favor and nail this motherfucker. I'd like to be there myself when you find his freak ass."

Nicklas stuck out his hand. "I'd bet a C-note that this guy'll put up a fight. Hell, what's he got to lose?"

"Certainly not his looks," Cawley said sarcastically.

Neither of the Middletown detectives had any idea that Sam Cawley's hunch was on the money.

Nor would Charles Dewey give either of them the chance to celebrate it.

Thirteen

~~~ ~~~

Watch Hill Harbor

While police in Connecticut, Rhode Island and Massachusetts were scouring the roads and countryside along more than one hundred fifty miles of coastline, Charles Dewey had followed Route 1 into Rhode Island. He saw signs for Westerly and Watch Hill and was intrigued by the latter, if for no other reason than he liked the name. He was impressed by his luck thus far following his escape, and figured he might as well let his instincts continue to dictate his actions.

The convict was feeling reenergized, having already had the good fortune to come upon a closed filling station just off the road near Wequetoquock Pond that also served as a general store for the local farmers and fishermen. He had pulled the Model A
~~~

behind the dirty white clapboard building, keeping an eye open for any signs of activity inside. There were none that he could see, and a large "Sorry, We're Closed" sign hung in the front door.

Dewey found a tire iron in the trunk of the car and tried to pry open a heavy lock on the back "Dutch" type door; but making no progress, he simply shattered a window in the top half and reached inside and released the upper deadbolt. The door swung open. He hoisted his huge frame over the bottom section and was inside the building in less than sixty seconds.

The convict went straight for the cash register but couldn't get the cash drawer open, even after he hoisted the two hundred pound device over his head and threw it against a concrete wall ten feet away. He decided not to waste any more time with it, opting instead to load his arms with several large boxes of 00 buckshot shells, a couple of heavy wool blankets, some rope, a heavy, police issue flashlight and some extra batteries. He threw the stuff into the car's trunk and went back for more, finding a thick wool mackinaw coat that barely fit him but would at least hide a portion of the filthy coveralls he wore. He wondered if this is what people meant when they said, "He's like a kid in a candy store," as he picked up a dark green cap with a *John Deere* logo embroidered on the brim.

As he was leaving, Dewey noticed a glass case in a corner that was chained and locked. It was filled with new hand guns, ammunition and a dozen or more hunting knifes. He smashed the case with his tire iron and grabbed a Smith & Wesson .38 and a long, polished, hunting knife with a serrated blade that looked like it could cut through oak. It felt good in his hand.

Finally, he grabbed a couple of five gallon cans of gasoline and headed the Ford back out onto the road, having found what he needed without discovery. A few miles up the road he left Route 1 and drove slowly into Watch Hill, hoping to find some place to hide out for awhile, knowing that he couldn't stay on the road much longer. The escapee stayed to the main road until he came to Bay Street, overlooking a sizeable harbor. With the car hidden behind a grocery store, Dewey turned up the collar of his new wool coat and pulled the lid of the hat low over his eyes, then began walking toward the harbor. Light rain was still falling so the streets were fairly deserted, but he could hear church bells pealing. The sound of carnival music and the smell of meat being grilled caught his attention and he went looking for it. A hundred yards ahead he found the source.

Dewey was starving, not having eaten since his lunch at the prison nearly two days before. He remembered the cash in his pocket which he had stolen from the liquor store and made straight for Louie's Dogs & Things. From behind the counter, Louie saw the lumbering giant heading his way and swallowed hard. The short order cook didn't think he'd ever seen a man so large. As the escaped convict got closer, Louie was sure of one other thing. He had never seen a man so cruelly ugly.

"What'll ya have there friend," he said in his most friendly voice to the behemoth looking down at him in the trailer. Dewey literally had to duck under a short, roll out canvas awning Louie had rigged for foul weather or a bit of shade. The owner would try anything to put the customer in a better frame of mind - and this was one customer he hoped was in a good mood.

"Gimme a couple of hamburgers," the man said quietly, almost mumbling the words. Louie wrote down the order on a pad and looked up into Dewey's face. The look in the man's black eyes, set back so deep in his skull in dark pockets startled the cook, causing him to involuntarily flinch. It was the look of a man tormented and wounded. He'd seen the same look only once before, when he had gone hunting for the only time in his life. He had dropped a huge, eight-point buck that he and a couple of buddies had tracked for hours with a rifle shot clean through the heart. When he went closer to examine his kill, the look in the poor beast's lifeless black eyes glistened with terror. The experience had shattered him and he was sick over it for weeks. As he stared into Dewey's face, Louie felt like he was looking into the eyes of another dead animal.

He quickly tried to recover from the start, stammering out, "Do you… I mean, do you want…"

The convict's face seemed to harden even more. "Is there a problem?" he asked quietly again, but with a bit of a growl in his voice.

"No, of course not… there's nothing… I just wanted to know if you wanted something to drink?" Louie managed to spit out.

"Coffee."

Louie turned quickly away from the huge man, terrified of him without really understanding why. He busied himself at the grill. "Coming right up, sir," he said trying to sound as matter of fact as possible, only turning around when the food was ready. The stranger paid him and left without another word. Louis shrugged it off and went about his business.

Dewey sat down at a table near the trailer and ate in silence, trying to keep as low a profile as possible. He looked around the area, seeing nothing of much interest. Three boys came out of nowhere and ran up to Louie's counter. They seemed to know him. Must be locals, he thought. He watched some more. The boys ate their sandwiches without giving the convict a second look, then began walking over to the docks. The huge man stood up from the table as discreetly as possible and followed them from a short distance away.

The biggest of the three seemed to be in charge, Dewey thought. He sized them up and concluded they were brothers, all with sandy brown hair and similar facial features. The boys ran down a long dock to a charter fishing boat that was pulling in after several hours of casting for bluefish about two miles off the Atlantic side of Napatree Point. The captain of the boat waved to the boys as he proficiently nosed the bow towards a pier at the end of the dock, then cut the power to one engine and swung the stern of the forty-five foot high-bridge cruiser neatly against the dock. A deck hand threw a length of rope to a waiting James who caught it on the run and tied off the stern with an expert "Waterman's Knot". Then the boy stepped quickly to the front of the boat where the Captain himself threw him another line which he tied around a pier with an equally skilled "Running Bow-line" knot. James beamed. He had become intrigued by the craft of maritime knot-making, and worked hard all summer learning from various charter skippers stuck in the harbor by the poor weather.

The Captain gave the boy a salute for his help and then waved all three boys aboard to help unload the morning's catch. Dewey looked on from the other end of the dock, careful not to look too interested. If not for his immense size, he might have been mistaken for a deck hand on any one of the large fishing boats tied up in the harbor. He lit a cigarette and looked out over the harbor.

There was money here, he thought, wherever the hell he was. He could smell it. The houses he saw on the drive through the village reeked of it. Dewey figured that they were mostly summer places for wealthy folks. The finely trimmed lawns and shrubs gave that away. He could see beyond the harbor that all along the coastline there were cottages - hell, wooden castles, he thought. Sailboats were everywhere. He might be the son of a southern dirt farmer, but he was smart enough to know that where there are yachts and mansions, there's money.

A plan was beginning to form in his head. If he could get enough money together, he might be able to convince some freighter captain to sneak him out of the country. Anywhere but here, he thought, where he had no future, except for a few minutes in the electric chair or swinging from a rope. The thought made him shudder.

His thoughts drifted back to the boys as he noticed them walking down the dock in his direction. The huge man lit another cigarette and waited patiently for them to walk by. He didn't have to. He saw one of the kids, the smallest one, pointing at him from twenty yards away. The boys slowed their progress towards him, obviously wary of him. At ten feet, they stopped and just stared at him.

Dewey made like he was looking out over the harbor and overheard one of them say, "Jeez, Louise - can you believe how big he is?" He flicked the butt off his finger tips and into the water, then suddenly turned toward them and said "Boo!", the word coming out of his mouth like a projectile. He laughed out loud when all three of them jumped and ran several feet the other way, as if he was going to chase them.

Still laughing, he called to them. "Now wait a minute, boys. I didn't mean to scare y'all. Just foolin', that's all."

Brian was the first to say something. "Man, you scared us. Just how big are you, mister? Are you mad at us?" The boy was plainly still frightened of him.

"Nah, I ain't mad, pretty much used to folks lookin' hard at me, being so big and all," Dewey said in as gentle a voice as he could muster. "I reckon you ain't seen someone's big as me before, huh?"

"No sir, mister," James said, trying not to show he was afraid too. "We didn't mean to stare." Geoff Jr., normally not afraid of anyone or anything, clutched James pants leg, holding on for dear life. He was trembling.

"No hard feelin's boys. Tell you what. How's about I buy you a soda to make up for scarin' you. What do ya say?"

Geoff Jr. and Brian looked up at their big brother, waiting to see what he would say. James felt their eyes on him and knew he couldn't show fear. "Sure," he said. The younger boys smiled, feeling more comfortable knowing that James wasn't afraid of the man.

"Lead the way, son," Dewey shot back. "Say, you boys live around here?" he asked as James led them to a small wooden shed on the docks that doubled as a bait and tackle shop and snack shack. There was no response. He told himself to slow down. "Tell the man what you want boys," he invited.

With a Coca-Cola bottle in hand, James invited the man to sit on the dock with them as they drank, their legs hanging off the edge above the water. Dewey took him up on the offer, but when he sat down and hung his legs over the side, his feet went into the water. That was all Brian and Geoff Jr. needed to see. Despite James giving them the evil eye, the two boys couldn't stop laughing. Even the convict laughed again.

"Hell, I guess I do look a mite ridiculous sittin' here with my boots in the ocean," he said, and laughed again. He took off his hat and pushed his long, greasy black hair off his forehead, tucking it back under the cap. "So you boys from around here?" he asked again, hoping they were comfortable enough now to feed his curiosity - and perhaps his plan.

James didn't hesitate this time. He was almost feeling sorry for the man. The guy needed a haircut and his pants were pretty dirty leading the boy to the conclusion that the man was poor along with being the ugliest, scariest person he'd ever laid eyes on.

"Yah, mister, we live in Westerly during the winter, but in the summer we move out here to Sandy Point. You can see our house from here. See it, it's out there near the tip of the land?" James pointed to the family's mansion across Little Narragansett Bay. The house was silhouetted against the gray sky and Dewey couldn't make out many details accept that the house was large. Very large.

"You mean with your family, right? You live out there with your family?" he probed.

"Yah," Brian chimed in. "With my mom and dad and my stupid sister, Kate."

"And Shelly," Geoff Jr. added, not wanting to be left out of the conversation."

"Oh," Dewey responded, trying not to appear too eager. "Who's Shelly?" he asked.

"She's our housekeeper. My dad works a lot and he's not around all the time so my mom needs some help during the day. Shelly lives with us in Westerly, too. She's just like family," the oldest boy explained.

"Almost like a grandmother," Geoff Jr. said. "But she's not dead like our other ones."

They all looked at the small boy. "Moron," Brian teased.

"What did I say?"

Dewey grinned. "You mean there's no man around during the day to help your mother? It must be hard for her with all you kids."

"Nope, just some times my father hires some college guys to help out on weekends and at the end of the season when the house needs to be shuttered," James responded, telling the convict just what he wanted to hear.

"I see. Is there a college boy out there now helping out?" he dug a little deeper.

"Yah, some guy named Andy; I don't know his last name. He goes to Brown. He's nice."

"Brown? " Dewey responded, unsure of what the boy meant. The three of them looked up at him quizzically.

"You're not from around here, are you mister?" Brian said. "Brown University. It's in Providence."

"Oh, that Brown," Dewey said, shaking his massive head up and down like he knew of the place. "Say, how old is this 'Andy'?"

"Geez, I don't know, mister," James said, caught off guard by the question. The convict realized he had gone too far, made the boy suspicious.

"Aw, doesn't matter. It's just that I have a boy of my own in college, I was wonderin' if they might be the same age." Dewey lied, congratulating himself on the quick recovery. James nodded and let it drop.

The four finished their sodas in silence. "We gotta get back now, mister, my dad will be looking for us," James said.

"Sure," Dewey said. "Well it was nice gettin' to know you boys. I hope you do good in school this year. Maybe I'll see you out there on, what is it again, 'Sandy beach'? Is there a road out there to your neighborhood?"

"It's Sandy 'Point', mister," Brian responded. "And yah, Fort Road goes all along Napatree Point, then hooks a right onto Sandy Point right where the Fort is. It's paved and it goes all the way to the end where we live."

"The 'fort'? What fort?" Dewey probed again.

Fort Mansfield, mister," James said. "You aren't from around here, are ya?" There was no response. "It's an old abandoned military fort that used to have some big cannons. My dad says the Army built it about forty years ago to defend against anybody trying to invade Long Island. But they made some mistakes building it and closed it down a long time ago. All that's left now are some old concrete buildings and underground rooms."

"My dad says we can't play there anymore, cuz my mom thinks it's dangerous," Geoff Jr. said.

"That so..." Dewey said, already feeding the information into his plan. "Well, you boys better run along now. See ya round."

James ran off in the general direction of their car parked near the Carousel, with his two younger siblings close behind. Dewey got up and walked over to the shed, half hiding in the building's shadow, watching as the boys grew smaller in the distance. Then he watched as a man, perhaps their father, appeared and seemed to be scolding them. He saw the oldest boy point back in his direction, but his father ignored him and continued to scold him. Then they walked away together, the three boys walking behind the man, obviously having been chastised. Only Geoff, Jr. turned and looked back in his direction. The giant man raised his right hand as if it were an imaginary pistol and fired at the little boy. The child's eyes grew wide with fright. He turned his look away, quickly and grabbed his father's hand.

Dewey waited until they were out of sight and a few minutes longer. Sure enough, a dark colored Cadillac convertible pulled out of Bay Street and took a left onto Fort Road. As he watched, the luxury car drove out onto Napatree Point, past the huge mansions the convict had seen earlier.

He figured it was early afternoon by then and slowly walked back to his car. The hulking man looked almost clownish behind the wheel of the Ford. He was so big it almost appeared that he was wearing the car. He thought for a few more minutes before starting it, plotting out a plan that would bring him out to Sandy Point later tonight. But first he needed a place to hide. It was just a matter of time before the police found him in the stolen car.

He pulled his hat down lower over his brow, put the Ford in gear and turned down Bay Street to the entrance to Fort Road. Fort Mansfield, he thought. Underground rooms. It sounded like just the kind of place he needed to hole up in for awhile. He reached under the front seat to make sure his shotgun was still where he had hidden it.

He'd need it when he began his own invasion.

Fourteen

~~~ ~~~

Chelsea Piers, New York City

The *RMS Carinthia* rocked gently at Pier 54 of the Cunard-White Star Terminal in New York City, the motion all but imperceptible to the six hundred passengers who had spent most of the morning boarding the magnificent passenger liner. They were preparing for a two-week cruise to the Caribbean that would make port in Kingstown, Havana, and Nassau. The weather had not been cooperative; it was rainy and cool, and the mostly well heeled patrons who had booked passage on *Carinthia* were eager to depart for the sun and warmth of the islands to make up for the summer's wretched weather.

As tradition would have it, the ship's Captain greeted each and every one of the First Class
~~~

passengers as they stepped off the gangplank and onto the pristine "A" deck, where the wealthiest of the *Carinthia*'s passengers were quartered in luxury staterooms. The twenty thousand ton steamer could actually accommodate more than sixteen hundred passengers, but the Great Depression had dimmed the popularity of the autumn winter cruises. Nonetheless, a full compliment of crew was aboard to wait on every passenger's whim for the duration of the cruise.

The decidedly Australian parlance of Captain A. C. Greig's "British" accent was essentially lost on the majority of the American passengers whom he greeted with a cheery "G'day, sir!" But those few Brits making the trip almost immediately wrinkled their nose at the good Captain, despite his Hollywood-like, chiseled handsomeness, and wondered in whispers how it was that an Aussie had come to skipper one of the Cunard-White Star Line's most elegant ships.

"I'm afraid the gentlemen from down under have never quite mastered the length of their vowels, my dear," explained a representative of the British Ambassador's New York staff to a fellow guest at dinner that same evening. "Pity. The country has enjoyed entirely unexpected success in the face of its humble roots as a penal colony of the British Crown," he said to a lovely twenty-something Manhattan heiress who had instantly captivated him and whom he was desperately trying to impress. She was one of a number of wealthy young American beauties on board. They were unmistakable with their finely made up faces, a bloom of pink or peach on their cheeks and their hair coiffeured in the silky wave that had become high society's fashion rage. Typically they were draped in mannequin-like couture, which most of the seamstresses who were buried in the bowels of Fifth Avenue had liberally interpreted from Parisian designs. But the complete look simply glowed of youth, fashion and femininity and lent a somewhat seductive ambiance to the *Carinthia*.

Captain Greig was not quite as smooth as most of the grand masters of the British ocean-going passenger liners. But what he lacked in aristocratic polish that made some of his constituents more popular, he more than made up for with his extraordinary leadership and seamanship skills. He was a no-nonsense man of somewhat slight build yet he rarely had to repeat an order as he was remarkably well liked and respected by his crew. Most of them had experienced the Captain in action in severe weather of some sort or another plying the Liverpool to New York run across the treacherous North Atlantic.

Greig was proud of his charge; and indeed, the *Carinthia* was a grand lady of the oceans. Passage on her was coveted by those fortunate enough to have escaped the infectious ruins of Wall Street after the stock market crash of 1929. Admittedly, she was not quite as impressive as the "Olympic" class liners that had been the unofficial flag ships of the Cunard-White Star Line following a merger of the two giants of the shipping world in 1934, when each had encountered serious financial difficulties. But *Carinthia* more than made up for her more diminutive scale with fittings and accoutrements worthy of the opulence of the legendary White Star Line's *Titanic.*

Carinthia was a floating luxury palace, complete with swimming pools, a gymnasium, a five thousand square foot arena for sporting events, a theater, racquetball courts, massage and shower facilities, instant running hot water in spacious paneled suites with oversized beds and silk sheets. On "A" Deck, Cabin Class patrons could enjoy a cigar in a smoking room which emulated the expressionist style of the famous Spanish painter, El Greco.

Despite her regal trappings, *Carinthia* also represented the challenges of a tiring industry, beset with overcapacity in a dwindling market but banking on a recovery that would support the return on investment required by the ongoing construction of the Cunard-White Star Lines' new "Queens": the juggernauts *Elizabeth* and *Mary.* Consequently, the *Carinthia* was removed from the transatlantic route on which she had built her fame, and was now deployed as the ultimate in luxury winter cruise vessels.

Shortly before casting off, one of the last passengers to board the ship found the welcoming hand of Captain Greig at the entrance to "A" Deck, his handsome wife and children in tow.

"I say, Mister Revson, it is indeed a pleasure to have you sail *Carinthia* again," Greig said, energetically pumping the outstretched hand of his frequent and very important passenger. "And, my dear Mrs. Revson," he turned to the millionaire's wife, "I dare say that you have that unique quality of growing in beauty with every passing day." The portly woman blushed.

"Why Captain, if you are half as gracious to the rest of the women on this boat, then you must have to padlock the door of your quarters at night," Ancky Revson replied. Her husband, the rotund Charles Haskell Revson laughed aloud at the unabashed flirting between the two and wrapped a heavy arm around his wife's shoulders.

"I regret to acknowledge that you are a slight more fit than I am, Captain Greig; but I promise you my lack of muscle will not stand in the way of my determination to hold on to the girl of my dreams," Revson said, laughingly. "In short, old fellow, you shall have to wrest my bride from me."

"Well, then, if I shall have to resort to force, so be it," Greig responded in mock determination. "Please join me at my table at eight sharp tonight, sir, and we shall divide and conquer." He paused for affect. "You should anticipate two bottles of a rare 1921 Dom Pérignon that I recently happened upon in Havana, of all places. I cannot think of two other people with whom I would rather share them."

"Delightful, old man," Revson responded, playfully slapping the back of his old friend who had invited him to dine at the Captain's table more times than he could count over the last decade.

Charles Haskell Revson was a driven, hard charging millionaire who ruled the US cosmetics industry. He had come to know Greig from his frequent passages on the transatlantic route to Europe, where he bought and sold cosmetics and fragrances for the company he founded that bore his name, an emerging darling of post-crash Wall Street. He was renowned for his high-handed and often grossly imperious behavior in the corporate boardroom. However, when aboard a ship under Greig's command, the wealthy man displayed an almost reverend-like respect for the Captain, much to the amazement of Revson's business associates.

"Well, then, we shall see you tonight, my friend," said Revson. There was a twinkle in his eye already. "Come along children before the Captain tires of your behavior and throws you overboard like so much chum." He turned to go, then remembered something.

"Captain Greig, if I may," he said, suddenly serious. "Before leaving this morning I caught a bit of news in the *Times* that talked of the makings of a dreadful hurricane approaching Florida sometime within the next several days."

"You are correct, Mr. Revson, and please note that my crew are keeping a watchful eye on this storm, and regularly apprising me of its progress."

"Oh, I have complete faith in you, Captain," he said, smiling. "It is nature I distrust. I should guess that there is little chance that the *Carinthia* will encounter this storm, no matter its track?"

"Again, you are correct. We will steer along the coast on a decidedly western track, which will keep us, at a minimum, at least one hundred miles distant from the hurricane at all times," Grieg informed him. "At any rate, old friend, this beast shall more than likely turn north and avoid southern Florida completely. I further predict that it will then blow harmlessly into the North Atlantic. They almost always do."

He turned to Mrs. Revson and bowed. "And so my dear, all you need concern yourself with over the next two weeks is the watchful eye of this admirer, and I dare say the possibility to steal a kiss when the old man isn't looking."

She squealed with laughter. "You are incorrigible, Captain," Mrs. Revson said.

"Yes he is, my dear, and he worries me," her husband said. "I dare say if the man is as good a philanderer as he is a sailor, I should fret for the safety of your virtue."

At precisely noon, Captain Greig gave the order for *Carinthia* to cast off her lines. The great vessel was then slowly maneuvered by four heavy tugs into the deep waters of the Hudson River. Passing by the Statue of Liberty some minutes later, she blew her horns in tribute, and Grieg saluted from the Bridge as he always did when entering or departing New York Harbor.

Then, he called out a course that would take *Carinthia* due west, where the United States Weather Bureau assured him he would find only mild wind and precipitation as the consequence of the approaching hurricane.

But certainly, he thought, absolutely nothing to worry about.

Monday
September 19, 1938

Fifteen

~~~ ஃ ~~~

Jacksonville, Florida

Despite the oppressive heat, every one of Grady Norton's two dozen meteorologists and forecasters showed up for work on Monday morning, and as usual wore their ties pulled up tight in their collars and their suit jackets buttoned as they entered the office. Although Norton did not crack the whip on formality, he didn't have to. His men were professionals, for the most part well educated and intensely serious about their work.

Nevertheless, wearing a business-type suit and tie had a certain symbolism for the men, known only to them. Looking as crisp and professional as any doctor, lawyer or judge was just one of the silent ways they fought back against the criticism that had been building up against the United States
~~~

Weather Bureau for the last several years, primarily sparked by the agency's blown call in the 1935 Florida Keys fiasco. The criticisms were pointed. The United States Congress simply thought the Bureau lacked professionalism. By the end of the day, the tropical heat of Florida had wrung them out, and the ties became a little looser, the jackets hung on the back of a chair and shirt sleeves were rolled up. That was alright with Norton, though. Late day in the Weather Bureau Hurricane Center just looked like it was inhabited by sweating, hard working professionals.

In the days following the 1935 Labor Day hurricane, congressmen whispered to the media about the Bureau's practices, especially the lack of a visible training program, and the inferior management of the Department of Agriculture to which it reported. The criticisms were harsh but not untrue. Secretary of Agriculture Henry Wallace was more concerned with selling to Congress his unpopular strategy of slaughtering pigs and plowing up crops to increase prices for the commodities of financially desperate farmers than he was about improving the performance of the Weather Bureau.

The nation's elected representatives also had other things to worry about. Both sides of the congress were busy fighting FDR's supposed blatant disregard for the Constitution as the President took bold actions designed to lead the country out of depression. Career men like Grady Norton knew that it would only be a matter of time before Congress took a bead on the Weather Bureau, and shuddered at the thought. He often said to anyone who would listen that if there was anything that could make his agency less efficient, it was congressional "assistance".

On this Monday morning however, which had begun for Norton and half his crew long before sunrise, there was a more ominous threat to consider. The killer hurricane now bearing down on a hard track for Miami at fifteen to twenty miles per hour occupied every thought of the men inside the nondescript Bureau headquarters in Jacksonville. The forecasters and meteorologists pored over oversized charts spread on long rows of draftsman-like tables that filled the offices.

The obvious order that ruled the office was overtly ironic considering the chaos the men were tracking, which was whipping the ocean off the Florida coast into a maelstrom of destructive force.

Shipping reports of the hurricane's progress were getting harder to come by now that word had spread amongst seafarers to avoid the storm, which was roughly five hundred miles off the coast. Still, there was enough information coming in to convince Grady Norton and Gordon Dunn that the hurricane was continuing on to the southern Florida coast with winds packing a punch of one hundred fifty-five miles per hour. Devastation was inevitable if the storm held its current path.

"Hell, Gordon, twenty-four hours ago I might have thought this damn thing would turn. So many have before," Norton said to his friend and colleague. "But she ain't giving me any reason to think she's planning on heading north and acting more like a lady."

It was true. Instead of slowing down, as most Cape Verde hurricanes did as they cleared the Caribbean waters, this storm was accelerating. Its unusual behavior convinced the two men that this hurricane would not veer north as they hoped, but instead would pick up speed and slam into Florida.

"I agree, Grady," Dunn responded, fatigue and worry etched into his lined face. Neither of the two men had had more than a few hours rest since Friday and they were both ready to drop. Only adrenalin and the burden of responsibility they felt kept them going.

"We're just not getting any help from the 'Bermuda High', so there's nothing in the way between goddamned Cuba and Miami. I think we need to take this to the next level, boss. It's called for," Dunn continued.

The 'Bermuda High' Dunn referred to was a huge high pressure system - several thousand miles in diameter and as much as eight miles high - that sat over the western Atlantic Ocean predominantly over the summer months. Moving in a clockwise rotation, the system was generally centered over Bermuda, and naturally pushed air from as far west as the Gulf of Mexico north across the southeastern portion of the continental US coast. Sometimes it would even continue into New England before veering east out into the Atlantic Ocean. Cape Verde-type hurricanes usually ran smack into the

Bermuda High, which often would slow the storm's forward progress and slowly force it to turn northward. In that event, the hurricane would eventually smother itself over cold waters.

"Just once, Gordon, I wish y'all' would tell me I'm crazy," Norton chided his friend with a tired grin.

Dunn took a deep drag from his cigarette, mulling the comment. "Hell, Grady, if I did, that would make me crazy too."

Resigned to the inevitable, Norton picked up the microphone to update the thousands of Florida listeners who were by now hanging onto the senior meteorologists' every word as the hurricane approached. Already, stockpiles of water, blankets, lanterns and batteries, canned goods and other necessities of life in a hurricane belt were being depleted across the southern tip and eastern coastline of Florida as wary residents prepared. They'd been through this drill before. Traffic across interstate routes was also increasing as some folks thought better of waiting out the huge storm and took the decision to evacuate, moving south to safer ground. Norton was careful to keep his voice even as he spoke into the microphone. Any sense of alarm in his words or manner would spook the state even more and make matters worse.

"Good morning, this is Grady Norton of the United States Weather Bureau reporting from Jacksonville," he began. "As reported, the severe hurricane approaching Florida is now located about five hundred miles east-southeast of Miami. The storm is currently tracking towards the mainland at fifteen to twenty miles per hour, and sustained winds of more than one hundred fifty miles per hour have been reported. The entire Florida coast, from Melbourne to Key Largo should take preliminary precautions to prepare for this dangerous hurricane, which, on its present course should reach the Florida mainland in about twenty-four hours. Residents are advised to take all precautions in advance of this storm, including evacuation of the coast and low lying areas. Further advisories will be issued continually as new information on this storm becomes available."

Norton slowly put down the microphone and sat wearily behind his desk, looking out the window at the hot sun rising over the horizon, which was already pushing the mercury well into the upper nineties. There was silence in the room, broken only by the continual chatter of the station's multiple teletype machines.

This was the time the career forecaster hated the most. He was all-powerful in predicting the storms' path, but completely powerless to stop it. The tired Norton clenched his fists in quiet frustration. Then he composed himself and turned around to face his men, who seemed to be waiting for him to say something. Norton lit yet another cigarette, took a deep drag and blew the smoke out slowly.

"Well, hell y'all… it ain't rainin' yet, is it? Let's round up as much new data as we can before the noon briefing," he said steadily, digging down into his inner reserves to appear calm, sharp and in charge. "We've still got time, boys."

There was silence in the room other than the steady rhythm of the teletype machines.

"Well, goddamn it... what's wrong with you boys?" Norton bellowed. He had suddenly realized they were afraid.

"Why ain't one of y'all trying to prove Grady Norton's a tired old coot with his head up his ass?" he hollered out to them. "Shit, when I was your age I'd do just about anything to prove the boss was wrong." He turned and looked to Dunn looking for corroboration. "Ain't that right, Gordon?"

Dunn smiled, knowing what his friend wanted.

"Well how would I know, Grady? I'm younger than you," Gordon Dunn replied. Someone laughed. "But I sure would like to take you up on that offer to prove you're full of shit... 'Boss'." Before Norton could respond, the room erupted into laughter and you could almost hear the pressure of stale air being released from the room.

A smile across Norton's face further eased the tension. "Why you sound like a man bucking for a promotion, Gordon," Norton replied. He leaned back into his chair and put his large black wingtips up on the desk. "Only trouble is..." The room exploded again at the tit-for-tat exchange between the two administrators.

"But I'll tell you what, Gordon, and you can pass on the offer to your friends here. Any man who can prove my forecast wrong gets a twenty dollar bonus on the spot and free beers for a month." A nervous titter came from the audience this time.

"And trust me boys, this is one time I'd be happy to be wrong, he added."

"Hell, Mr. Norton," a voice suddenly interrupted from a desk near the back of the room. A young man, beads of perspiration on his face, slowly pushed back his desk chair and stood up. All eyes in the room were upon him. "With all due respect, sir, you can stick your twenty."

Norton, taken aback, did not respond.

"My folks who live in Key Largo, just barely made it the last time," he said, his voice dropping off. "They found my Grandfather's body…what was left of it. He was sandblasted to death, flesh all stripped off his bones."

The young man balled his fists in anger as he spoke. "We ain't gonna make the same fucking mistake again, Mr. Norton."

"Hell, no sir."

Sixteen

~~~ ~~~

The Elm Street Elementary School, Westerly

"Katherine Lapkin, you are sorely trying my patience, young lady!" the teacher admonished the student, in truth, having finally lost her patience with the obnoxious child.

"I have warned you repeatedly about chatting with your friends in the classroom as if it were a Sunday afternoon at the beach. Now be still, do you hear?"

Kate slunk low in her seat at her wooden desk which at times seemed like an anchor tied to her waist. She fidgeted in her seat for a second, pausing to consider a very unlady-like response of which she was entirely capable of devising and delivering with a razor sharp tongue. The girl opened her
~~~

mouth to speak but was rescued from making another mistake by the ringing of the lunch bell. Instead, she coyly smiled at her gray-haired teacher, Mrs. Carol Crandall, effectively signaling the exasperated woman to stuff it. But the veteran of thirty-odd years of classroom skirmishes was not about to let the impolite little girl have the last word.

"Kate, I think the two of us will have lunch together here in the classroom today. The rest of you may go," Crandall said in a more composed voice. "Now be careful on the playground after lunch, and boys, no fighting." The classroom of thirty-eight students at the Elm Street Elementary School in Westerly emptied quickly as the children in Crandall's second-grade class fetched their paper lunch bags or metal pails from under their desks, formed a single line and marched to the lunchroom. After a fifteen minute break to eat the sandwiches and sweets prepared by their mothers earlier that morning, the class would join the other two hundred seventy-nine students of the school on the playground where they would be allowed to play for a half hour, rain or shine. For an unbridled thirty minutes, all the children would run, scream, holler, sweat and essentially do whatever else compelled them to release the pent up energy that came with being cooped up for several hours in an unventilated room. All but Kate, that is.

Mrs. Crandall sat at her desk for several minutes after the classroom emptied, making several notes on the fastidious records she maintained of the academic performance of each child in her charge. The kindly woman had been at her trade long enough to welcome to second grade the children of students she had instructed much earlier in her career. Such was the case with Kate Lapkin, whose father Geoffrey had been her student when Crandall was a just a year removed from her two-year certificate studies at Mount Ida College in Newton Corner, Massachusetts, a stones throw from the Brighton neighborhood of Boston.

She married within weeks of her graduation, moved to Westerly where her husband worked, and began teaching at the Elm Street public school that very year. The couple had been unable to have children, so Carol Crandall dedicated her motherly desires to doing the best job she could in helping generations of children learn to love to learn. Parents clamored to place their children in her class, not only because of her remarkable skills and kind manor, but also because she was brilliant at guiding young boys and girls through the vitally important second year of school, where learning to read fluently was the utmost objective.

In all her years of teaching, Carol Crandall had been challenged by more than a few "Kates" - children who were exceptionally bright for their young age with social and language skills far advanced over their peers. These children were labeled "precocious" by adults, but in truth they were often behavior problems, whose constant grating against authority and instinctive glibness routinely landed them at odds with their elders.

Worse, their peers tended to shun them, put off by what they interpreted as haughty and condescending behavior. Kate Lapkin was a classic case who had already crossed swords with Crandall even though the school year was only weeks old, and she appeared to have few if any friends.

"Kate, why don't you come up here and sit next to me for awhile," Crandall said kindly to the girl, still sitting alone at her desk. "Let's have our lunch and talk for awhile, okay?" Kate was unresponsive, but slowly approached the teacher's desk and took a seat in the chair beside it. The young girl silently opened her brightly painted pink lunch pail, a gift from her father on which he had drawn the letters K-A-T-I-E in bright red block letters. It was one of Kate's most treasured possessions.

Crandall took an apple from her desk drawer and began polishing it with a handkerchief. "I wonder if something is troubling you, Kate," she said in a matter-of-fact tone, hoping the child would take the bait and open up. The girl remained silent. "We really do need to talk about this, Katie…"

"There's nothing wrong, Mrs. Crandall. No, there is nothing wrong indeed," Katie suddenly shot back, irritated. The teacher caught the edge in her voice and the obvious fire in her eyes. She didn't respond immediately.

"Well, there must be something on your mind, Kate. Here it is only the third week of school and this is the fourth conversation I've had with you on your behavior," Crandall said. "Now, either you or

I are going to talk about this, or I'm going to discuss it with your parents." Kate flinched.

"Which will it be?"

The seven-year-old girl sulked, hating to be cornered. "Okay," she said quietly.

"Okay? That's not telling me much. What I want to know, Kate, is if there is something bothering you that is making you angry," the teacher prodded. "That's exactly how you behave - you seem angry with me and your classmates. In fact, you seem angry with the whole world."

Kate looked up from her lunch pail, a deep frown on her face.

"Whoa," Crandall said. "Let's hope your face doesn't freeze like that!" she said laughingly, attempting to elicit a smile from the girl. Katie's eyes narrowed. She wasn't in a smiling mood.

"My brothers make me mad!" she suddenly blurted out. "For heaven's sake, they're always making fun of me and beating me up. I'm just sick and tired of it."

Crandall was silent, hoping the child would continue.

"In fact, I'm thinking of leaving Napatree Point and going to New York City," she continued, doing her best to look serious. Crandall had to stifle a laugh at the look on her small face. "I'm going to get as far away from my brothers as I can. Why, I'll just get my own apartment near Central Park." Emily and Geoff had taken the whole family to the city at Christmas time. The memory of riding through Central Park in a horse-drawn carriage was still fresh in her mind. Crandall raised her eyes in surprise.

"No one will miss me," she added.

"Well, it certainly sounds like you've been thinking about this problem. Is that what's bothering you, dear child?" Carol Crandall said. "You mean to tell me that you're letting your brothers make you unhappy? Why, I'm very surprised, Kate."

The girl looked up at the teacher. "Why?"

"Because you are simply too smart to let them get the better of you, " she said, positioning herself as a friend to the child. "You know, I'll bet they make fun of you because they're jealous."

Katie looked puzzled and disarmed. "Jealous of what? What could they possibly be jealous of? I'm smaller than they are, they have more friends than I do…for jiminy sakes, I'm a girl!" she added in frustration.

Crandall was actually relieved at the source of the girl's tension. Sibling rivalry was more real and painful than most adults understood and she shifted her tone to steer the conversation where she knew from experience it needed to end.

"Now Katie Lapkin, you listen to me," the teacher said firmly, in mock indignation. "First, you should be proud to be a 'girl' - a very smart and pretty one, I should add -- who will someday be a fine lady just like your mother. I never want to hear you say that you're 'just a girl again'." Katie's eyes widened.

"Second, size doesn't mean a thing, young lady. They might be bigger than you physically, but what really counts is how big your heart and your brain are. Why some of the most famous and accomplished people in the whole world were little people. Take me for example," she said, chuckling. "Why I'm only five-feet-one-inch tall and there probably isn't one student or parent in all of Westerly who doesn't know my name enough to say hello." She paused for a moment, letting her words sink in. "They always greet me with a smile, too."

Finally, Kate smiled. "You are famous, Mrs. Crandall. My dad says you were the best teacher he ever had. The prettiest one, too."

The gray-haired teacher laughed out loud. "Well, I always did say your father was one of the smartest students I've ever taught. No wonder he's so successful. Now you go home tonight and tell your brothers to stop picking on you or they'll have the famous Mrs. Crandall to answer to. Got it?"

Katie beamed. "Yes, Mrs. Crandall. You're not going to tell my mother about this, are you?" she asked hopefully.

"I don't think so, Kate. It will be our secret. I don't believe you and I will have any more trouble getting along this year. And that's good - we have so much to accomplish in such a short time. Now when you finish your lunch, you can go outside and play for the remainder of afternoon recess," she added, smiling. Kate jumped up from her chair and ran to put her lunch pail under her desk.

She turned back to the teacher. "Thanks, Mrs. Crandall, I feel better now."

"You're welcomed child," she responded. "But Katie, before you go, would you make me a promise?"

"Sure!" she said without an ounce of insincerity.

"Someday when you really get an apartment in New York City, will you invite me for tea at the Waldorf Astoria? I just love their crumpets."

"Wouldn't that be fun?" Katie squealed. "And we could invite my mother too. Just the three of us! Well now I can't wait to grow up and have our date!"

Crandall laughed aloud again. "Don't hurry child, don't hurry."

The afternoon passed without a trace of hostility from the girl, and Carol Crandall was no longer concerned with Kate Lapkin's behavior. At day's end, as she stood watching from a large window of her second floor classroom, the children climbed into a school bus to go home. She was surprised when Katie stopped at the door of the bus, turned and waved up at her. Crandall blew a kiss and waved to the elated little girl who suddenly adored her teacher.

Katherine Lapkin grinned from ear to ear as she took her seat in the bus. There was nothing she liked more than making a new friend. Especially, a "secret" friend.

The school bus lurched into gear and began its circuitous route through Westerly. The driver, "Old" Pat Collins, had driven the same path every afternoon for the last seventeen years. He barely had to glance at the road he knew the route so well; and with light traffic during the school year, Collins often found himself watching the antics of his young riders in the rear view mirror. A lonely widower long retired from the docks, Pat Collins looked forward to the hour he spent each morning and afternoon picking up and delivering the elementary school students of families throughout Westerly, including the village of Watch Hill and down along Napatree Point to Sandy Point. He had little else to occupy his time since his beloved wife, Rosalyn, had passed some eight years prior. The bit of time in the school bus with his rambunctious cargo helped him get through the long winters he faced alone in his small house on the Westerly bluff overlooking Watch Hill Harbor.

The small cottage had been his wife's passion; she had so loved the salt air and the feel of the nearly constant ocean breeze that enveloped it. For Collins, the stone and slate-roofed home was a constant reminder of their days together that nipped at his soul. He knew he needed to leave the place for his own good; but at the same time, he could not bear the thought. Tending to the children gave him a much needed reprise from his sadness.

During the first few weeks of the school year, before the Lapkins moved back to their home in Westerly at summers end, Brian, Geoff Jr. and Katie were the first students he picked up in the morning way out on Sandy Point. In the afternoon, Katie was the last one off his bus. Her two brothers always took a later bus home after sports practice -- football in the fall, basketball in the winter and baseball in the spring. On the ride home with Collins, Katie always sat directly behind the driver's seat to make it easier for the two of them to chat for the few minutes they were alone together each day. He looked forward to their conversations.

Today, he noticed right away a happier look on the little girl's face. She must have had a good day at school, Collins thought. He liked seeing her so happy and animated, busy in conversation with a schoolmate sitting next to her.

The old man laughed to himself as a thought crossed his mind that just as a picture was a thousand words to some folks, a word was a thousand pictures to the little girl. She could strike up a conversation with just about anyone. Yep, Katie Lapkin could probably charm a Trappist monk into singing Christmas carols with her, he reflected, stifling a chuckle. Then he winced, for just as quickly, another thought came to his mind, a troubling one. For all her intelligence, the little girl was far too naïve to understand that there are certain people in the world she shouldn't talk to, the kind of people who are just too mean and evil to share words with. The school bus driver made a mental note to speak to her about the danger of talking to strangers.

Unfortunately, by the time he dropped Katie off on this rainy Monday afternoon, Pat Collins was preoccupied by a faulty spark plug that was causing the school bus engine to miss, and the lecture temporarily slipped his mind. It was unfortunate for Kate, perhaps, but good fortune for just the kind of person that Collins' worried about.

And he was sleeping not more than two hundred yards from the spot where Katie Lapkin stepped off the bus.

Seventeen

~~~ ~~~

The Westerly Police Department

"We found the car in the Yacht Club parking lot. The son of a bitch is here alright," Westerly Police Chief Gil Cianci told the two Middletown detectives, not even attempting to hide his aggravation at the discovery of the black Ford Model A earlier that morning. A patrolman who had stopped at the Club's back entrance for his daily coffee saw the nondescript automobile parked in a corner of the lot adjacent to the beach and recognized it from the Connecticut license plate numbers. The plates had been noted on the APB that had been revised following the discovery of the bodies of the two murdered college students in Stonington, Connecticut.
~~~

"At least it ain't the tourist season, Gil," Irv Nicklas said to the police chief, trying to lighten the mood. "You must be pretty much down to the locals now."

"Yah, and from what you've been telling me about this creep, picking him out of a crowd shouldn't be too hard. But why the fuck did he have to perch in Westerly," Cianci responded sullenly.

"Just think of it as your chance to grab the headlines, Chief," Sam Cawley responded in a tone that suggested he didn't have much time for whiners. "What say we get down to business here before this asshole gets a chance to reduce your population - okay?"

"Yah, yah, keep your shirt on," Cianci said, bristling under his collar. He had to cooperate with these two pricks from Connecticut, but he sure didn't have to like it. "What do you want to know?"

"Well for starters, are your guys looking for him? I mean this isn't a very large town…"

"Of course we're 'looking' for him," Cianci answered, not even attempting to hide his irritation. "We don't all clean fish for a living here."

Cawley shook his head in resignation. "Okay, okay, I'm sorry. Just a little cranky after sleeping in the car all frigging night with my partner."

"Was it as good for you as it was for Irv?" Cianci chided the detective. The three men all laughed, taking the chill off the conversation. "Well, for starters, I've got two patrol cars specifically looking for this ape. As soon as we finish here, I'm going to send a couple of men to the docks and a few more to check house-to-house along the waterfront. Tell you the truth, that's about the limit of my resources."

Nicklas pulled a handkerchief out of his jacket pocket and wiped his brow. It was still raining but the humidity was awful. He walked over to an open window of the chief's downtown Westerly office and looked down from the second floor to the street. There wasn't much activity to see in either direction.

"I take it Westerly rolls up its streets come the cool weather, hey Chief?" he said stoically to Cianci. "Don't think we're going to find our man out taking a casual stroll. What say we get those two patrol cars to take a closer look in the places he might be hiding? Like you said, a man the size of the state of Rhode Island should be easy to pick out. Well, you can bet he knows that too and is laying as low as possible. Unless you got any other ideas."

Cianci mulled it over for several minutes before responding. "I guess our best bet is along the docks, and maybe Napatree Point. A lot of the places out there are boarded up now for the season or in the process of being shuttered. There's a lot of beach out that way, plenty of places to hide, especially out by the old Fort."

"Fort? " Cawley asked. "Westerly has a fucking fort?"

"Like I said, Sam..."

"Aw shit, I didn't mean to be insulting. What 'fort'?" he repeated.

Cianci took in a deep breath trying to maintain his composure. These two were really getting on his nerves. He lit a cigarette and leaned back in his worn leather chair.

"Fort Mansfield. It's out at the end of Napatree, right at the bend for Sandy Point. Or I should say, its remnants. There's not much left of it."

"Go on," Nicklas said, intrigued.

"Goddamned government built it around the turn of the century, some kind of artillery placement designed to protect Long Island Sound from invasion," Cianci continued. "Apparently it wasn't worth a shit because it was only opened about five, maybe six years. Story goes that they found some kind of flaw with it and shut it down quick. It was a complete waste of fucking money, as usual."

"So what's left of it?" Cawley asked.

"Not much. Guns are all gone, of course, and there are some old buildings and underground rooms and tunnels. It's pretty much grown over and has been flooded a few times. Can't imagine our friend would find it very cozy."

"Yah," Nicklas said. He had a feeling that by now the convict was cold, hungry and exhausted, which would make the shuttered up houses a better place to hide. "Chief, you got a fire department in this town?"

Cianci cringed at the slight. "Yah, running water and toilets too. What'll they think of next?"

he said, sarcastically. Nicklas acted like he didn't notice the Chief's irritation.

"Well, maybe you could enlist the fire department guys to help out with the door-to-door checks," the Middletown detective offered. "Otherwise, I'm afraid our boy's going to get all snuggled up out there and we'll never find the motherfucker."

The man might be an ass but he wasn't a complete idiot, Cianci thought. "Good idea. Chief is a friend of mine. Jero Panciera. I'll give him a call right away, see what help he can give us."

"How about swinging a car out by Fort Mansfield?"

"It's quite a bit off the road, better to see if we can get some of the firemen out there," Cianci said.

"Make sure you tell the Chief this asshole is assumed to be armed," Cawley added, not at all sure about the fire department idea. "He hasn't hesitated to get nasty, Gil."

"In fact, I've got a hunch he's a real sick bastard. The more he hurts people, the more he enjoys it."

Eighteen

~~~ ~~~

Fort Mansfield

Beachcombers enjoyed rainy days on Napatree Point, especially when working the Atlantic side. The mild surf brought all kinds of treasure to the beaches, which were separated from the grand mansions by three- to four-foot high concrete storm walls. It was a beach picker's paradise.

Along with a daily wash up of shells and multicolored sea glass, the numerous wrecks off the coast supplied a continual stream of flotsam and artifacts from ships sunk as far back as the seventh century. Perhaps the most famous of the ships lost off the peninsula was that of the *SS Larchmont,* a two hundred and fifty-two foot long wooden paddlewheel steamship that went down four miles southwest of Watch Hill on February 12, 1907.
~~~

Steaming through heavy seas in a blinding snowstorm, the *Larchmont* was rammed by the coal laden schooner *Harry P. Knowles* and sank in less than ten minutes. Only nineteen men were saved from the disaster, which saw the loss of as many as three hundred thirty-two passengers and crew. Many of them had smade it into lifeboats but perished from exposure in the zero degree weather. Bodies washed up on the shores of Napatree Point for weeks after. More than three decades later, china and silverware, ships hardware and personal belongings continued to wash ashore.

Tyler James Griswold, a drifter who had walked the beaches off Watch Hill for more than two dozen years, knew what to look for and what it was worth. No one knew his age or much else about him, but he was well known to property owners along the spit of land jutting out from Watch Hill Harbor, and most folks just gave him a wide berth as he walked the shoreline. He was harmless, never seemed to bother anyone and never asked for anything. "Tiger", as he was known, was more an enigma than a problem. No one knew where he came from or even where he went each evening after hours of sweeping the beaches in search of treasure to pawn or barter. No one really cared.

On this rainy Monday afternoon, Tiger's olive-green rubber poncho was slick from the ocean spray kicked up by the surf and a strong breeze. He didn't mind being a little wet, although the salt water did make a gnarled mess out of his long, unkempt beard. Griswold hadn't had a shave or a haircut in years, and with the hood of the poncho pulled up over his head, there wasn't much of his face to be seen. Having combed the Bay side earlier in the day, he'd been walking the Atlantic side all afternoon and had only robbed the ocean of a few of its prized shells and a few interesting pieces of sea glass. Although, he had found something else that puzzled him -- a curious set of very large foot prints along the upper beach, far from the beachcomber's normal path at the edge of the surf.

From time to time, he studied the huge footprints which tracked all the way from the Watch Hill Yacht Club (which he visited each morning to scavenge food out of the trash) right up to the bend where Napatree Point took a sharp turn to the north and became Sandy Point. It was there that Tiger noticed the tracks left the beach and went off through the brush and trees that marked the bend, right where the remains of Fort Mansfield were supposedly located. There were no mansions here and no sea walls. This portion of the beach was still uninhabited even thirty years since the government had abandoned it. Tiger liked it that way.

The footprints worried him, not because of their size, but because they seemed to be heading directly toward the remnants of the Fort. That could mean trouble for the weather-beaten drifter. He dug inside a pocket in the poncho and retrieved one of his few personal possessions, a folding "Buck" knife with a six-inch steel blade. Griswold had traded for it years before at a pawn shop after he'd had a particularly lucrative day on the beach. He used it as a tool of his trade and had never thought of it as a weapon. Today, as he carefully unfolded the shining blade from its walnut handle, the thought occurred to him that he hoped he'd never have to use it as one. Silently, he left the beach and entered the underbrush.

Moving inland, Griswold stopped, having picked up a scent. He'd learned to trust his nose. On a battlefield in France twenty years before, he had ignored an odd smell that hit him almost immediately after he had climbed out of a sandbagged trench, following orders to take back the thirty yards of scorched and barren ground that his platoon had lost the night before in a brazen raid by the enemy. What little he remembered of the incident was his surprise at the smell of fragrance - similar to a woman's perfume - that struck him as he raced across the patch of land, and the sickening sweetness of the air. He remembered little else.

Griswold awoke hours later in a field hospital several miles back from the front, his face and hands covered with oozing burns and yellowish blisters, and his lungs full of deadly mustard gas. Tiger somehow survived but spent more than a year in a French hospital recovering. His injuries left a terrible toll. Now, the quiet man had only about forty percent capacity in his lungs and still wore the scars of horrible burns, only partially hidden beneath his beard.

This wasn't anything more than smoke from a camp fire, he guessed, but the smell was definitely coming from the area of the Fort where one of the

Crozier eight-inch disappearing artillery guns had been placed. Crouching low, he made his way forward, taking great pains to remain invisible in the brush. He stopped about seventy-five yards away from the concrete frame that stood as an entrance to a series of underground rooms and tunnels beneath what was left of the surface buildings. It was hard to make out the structures as a former military post. They were so overgrown with brush and wild vegetation to be almost hidden within the oasis that was surrounded by dunes and beach on two sides. On the backside of the installation, Fort Road ran through the bend about fifty yards off.

The burning smell became more intense as Griswold finally spotted a plume of gray smoke wafting up from one of the underground ventilation shafts that dotted the entire military complex. Either someone was cold or hungry, he thought, or maybe both. Either way, that was a problem.

Griswold retreated about twenty yards and made his way west back to the beach before turning north and then returning inland to the backside of the ruins. He knew of another entrance to the underground rooms, another entrance which would offer him the best chance of surprising whoever it was that had invaded his own hiding place.

Tyler James Griswold had been living in the ruins for more than five years, in a small underground room that he had blocked off from the labyrinth of tunnels running throughout the Fort. The small chamber offered him shelter and peace from the prying eyes of people who had a difficult time with his disfigurement. He didn't mind being a hermit who shuttered out the world. In fact he was quite comfortable with his life of solitude. However, he had no intention of giving up the little space he had claimed for himself. It was a place where he could endure his nightmares on his own terms.

The drifter was lean from his harsh lifestyle and still relatively agile and quick for his age. After checking the brush all around him for signs of danger, he dashed some forty yards along a path that was barely visible and heavily overgrown to the back entrance of the building. The door itself had long ago disappeared and the light on the stairs below him quickly disappeared, so he paused for several minutes to allow his eyes to adjust to the darkness. He was quite experienced with the art of finding his way through the maze of tunnels below in which there was virtually no light. Although he used the stubs of candles that he scrounged out of the Yacht Club's trash to light his private chamber, he knew the tunnel leading to it by feel and required no light. Silently, he began to descend into the staircase, the big knife firmly in his grasp.

At the bottom, more than twenty feet down, he paused for another moment to listen. Hearing nothing, he began to creep slowly through the tunnel that would take him to his room. His hands occasionally brushed the concrete block walls and he stopped every few strides to listen again. There was silence. Only the odor of smoke told him there was anyone inside.

When he got closer, a soft light began to show at the point where the shaft emerged into a large vestibule which must have served as a muster hall when the Fort was operational. The light came from ventilation shafts, now uncapped, which allowed slivers of light to penetrate the underground blackness. Various tunnels shot off this damp cavity beneath the earth, creating a virtual labyrinth of hallways and smaller rooms that had been sleeping quarters and for the storage of provisions. They were all empty now, except for the small compartment that Griswold had staked out for himself and which he had carefully hidden with discarded lumber and wooden crates left behind by the military. Even with a flashlight, the entrance would be hard to discern amongst the rubble.

Griswold clutched the wall just outside the atrium, staying away from the light. He held his breath, listening, but still found only silence except for the slight howling of the ocean wind that perpetually blew through the tunnels. Turning to the left, he inched forward into the vestibule, hugging the outer wall, and crept closer, mindful of the number of steps he was taking. He had long ago memorized the exact number of paces that would take him from the end of the tunnel and around the outer edge of the great room to the opening of the shaft leading to his private chamber. He didn't need light to find his way home.

A little more than twenty yards away, a huge, lone figure of a man sat hunched in front of a roaring fire that he had built in a pit beneath a large ventilation shaft. Several candles lit the small, cave-like room Dewey had discovered earlier that morning when he had spied Griswold emerging from the underground complex. The visitor had watched the gaunt-looking man walk off in the direction of Watch Hill. It didn't take him long to discover the secret of Fort Mansfield, and armed with the flashlight he had stolen from the general store in Wequetoquock the day before, he eventually stumbled into Tiger Griswold's hidden room.

Even after hours in front of the fire, Charles Dewey still couldn't shake off the cold that had enveloped him during the long night on the beach. At least he hadn't been discovered, and the military ruins the boys on the Watch Hill Harbor docks had told him about fit his immediate needs perfectly. In fact, Dewey had found a lot more than he had expected.

It certainly wouldn't pass for luxury, but the room he found was at least as comfortable as the prison cell he had previously called home. There were plenty of blankets and a straw mattress, enough candles to light the entire space, some books, containers of food and water and even a shotgun with several boxes of ammunition. Dewey had no idea who the man was who lived here, didn't care either. He expected whomever it was living in the underground crypt would return at some point, and the convict knew he would have to deal with the man.

The giant gazed into the fire, pondering his next step. He could stay here probably no more than a couple of days, although the chamber was hidden well enough that a search party might miss it. But if he could find it, someone else sure as hell could too, so he knew he would have to move again and soon. Dewey wondered if the cops had found the car he had abandoned last night.

His contemplation was interrupted by the slightest of sounds, his nerves frayed to the breaking point by extreme anxiety. Another man might not have heard the faint crunch of dirt beneath one of Tiger Griswold's worn leather boots, but Dewey sprang to his feet, the sawed-off shotgun he'd stolen from the old man in the liquor store in his hands. He had taken off his own shoes to dry them so he made his way silently to a spot adjacent to the hidden opening, out of view of anyone coming through. The convict didn't have long to wait.

Griswold, thinking he had the edge of surprise and his courage inflated by the feel of the hunting knife in his grip, made the decision to burst into the room and physically confront his invader. It was a mistake.

At the instant he emerged through the doorway, Dewey crashed the butt of his gun down on Griswold's head. The drifter never knew what hit him and dropped, motionless, to the hard cement floor, the knife still in his hand. The convict reached down and pulled back the hood of his victim's poncho, revealing the grotesquely disfigured face. He stared at the man but was unmoved by what he saw. Instead, he kicked the knife out of his hand, grabbed the stranger by the collar of his heavy sweater, lifted him off the floor and dropped his body onto the straw mattress. Dewey wasn't sure if he had killed the man, but didn't think so. He sat back down in front of the fire to see if the stranger would wake up.

Some minutes later, the convict watched as Griswold stirred on his bed. Eventually, he pushed himself up to a sitting position. Through bleary eyes, only then did he see the huge attacker who had knocked him nearly senseless. For a moment, Griswold thought he was imagining things as his vision slowly cleared. The blurry shape in front of him was simply too enormous to be real. Rubbing his eyes furiously, he looked again to find he was not mistaken. He sucked in his breath with terror as he made out the ape-like appearance and coal black eyes that alone could scare a man to death.

"Shit," he mumbled, trying not to show his fear. "What the fuck do you want? This is my stuff… just leave, will ya?" Griswold said shakily, hoping the beast in front of him would just get up and go.

Dewey sat silently, eyeing the smaller man. "I don't want your crap," he growled. "Just looking for a place to sit for a while." The murderer had been studying the unconscious drifter, wondering about the scars.

"What the fuck happened to your face..." he asked Griswold without emotion. The words came out more as a statement than a question.

"The war... German mustard gas."

"Fuck."

"Yah." The two men lapsed into silence, studying each other.

Tiger spoke first. "What's your excuse?"

"What do you mean," Dewey responded, unsure of the question.

"Why do you look so fucked up... at least I have an excuse."

A smile came to the convicts' face, but his features were so bizarre that it seemed to take the shape of a snarl. Griswold felt fear creeping up his neck as he looked into the giant man's face and his soulless eyes.

That was the moment when he knew he was going to die.

Dewey let out a chilling laugh, the deep rumbling of it resounding off the hollowness of the chamber. "Well, so much for small talk," he said, then casually aimed the shotgun at the drifter's head and pulled the trigger. The blast hit the smaller man before he could say another word, lifted his body off the mattress and slammed him against the wall behind him. An obscene mixture of blood, bone and brain matter sprayed the damp concrete, mixing with the powdery efflorescence of free lime that coated it. Rivulets of the gore ran behind Griswold's nearly decapitated corpse as it slid back down onto the mattress.

The killer sat motionless for a few minutes taking in the scene as an artist would his canvas. Then he stood up, slowly walked over to the dead man's body and unloaded the shotgun's second barrel point blank into Tiger's chest. A red mist rose from the stone floor.

Dewey hovered over the body, looking down at the violence he had sundered and felt a rush of adrenalin in his veins. The spontaneous act of killing made him feel all powerful. When he murdered, he felt supreme over those who feared and mocked him for his grotesque appearance. It was the only time in his life when he felt comfortable in his size. In his jubilation, he reached down and picked up the remains of the corpse with one hand and heaved it across the room as if it was a bundle of dirty laundry. With a sickening thud, what was left of Tyler James Griswold bounced off a concrete wall and fell to the floor in a twisted pile, just another bit of rubble in the ruins of Fort Mansfield.

Without another thought to the senseless murder, the mad man grabbed the straw mattress and flipped it over, hiding the disgusting mess he had caused. Then, as his adrenalin rush subsided, Dewey finally reached a point of exhaustion and dropped to the cushion.

He fell asleep within seconds, completely at peace, oblivious to the stench of death that seemed to follow his path.

Nineteen

~~~ ~~~

U.S. Weather Bureau Headquarters, Washington, D.C.

Charlie Pierce could hardly hear what Gordon Dunn was telling him over the telephone. In the background, the junior meteorologist could hear a loud celebration of some sort. He wondered if Dunn had finally cracked under the pressure of tracking the monster storm barreling towards Florida.

"The son of a bitch turned, Charlie, can you friggin' believe it, son?" Dunn yelled into the telephone when Pierce questioned the background noise. "Of all the hurricanes I've worked with old Grady Norton, this one takes the cake. I've never seen a monster like this one to wait so long to make up it's mind. We're in the clear, Charlie, do you
~~~

hear? Grady wanted me to advise you immediately."

Pierce checked the row of clocks hanging over the teletype machines, seeking out local time. It was nearly ten at night and Norton was preparing to issue a weather bulletin for the people of the State of Florida advising them that the hurricane had indeed turned north and would not directly impact the Keys as expected. The phone call to the Weather Bureau's Washington D.C. headquarters served to warn it that the Jacksonville Hurricane Center would soon turn over the responsibility of tracking the storm since it would no longer pose a threat to Florida.

Pierce, who had been on duty since before dawn, was filling in for two more senior forecasters who were on vacation. He was tired, but reminded himself that what ailed him was nothing in comparison to the marathon effort his Jacksonville colleagues had performed. Most of Grady Norton's people hadn't had more than a few hours of sleep at one time since Friday afternoon.

"That's great news Mr. Dunn; we'll be happy to take the ball when you throw it our way," Pierce responded. "She'll probably just blow herself out over the North Atlantic now, but I'll personally stay on it and keep you informed."

The stunning turn of the weather shocked everyone because earlier in the day, all signs continued to indicate that Florida was in for a direct hit. As the morning sun rose over the Keys, the hurricane was some six hundred fifty miles east of

Miami, moving in a west-northwest direction at approximately twenty miles per hour. Reports coming in from the few ships anywhere near the storm area indicated the hurricane was still mean and growing, continuing to take a direct bead on Florida's southeast shores. From all evidence, it appeared that Norton and Dunn had accurately forecast and mapped the storm, and the outer edge of the hurricane would begin to barrel into the Florida coast on Tuesday morning, the twentieth of September. Grady Norton had issued another urgent advisory to the state population, this time a formal hurricane alert. There was fear in the air.

However, just after one in the afternoon, Norton received a telephone call from the station chief at Cat Island in the Bahamas.

"Grady, we're getting barometer readings of 29.60, so the pressure is definitely rising," said Willis Shipman from the lonely outpost. Norton and Shipman had only met once in Washington, but routinely talked by telephone. "You would expect it to be dropping faster if it was still running for Miami, agree?" Shipman asked.

"Agreed," Norton responded. "Willis, I think we've just seen the first sign that this thing might be turning north," Norton said, feeling the first twinge of relief. But he would have to find far more conclusive evidence that the storm was recurving before he could relax.

By four o'clock, the evidence was starting to pile up. Reports from the Bahamas, Cuba and the outer islands began trending differently. Barometric pressure readings were slowly rising and winds had dropped down to about one hundred thirty miles per hour, still plenty dangerous but suddenly not as terrifying as earlier reports of wind speeds nearing two hundred miles per hour. The Jacksonville Weather Bureau didn't quite know what to make of the changes, but they all appeared to be positive.

Two hours later, reports from Cuba indicated a near miss - which Jacksonville believed was only possible if the hurricane had indeed begun to recurve to the north. Grady Norton and his staffed collectively took a deep breath in the stifling office and watched and waited, hoping against hope that the next report would be more decisive. By nightfall, the air suddenly felt cooler for the exhausted meteorologists and forecasters. It wasn't that the temperature had dropped. It was just the collective sigh of relief in the Jacksonville office that seemed to take the heat off. They'd ducked a major disaster. Shipping reports confirmed that the hurricane had indeed recurved, and was now clearly headed north where it was expected to slowly peter out until it became nothing more than a mild shower somewhere off the coast of Maine.

In a last burst of energy, Norton and Dunn worked feverishly to analyze, check and recheck all available data to be absolutely certain that the danger had passed. At ten fifteen that night, following Gordon Dunn's call to Washington, Norton picked up his microphone for the final time that day.

"This is Grady Norton at the US Weather Bureau Hurricane Center in Jacksonville," he began, lighting a cigarette as he spoke, a slight grin coming to his face. "The severe hurricane tracking towards Miami and the Florida coast has veered sharply to the northeast and is moving towards the eastern Atlantic. Consequently, the storm threat to Florida's east coast has greatly diminished. The hurricane is now situated about four hundred twenty miles due east of Miami with further turning in the northern direction expected over the next twenty-four hours. The coast line from Melbourne to Key Largo should expect heavy rain and gusting winds as the storm blows out to sea.

"I repeat. The hurricane warning posted at two o'clock this afternoon has been rescinded. The hurricane warning is no longer in effect." A resounding cheer went up all across the station house as Norton set the microphone down and turned to his men.

"Gentlemen, y'all have done good work here. I'm mighty proud of y'all," he announced to his weary staff. "Now, I suggest we post some small craft warnings and try to convince our neighbors it might not be good sailing for about twenty-four hours. We need to watch this bastard for the next day or so before we hand it over to Washington. Gordon here has already advised them of the change. I reckon by day after tomorrow, this monster will more likely resemble one of them 'April showers'." A few laughed, but most were too tired to do much more than smile. "Now, finish up so you boys can git out of here and get some rest," he continued. "Y'all sure deserve it."

Norton slapped his pal Gordon Dunn on the back and grabbed his coat. He envisioned his wife waiting for him at home, knowing she'd have dinner on the table waiting for him after hearing his last broadcast. Right now, all that the station chief wanted was a cold beer.

As they walked out of the office together, Norton and Dunn were silent. They'd done good work, but also ducked a big one, and knew it.

"Well, let's hope that 'sum bitch strangles itself real fast, hey boy?" Norton said.

"Don't think I'd worry about it," Dunn replied, rubbing the back of his aching neck. "It's a pretty good feeling to stare down the devil, Grady. I just want to soak it up for awhile. God knows it won't last long."

As the two men went home to their families, neither one could have known that the devil had merely blinked.

Tuesday
September 20, 1938

Twenty

~~~ ɕ ~~~

The Lapkin Mansion At Sandy Point

The constant, dreary rain was finally getting on Emily's nerves as she worked with Shelly to pack up James for his return to Choate on Thursday. The oldest of the Lapkin brood wasn't contributing much to the effort. In fact, he'd disappeared. Emily was actually a little relieved that he had gone off. His sullen mood at the thought of starting school again found an easy target in his mother.

"One last time, will you please tell me why you and Dad are making me go away to school? Why can't I just go to Westerly High like my friends?" James whined. He despised returning to school each year and was absolutely despondent about leaving Sandy Point. Like his father, he lived for the
~~~

surf, sailboats and sun of Napatree Point and Watch Hill. After only a few days back at Choate though, his mood would improve dramatically and he actually enjoyed the school and the friends he'd made there. The worst part was not being able to come home until Thanksgiving, although his parents would drive up several times during the fall semester on a Sunday to spend the afternoon with him.

"He's almost a man, Emily, but leaving home is one of the hardest things he'll ever do, young or old," he had told his wife after she received a letter from James in October of his freshman year, begging her to let him come home. He was painfully homesick, and Emily was worried about him. "He'll be okay, sweetheart, he's just got to gut this out until Thanksgiving. Then it will be better for him, trust me," Geoff had reassured her.

Emily had struggled for months with second thoughts about their decision to send James away to school before he actually left. Part of it was her own emotional difficulties in letting her oldest son go, but she also worried for his happiness. Geoff had convinced her that the private prep school would give their son an education and opportunities he just couldn't find in the public school system. She'd learned long ago that once her husband was convinced of something, he was a difficult man to persuade differently. In her heart she knew Geoff was right, and that when it came to their children, every decision was well and completely thought out. Not that made packing him up for the return any easier. The rain simply made the last couple of days before he left home again all the more miserable.

Actually, James was feeling better after slipping away from the two women who were fretting about his underwear and socks and how much they could fit in a single steamer trunk. He'd gone outside to the porch and found Andy Popillo, the second year student at Brown University who his father had hired to help close up the mansion for the winter. Popillo was taking down the dozen canvas awnings that shaded the ocean-front, oversized windows from the glaring sun. They'd been wasted this summer on the rainiest season in memory.

"Whatcha up to, sport?" the twenty-year-old college boy asked James. Despite the rain, Popillo had stripped off his shirt, finding the damp humidity oppressive. Like his father, a Sicilian mason in Providence, he didn't need much of an excuse to work bare chested. His father once told him that wealthy people didn't believe a man was working hard enough if he wasn't sweating, and even a thin tee shirt hid the proof that he was. With the muscular build that the older Popillo had passed down to his son, Andy had nothing to be ashamed of.

Lean, muscular and tall at six feet one, the boy also had a work ethic like his father's. "If a man pays you a day's wages, then you give him a day's work, Andrew, no shortcuts," Mr. Popillo had schooled his son, and he had set an example for him every day of his life. Unfortunately, the man also worked himself into an early grave, succumbing to a stroke at just forty-seven. The tragedy left his young son grief stricken but intensely motivated to find a better life for his widowed mother and his two brothers. The young Popillo had supported his family by working two jobs all through high school, while somehow earning grades good enough to land him a full academic scholarship to the renowned Ivy League university, Brown, located on College Hill on the East Side of Providence.

Andy was smart enough to know that breaking your back working didn't necessarily mean you had to do life-shortening physical labor. He not only had a brain, but his looks caught the attention of more than a few of the Westerly summer girls - and some of their mothers, as well. He had the matinee idol looks of a Clark Gable, although with a sort of Mediterranean darkness, and his slightly olive complexion and curly jet black hair seemed to soften his deep brown eyes. The teenage waitresses at the Yacht Club whispered and giggled over his "bedroom eyes", and some of them privately fantasized about Andy visiting theirs.

James had overheard some of this rather sexually charged but innocent chatter among the girls at the Yacht Club. That made Andy Popillo a man of great interest to the younger boy, who, in the last six months, had begun taking notice of the girls and certain of their blossoming attributes. James wasn't aware of the epic hormonal upheaval going on in his own well toned and tanned teenage body, only that all of a sudden he was seeing girls a lot differently. He jumped at the chance to spend some time with Andy, whom, judging from his looks, was probably experienced with older women. Nothing could have been farther from the truth, as Andy was much too busy studying and working to have time for girlfriends, but he wasn't about to let on. He rather enjoyed the aura of being a ladies' man, even if it was a myth.

Popillo had met Geoffrey Lapkin at the Yacht Club where he worked not only as a waiter during dining hours, but also as a dock hand, maintaining the small fleet of sailboats the Club owned. The money was better than anything he could make working in the city and besides, working at the beach all summer was a sort of vacation for him no matter how many hours he put in. At the least he was away from the stifling and slightly suffocating heat of the city and working against a backdrop of the sea and Little Narragansett Bay, pristine beaches, and the continual ocean breeze. The young man sent nearly his entire earnings home to his mother, holding back only enough to live on. It wasn't an easy life for him; but he was satisfied, believing that his father would be proud of him. That kept him focused.

"I'm getting ready to go back to frigging school," James said. "I hate it. Connecticut is like living in the Antarctic, they get so much snow and ice," he continued, forgetting that Wallingford was only seventy-five miles away. For the young teen, it at times seemed like a thousand.

"Aw, it can't be that bad, James," Popillo said. "I mean it could be a lot worse. I used to have to go to high school and go right to work every afternoon and night. I'd do that five days a week, and on weekends work two jobs. Betcha' Choate isn't worse than that, hey sport?"

James winced, hating it when Andy called him "sport". "Yah, I guess not, but it's so boring, ya know? It's all boys... I mean 'guys'. There's no girls, nothing to do...."

Popillo stopped what he was doing and turned to James. "Oh, so that's what this is all about. No dames, huh?" he said grinning.

James hesitated. "Yah, there's no... dames. It seems kind of strange sometimes going to school with all boys... guys," he corrected himself. "I mean at Westerly High there are tons of girls. Not that having girls around is all that important, I mean, it's just that... you know..." He looked up at the older boy, hoping he'd finish his sentence. Popillo let him run on, somewhat enjoying the kids' discomfort. It wasn't so long ago that he felt just as confused about women. Actually, Popillo thought, "girls" had confused him too. Women were a lot easier to understand. All you had to do was be attentive, honest (as long as it didn't hurt her feelings), kind, sweet and caring and you'd find all kinds of treats lay in store.

He felt kind of sorry for the boy. For all the kid's money, he thought, the kid would still have to suffer the pains of growing up, and that wasn't easy, rich or poor. "I know where you're coming from, James," he said, sitting down next to him. "You can't live with 'em, but you sure as hell can't live without 'em," he laughed. James laughed too. Popillo suddenly felt a lot older, like he did when he was around his younger brothers. It didn't feel like being a big brother, he thought. It felt more like, you know, being responsible for someone who needed your help. He actually liked the feeling. In a way, it was what gave him satisfaction from supporting his family since his father passed away.

Popillo dug into his pants pockets and pulled out a pack of "Lucky Strikes". He tapped the pack against the back of his hand several times, then ripped open half of the top, raised it to his lips, locked on to a cigarette with his teeth and slowly drew out a cigarette. He'd seen "Major Geoffrey Vickers", Errol Flynn's heroic character in *The Charge of the Light Brigade* make the same move on the big screen a couple of years ago and thought it was quite manly, and even a bit provocative. Actually it was the only movie he'd ever seen because he felt guilty afterwards about spending the two bits on himself. But Flynn's romantic characterization of the "Major" gave him a glimpse of how a sophisticated and educated man should behave around women.

James was going to have to figure all that out himself, Popillo thought, but offered a cigarette to the teen. Startled, the younger boy looked up at his older friend and smiled, as if he'd made a mistake. Then catching himself he stammered, "Uh, no thanks, I don't smoke. I mean I used to but I gave it up." Popillo smiled and put the cigarettes back in his pocket, satisfied that he'd given the kid a little taste of what being older felt like. He lit up with a metal lighter that had been his father's.

"You got a girlfriend, James?"

"Nah, I've been sort of busy," the teen said awkwardly. "But there is this girl I met that..." He didn't know how to finish the sentence.

"Gotcha," Popillo said, being merciful. "She's special, huh?"

"Yah, I think so. Really pretty."

"Well, you're a good looking guy. Why don't you ask her out sometime?"

James dropped his gaze to the porch floor. "I dunno. I get kind of confused when I'm around her. Don't know what to say..."

The two were silent for a moment

"Yah, I know how that feels, sport. Women can sure make you feel stupid," Popillo said. "But you know, James, women aren't all that hard to understand," he offered.

James' eyes narrowed. "Yah, sure, you've never had to eat dinner with my sister," he whined.

"Kate? Little Kate?" Popillo feigned surprise. "Why she acts more grown up than most of the women I know."

"Yah," James replied. "That's the problem."

"Well, looky here, James, let me give you lesson number one," the college man offered after taking a deep drag from his cigarette. "Never, and I mean never, let a dame get under your skin. If the girl knows she's got your attention, you're in trouble. Just ignore her."

"Yah?"

"Yah. Trust me, I've got a lot of experience in this," he exaggerated. Popillo took another drag, then exhaled smoke rings to impress his student. He blew out one final giant circle and watched it begin to drift away. Before it dissipated, he flicked the glowing red cigarette butt through the center of the ring.

"Wow," James said.

Ignoring him, Popillo closed out the day's lesson. "James, if you really want to make a girl like you -- hell, love you -- it can be done, ya know."

The teen sat motionless, anticipating Andy's every word.

"First of all you have to show her that you're smart. You have to prove to her that you're an educated man and that you're sophisticated, that you know how to talk and walk in a way that's not flamboyant, ya know, showboat like, but just easy, like you're comfortable in your own skin. You know what I'm saying?"

"Oh, yah, sure," James said, but not at all sure. No one had ever talked to him like this, like he was an adult for cripes sakes, and he was hanging on to every word.

"You have to show her you've got brains and style without being a jerk," Popillo preached. The words amounted to thoughts he'd had for a long time, but he'd just never had anyone to share them with. He was enjoying the opportunity. "And if that alone doesn't make her sweet on you, then just treat her nice. Be polite, always be a gentleman and talk to her softly," he said, adding quickly, "after you've listened attentively to whatever it is she has to say," he said. "That last part is real important, sport."

James continued to stare at Andy even after he'd stopped speaking, as if he was waiting for more.

"Geez, thanks, Andy," the teen finally said. "I never thought about it that way," he stammered.

"Yah, well now you know," Popillo said. "That's why school is so friggin' important. So be happy you're going back to school. Just think of all you're gonna learn and how impressed the dames will be this time next year. Damn, you'll be swatting them off like flies on sugar, sport.

"Yah, you're right. I probably ought to get back upstairs, help my Mother. Thursday's a big day, ya know?"

"Yah, I do know James. I'll be going back to Brown myself in a few weeks. Buncha' women waiting for me," he joked and punched the teen lightly in the shoulder. James got up to leave, a smile on his face.

"Hey, sport…" Popillo said. "So you gotta tell me. What's her name?"

"Promise you won't tell anyone?"

"Me? I'm too sophisticated for that, sport. Real men never tell bedroom stories," he replied, suddenly turning straight faced.

"It's Olivia."

Popillo lit another cigarette. "Olivia," he repeated, slowly sounding out the name. "I like that, very sophisticated. Like 'Olivia de Havilland'. You two will make a great couple. So go get smart, sport. We'll talk again next year."

James bounded into the house, yelling to his mother. "Mom, we gotta get ready. I want to get to school a little earlier, okay?" he said, the sound of his voice fading as he ran up the stairs to his bedroom.

Andy Popillo took a last drag on his cigarette and flicked the butt down to the beach. He climbed down from the porch and let the rain fall on him for a minute, reveling in the cool sensation. The talk with James was good for him too, he thought. He wished he'd had a big brother to talk to. Or his dad. "God, I miss him," he said aloud. Only a flock of seagulls, scavenging on the beach, were near enough to hear him. They didn't seem to care.

For all Andy Popillo's bravado and his studied confidence, the young man was actually very lonely. He hadn't had much time to be a young man like James, and inside his heart ached to be a boy, to fall in love, to have someone to care for who cared for him. There just wasn't time.

Like he always did when his true feelings temporarily escaped the discipline and burden of his responsibilities, Popillo shook off the melancholy and plunged back into his work because he knew it did no good to feel sorry for himself. He hurried back onto the porch and began wrestling with the awnings again.

As he worked, the thought occurred to him that he hadn't seen Tiger Griswold at all today, which was unusual. He and Tiger had become friends over the summer, after Popillo began leaving carefully packaged kitchen leftovers for the drifter in the trash cans behind the Yacht Club. It was a kindness the battle-weary veteran had never known before and it wasn't long until he and his new friend Andy were combing the beaches together on early weekend mornings. They became so close that Griswold actually brought the young man to his hideout at Fort Mansfield after swearing him to secrecy.

It was strange that he hadn't seen him today, Popillo thought. Tiger knew he was working at the Lapkin mansion, and the family had always treated the drifter kindly. If he didn't see him by the end of the day he'd make a point of going out to the Fort to check on him after work.

You never know, he thought, suddenly feeling chilled. He reached for his shirt. The old fella might have gotten sick or something. It nagged at him the rest of the afternoon. By then, Tyler James Griswold's mutilated body was laying stone cold dead amidst the rubble and ruin that he had called home. The man who lived there now, like Tiger, was also desperate to escape from a world that shunned him. But there the similarities ended.

For the new owner was hardly as friendly.

Twenty-One

~~~ ~~~

Marsh Harbour, Great Abaco, Bahamas

Less than a mile off shore, two fishermen with the fiercely hot sun on their backs, diligently cast heavy, hand-knotted nets again and again into the clear blue waters off Marsh Harbour on Great Abaco, largest and most northern of the Bahamian Islands. The work was hard, and on this day, very unrewarding. All they had to show for a morning of backbreaking labor were a few ugly, diamond shaped skates with their sharp barbs and other worthless bottom fish.

The eldest of the two tired fisherman, Roosevelt Ferguson finally signaled it was time for a break, and sat down heavily in the bow of the brightly painted wooden boat, its royal blue and sunny
~~~

yellow markings typical of the festive appearance of most local fishing trawlers. Ferguson was proud of the boat he had built with his own two hands decades before. But that was typical of the black man whose roots dated back to the slaves who had accompanied six hundred British Loyalists from New York in 1783 when they fled the newly independent United States.

He was enormously proud of his heritage, dating back to the struggles of his great, great grandfather and his own father's father to win their freedom from slavery. Today, Roosevelt Theodore Ferguson sustained that birthright in his own independence. He was his own man, his own boss, and damned proud of it, albeit in his own humble manner. He was deeply religious, and the only higher power he recognized was that of his Lord and maker.

Though he barely made a living off the bounty of the Atlantic Ocean, the sea was his home. It was the only place in his small world where he felt truly without master and, without arrogance, almost invincible. Ferguson truly believed that there was nothing the sea could throw at him for which he was not prepared or that he could not overcome.

His son, George, who worked the boat at the side of his father every day of the week, was the oldest of his nine children, and shared in the old man's quiet confidence. When he was with his father, no matter how far from the harbor they might wander in search of fish, the thirty year old felt no fear. Roosevelt Ferguson was the backbone of his large family; and he believed that despite his humble place in God's order, he was genuinely important to those who loved him and depended on him.

However, on this otherwise beautiful and cloudless day, his spirits were uncharacteristically low and he felt unusually tired. The ocean had provided little over the last several days, barely enough to put a meal on the table for his brood. It was as if the fish had gone into hibernation, hiding from something that he could not see. His instincts told him something was wrong. Why else would God forsake him?

"I don't know, Dad," George said to him after they had pulled yet another empty net from the sea. "I think we're wasting our time. The damned fish have just disappeared."

Ferguson frowned at his son's curse. "George, the fish always expect us to be polite. Cursing will not fill our nets," he said.

George loved the old man, but he worried over him. His father had just turned seventy-six and was too old to be tending to nets -- especially empty ones. But no amount of talk or reason would convince the old man that he should retire from the sea and let his strong sons manage the responsibility of caring for him and their beloved mother. There was no shame in growing old, he thought. Was there?

"Let us cast the net once more, George. Perhaps our Savior will smile upon our effort this time," the elder Ferguson said. There was no arguing with him, George thought. Not even his beloved wife, Martha, could sway the old man. Without another word, the two men set about preparing the net to be cast.

Out of nowhere, a large swell hit their small fishing boat broadside, rocking it violently. The old man had been walking toward the bow when the wave hit and he lost his balance. George watched in disbelief as his father fell overboard. In all his years of tending to the nets with him, he had never once seen the old man do such a thing.

"Dad, are you okay?" George screamed, hurrying to the port side where his father had fallen overboard. He was alarmed and quickly threw the old man a rope with which to pull himself back to the drifting boat which had already moved several yards away. Then he almost laughed at the thought of his father being in trouble. Why, his father could still swim rings around him.

As if to confirm his son's wasted concern, Ferguson let loose with a hardy laugh, his voice hoarse from the salt water that he had swallowed while falling. "Jesus, Dad, are you trying to scare the shit out of me?" George bellowed. The old man laughed again, despite his son's cursing.

While he waited for the old man to pull himself aboard, George caught a movement out of the corner of his eye. He swung his gaze towards the commotion and his eyes widened in disbelief. Coming at them were dozens, if not hundreds of dorsal fins, slicing through the blue offshore waters at tremendous speed but leaving almost no wake.

George's mouth fell open at the chilling sight of the huge school of sharks. Tiger's, Hammerheads, even Great White sharks were bearing down on the boat with his father still in the water. It appeared that the old man was the only meal in the ocean.

"Dad, hurry, hurry, get in the boat for Christ's sake," George screamed to his father. "There are sharks heading this way - a lot of them!"

Ferguson stopped pulling on the rope and looked over his shoulder. He wasn't particularly concerned about dealing with a shark or two. He'd done that many times in his days as a fisherman. He laughed, then turned to see the huge sharks racing towards him. Instantly he knew that he would never make it back into the boat in time. "George, brace yourself, they may hit the boat," he screamed back to his son. Then he began to pray, watching in horror as the terrifying predators came at him.

Roosevelt prayed while waiting for the inevitable. "For thine is the Kingdom, the Power…" he said, his voice elevating with each word as the sharks came near. "…and the Glory, for ever…" The old man looked down into the clear water just as the first shark came on him. He waited for the bite he knew would come, from the savage teeth that could cut a man in half in a split second. Ferguson saw that it was a Bahamas Tiger shark, at least twenty-five feet long, its open mouth large enough to swallow him whole.

"...and ever, Amen," he prayed silently now, resigned to a hideous death. The old man closed his eyes. Long seconds passed.

Nothing happened.

When he opened his eyes again, he found himself surrounded by hundreds of the killers but none seemed the least bit interested in him. The monstrous fish were simply racing away from the coast of Great Abaco and heading out into the open Atlantic. For five minutes or more, he tread water while the sharks swam passed him, heading southwest at breathtaking speed. Then it was over and the old man finally pulled himself back into his boat.

"What the hell, George," he said, shaking his head in disbelief and allowing himself a mild curse. "In the name of God, what is going on, where are they going?" George sat next to his father, shivering from the mild shock of the encounter, and hugged him. "I don't know, Dad, I thought you were a dead man," he said.

"Unless the sharks have suddenly lost their taste for old fishermen, I cannot imagine what..." He stopped in mid sentence and gazed up into the heavens. He and his son watched as the sky began to turn a sickly shade of yellow and almost immediately the wind began to pick up. The old man knew what it was.

"My God, they're running for deep water," he said in disbelief. "That's it... the sharks can feel the pressure dropping and they hear it coming...oh, dear God, protect them."

"What? Protect who, Dad?" George responded, completely confused. "What the hell is happening?

Ferguson ignored his questions. "George, hurry, start the engine. We've no time to waste, my son," he screamed. "We must get back to the island and protect the family! They will not see it coming..."

"See 'what' coming, Dad, what is it? George yelled while hurrying to start the engine. "Jeez, you'd think the world was coming to an end."

"It may be, George, it just may be," the old man screamed again. "Do you see the sky? How yellow it is turning? Do you feel the wind and how the boat is suddenly rocking? There is a storm coming unlike any you have seen before. Hurry, we must get back to your mother..." Ferguson began praying again as he stowed the nets and other fishing gear and George swung the bow around towards Marsh Harbour.

"Open the throttle wide, we have no time to waste," he bellowed. Then he turned back to the open ocean. The look on his face sent a chill through George. "What is it, Dad?" he yelled, turning around to see for himself. What looked like a huge fog bank, perhaps sixty- to seventy-feet high and as wide as they could see, was rolling toward them at an incredible speed.

"My God, what is that, Dad, it can't be fog, what...?" George implored of his father, a look of confused terror in his eyes.

"It's not fog, George," the elder man said, his shoulders drooping in resignation. He suddenly knew that he was to die on this afternoon, after all.

"It's water. A storm surge. It will wipe out Abaco... your mother and the children... they will not have a chance," he said solemnly, any hope of survival now gone.

"Water?" George yelled incredulously, "That can't be water, why its...." The rest of his words were lost in the cacophonous roar that was on them in the next instant. For a second, he thought the boat might ride the crest of the awesome wave, but then realized almost in the same moment that there was no crest. It was just a solid wall of water. An instant later, the incredible ocean surge crashed down on the small boat, shattering it as if it had been dynamited, and pounded its two occupants into the sea floor with the force of a pile driver. Mercifully, the concussion of the impact caused them to instantly lose consciousness as the bodies of Roosevelt Ferguson and his oldest son were tossed across the sea floor like torn kelp until they drowned.

The horrifying wave gained even more strength from the warm, shallow water and was rising higher as it approached land. Driven by winds of more than one hundred fifty miles per hour behind it, the wall of water sped unimpeded towards the unsuspecting harbor, its village and beyond. In seconds, it would pass over the entire island, destroying nearly everything in its path. What little remained of the quiet island and those few inhabitants who miraculously survived the storm surge would not have a moment to recover. For the ferocious winds and blasting rains following the surge would see to it that absolutely nothing survived.

The shocking roar that descended on Great Abaco was the only warning the Islanders had. In the small kitchen of a tidy cottage tucked behind Marsh Harbour, Martha Ferguson dropped a potato she was peeling into a porcelain bucket and ran outside with panicked thoughts for her husband and son. She looked up into the sky, at its hideously yellow pallor, then at the coastline off the harbour. Martha watched, horror-struck as the unfathomable storm surge pounced on the marina and tossed boats, big and small, flying through the air like children's toys. In an instant, she knew that her husband and her first born would not be home this night, or ever again.

The old woman reached for the gold crucifix hanging around her neck and clutched it. Before she could cry out in grief, the wave was upon her, at once stifling her anguish and suffocating the life from her body.

Only one thought came to Martha's tormented mind before the darkness engulfed her. It was not of her husband or her children. It came in the form of a question.

What had they done to deserve the wrath of Satan?

Twenty-Two

~~~ ~~~

Fort Mansfield

Pat Collins steered his school bus to the side of the road just after the junction of Napatree Point and Sandy Point on Fort Road. Behind him, still yapping on, Katie Lapkin was just finishing the story of how her big brother James had begun to teach her how to surf. As usual, she was wildly animated and the kindly school bus driver could barely keep up with her non-stop chatter. It was raining lightly, just enough to have to use the wipers, making it even more difficult for the old man to hear the little girl.

"And it was just so marvelous, Mr. Collins, I mean we were way out in the surf, the water was probably at least twenty-feet deep," she told him, not missing the slightest detail. "At first I was
~~~

frightened, but then James showed me how to sit up on the surfboard, and I did it without falling off. Then we rode this giant wave to the shore sitting on our surfboards and it was just wonderful. It was so much fun, I tell you. My big brother is so sweet."

A smile came to Collins' face at her sudden pause. It was not unusual for Katie to get so excited in her story telling that she would occasionally have to stop and catch her breath. He seized the moment.

"Is that so, Katie," the driver said. "Why, I'd like to see you up on that board, I would. Just you be careful, okay young lady?"

"Of course, Mr. Collins," she replied instantly with a fresh supply of oxygen in her lungs. "But James will keep me safe, he's so strong. Anyways, we won't have time to do any more surfing this week. He has to go back to school in stupid Connecticut. I miss him when he's away."

"Yah, but he'll be home for Thanksgiving before you know it. Now skedaddle you, I've got to get this old bucket of bolts home before it overheats," he said to her, gently ending their conversation. "I'll see you tomorrow morning, Katie."

The second grader said goodbye and jumped off the bus from the bottom step. Her house was still about a mile away, but Collins typically dropped her off at the junction because it was so hard to turn the long bus around at the end of the narrow road. The only time he drove to the very end of Sandy Point was when the weather was foul. Katie never objected; she told him that it was fun to say hello to all the neighbors as she skipped home. On clear weather days, their agreement was that she would wait on the side of the road until Collins backed up the bus and turned it around to head back to Westerly. Then he would honk the horn and Katie would wave to him as he drove off.

Pat Collins could not have known that their afternoon ritual was being observed by a man hiding patiently in the brush about twenty-five yards off the road. When the bus pulled away, the stranger watched as Katie waved to the driver and turned to begin the short walk home. Then, throwing caution to the wind, he stood up from his hiding place revealing himself to the little girl. Katie, startled by the unexpected movement in the brush, turned to look. Her eyes went wide with fright as she took in the man. He was a giant, with eyes as dark and glassy as the prized Black Widow marbles she played with, and he wasn't smiling. Katie froze in her tracks, afraid to run. She was terrified.

The man sensed her fear. "Hi, honey, don't be scared," Charles Dewey said to the girl, moving quickly towards her. "Don't be afraid, I won't hurt you, I just wanted to say hello."

Katie thought to run, but then, inexplicably held her ground, her fascination with this colossal person outweighing her fear. "Hello," she stammered.

"Well hello to you too," Dewey said with a smile on his face. "What's your name?" Dewey asked, softly. "Mine is Charles. Do you live around here?" The convict reached her at the side of the road and towered over the little girl. Katie bent her head back and looked up into the man's face. He had a scary face, she thought innocently, but sounded nice. "My name is Kate. I live in the last house down the street."

"Is that right?" he said, feigning surprise. "That really big one down at the very end of the road?" He pointed towards her house and shook his head. "Well, I'll be. Would you happen to have some older brothers, Kate? I think I might have met them on Sunday down by the docks. You know, near the carousel horse. That's the same house they said they lived in."

Kate nodded silently. Then her eyes went wide in recognition and she drew in her breath. "The ape man!" she blurted out without thinking. "I mean…" she hesitated, hoping he hadn't heard her. "Yes, my three brothers talked about it on Sunday."

"'Ape man', huh?" he said, averting his eyes from her so she wouldn't see the instant flash of anger in his eyes. He said nothing more. The moment passed.

"Can I walk with you a little way?" he said to the girl.

"Sure," Kate said innocently, and instinctively reached out and took the man's enormous hand. It was so big that she could do no more than hang onto one of his fingers. Dewey was shocked at the contact. He had never experienced the spontaneous touch of another human being.

"Oh," he said awkwardly, completely taken aback by the most innocent display of affection. Yet, even in that moment of confusion, the incongruity of the situation did not escape the killer. He became profoundly aware of his monstrous awkwardness as he looked into the face of the tiny child, full of innocence and so captivatingly beautiful. If Katie had been able to look into his eyes at that moment, she would have seen sadness. For Dewey had never before felt so odd and conspicuous, so completely uneasy in his own skin.

In the entirety of his life, Charles Dewey had hidden inside the menacing and intimidating body that had been so inequitably imposed upon him at birth. He had used it not only to terrorize others into having his way, but also as a defense against the knowledge that he would always be an outsider, that he would never fit in anywhere. The sense of self-assurance and security that his extreme physical manifestation had always provided him now betrayed him as well. He simply had no sense of how to react when another being showed him the merest, yet sincere, act of kindness. Consequently, he was an alien, deprived and devoid of any sense of humanity.

"Do you live around, mister?" Kate asked. "We only live here in the summertime. Then we move back to Westerly during the winter."

"Well, no, I don't live around here," Dewey replied.

"Where do you live?"

He felt odd talking to the girl, and inexplicably gave in to the urge to tell her the truth. "I actually don't have a place to live right now," he said quietly, surprised by the words that came out of his mouth.

"So where do you sleep?" Katie asked, perplexed.

"Oh, any old place. On the beach, sometimes." Katie looked up at him, the smile leaving her face.

"Even in the rain?"

"Yes, even in the rain."

"I've never met anyone who sleeps on the beach in the rain before," she replied.

"It's not so bad. I don't mind." He looked back over his shoulder and saw a car coming down Fort Road toward the junction. Panicking, he dropped the child's hand as if touching her was an obscenity. "I've got to go now," he spit out. "It was nice talking to you." Without another word he sprinted towards the shore and the obscurity of the tall brush behind the dunes.

"Okay, I guess," she said, calling after him, feeling a little disappointed that her new friend had left so quickly. "Maybe I'll see you tomorrow, Charles. I hope you don't have to sleep on the beach tonight. Do you have a blanket and a pillow?" she asked, genuinely concerned. But the convict did not reply and quickly disappeared from sight.

The car made the turn toward Sandy Point and slowed as it passed by Katie. It was Andy Popillo driving the beat up Chevy pickup that Geoff Lapkin kept out at the mansion during the summer to help with hauling groceries and trash for the large family.

"Hey, Katie, jump in," Andy said, cheerfully. "Had to run into town to pick up a tarp for your dad." She got in the truck and smiled at him, but didn't say anything.

"You okay?" he asked, not knowing what to make of her silence. She was never quiet. No answer. "Cat got your tongue?"

Katie finally smiled. "Yah, I'm okay. But I just met a man over by the junction. He was so big, almost like a giant. He scared me at first, but he was really nice after all."

Andy frowned, not bothering to hide his concern. "Geez, Katie, I don't think you should be talking to strangers like that. I'll bet your mom and dad would be upset if they knew. She turned to him with a sad look on her face.

"Oh, Andy, please don't tell them. It's just that he seemed so lonely and I don't want to get him in trouble. He was very nice. Please?"

"Yah, okay, but promise me you won't talk to him again, alright? What did he look like, anyway? You said he was a giant?"

She described the huge man and his dark and rather ugly face, sparing few details. The little girl actually frightened herself a bit as she remembered just how strange he appeared and how enormous his hands were. She shuddered as she finished.

"And where does this 'Charles' live? Did he tell you anything about himself?"

"Not very much, but he did tell me that he doesn't have anywhere to live right now. He said he sleeps on the beach - even in the rain!" she replied. "Isn't that awful? I guess I should have invited him to our house," she added, her conscience suddenly bothering her. "He must be very lonely."

"Life's not always fair, Katie. But that still doesn't make it okay to talk to this guy. We made a deal, right?" She nodded.

"By the way, where exactly did you first see him?"

"Right at the corner, you know, where the road passes by Fort Mansfield," she said, sure of herself. "Why?"

He didn't respond immediately, his thoughts turning to Tiger Griswold. "Oh, no reason," he said as he turned the truck onto the gravel driveway in front of the Lapkin mansion. "Just asking," he added, but now more anxious than ever to check on his friend living in the ruins of the old fort. "Well, that's about it for me today, Katie. I gotta go do something. Would you tell your Mom I'll be back in time for dinner? She asked me to come tonight."

"Oh great, Andy," Katie replied, then turned to him. "You know, maybe…" The little girl hesitated.

"What, Katie?" he asked.

"I was thinking that if you saw Charles…" She paused again and turned to Popillo. "I mean maybe you could ask him to come to dinner too. Wouldn't that be a nice thing to do for someone who lives on the beach?" she asked, genuinely concerned for the stranger. Then she jumped from the truck and ran into the house, anxious to change into her play clothes. "Mom, I'm home," she sang, letting the screen door slam as she always did.

Popillo parked the old truck off the road about fifty yards from the worn path that led to the remnants of Fort Mansfield. He took a flashlight with him as he always did when visiting Tiger. Unlike his friend, he couldn't get through the maze without the light to lead him. Besides, the musty old place gave him the creeps from the moment he entered the darkness.

Walking up the path, he found nothing unusual, just myriad tracks cast in the sand from local beach walkers. As he approached the ruins, the boy flicked on the torch and let its bright white beam play at the entrance for a moment, as if there was someone or something in the darkness that might spring out at the unwelcomed light. Nothing. He walked a few feet closer, still training the flashlight on the opening, but all was quiet. Popillo swallowed hard and pushed into the tunnel, fighting back against the immediate sense of claustrophobia that enveloped him. His skin was crawling as he took the first few steps inside, and he might have turned and run out if not for the concern he had about the drifter. Something wasn't right, he'd known it since early afternoon when Tiger failed to visit at the Lapkin mansion. Now his nerves were screaming alarms, yet he didn't know why. He was suddenly full of dread and apprehension.

Cautiously, the young man crept deeper into the tunnel, all the while scanning ahead of him.

Then he stopped, seized by a sudden urge to look down. He aimed the torch at the dirt beneath his feet. He stood motionless, seeing but not comprehending and his heart began to pound so violently he was afraid it could be heard. Below him were a set of enormous footprints stretching out as far as he could see, right into the great room. They were deeply etched into the gray soil, suggesting extreme weight. "Boot tracks," he thought, but couldn't imagine the size of the man who wore them. For sure, they weren't Tiger Griswold's. Popillo's hands shook. Someone had been here, someone very big. Then fear gripped him. Was he still here?

With his fear for Tiger growing, the young man continued forward at a faster clip, fighting his own anxieties with every step. He came to the great room and flicked the torch off, listening intently for any sounds. There was nothing. Popillo turned the flashlight back on, but just for a moment to get his bearings and get a fix on the entrance to the tunnel that would lead him to the drifter's makeshift apartment. He killed the light again, and hearing nothing, began to move around the outer wall of the great room, slowly inching his way to the spot where he thought the entrance was. Feeling the wall as he moved, he stopped every thirty seconds or so to listen. Still quiet.

When he reached the tunnel, he stopped, uncertain of how to proceed. He couldn't make out any noise. He smelled the remnants of a fire, but there was no smoke. He hope that meant Tiger wasn't inside. Dredging up his last bit of courage, he turned into the tunnel, waited a moment, and then turned the torch on. In front of him, the heavy wooden crates, piles of lumber and plywood that had hidden the drifter's private sanctuary were scattered around, tossed aside like so much trash. There was no light inside the room. Popillo took a deep breath. Tiger always left a candle burning whenever he strayed from the underground chamber. He called out.

"Tiger?"

The damp blackness was closing in on the boy as he waited for a response. He could feel the first pangs of terror creeping up his spine and the onset of a severe panic attack. He choked down the anxiety, his throat suddenly dry from fright. Popillo called out to the drifter again, but there was nothing. Just seconds away from being overwhelmed by claustrophobia, he forced himself to step through the doorway of Tiger's hideout. It was empty. With shaking hands, he lit one of the candles so he could save the batteries in his flashlight. It took a minute or so for the flickering soft light to penetrate the darkness. He sat heavily down on the soiled mattress where Tiger slept, and breathed deeply and evenly for a few minutes, calming himself. Then he turned around to see if the bed had been slept in and gasped with horror.

The college student jumped off the bed and staggered away, his eyes absorbing the rivers of blood and gore still dripping slowly down the wall behind it. Uncomprehending, he leaned forward over the mattress and held the torch closer to the wall. He put his left hand down to support himself, but jerked it away as if he had been shocked. The mattress was wet. Popillo put his hand in front of the light and saw blood on his fingers, then realized his clothes were also wet from sitting on the bed. Horrified, he leapt backwards and moved slowly away from the bed, cognizance of what he had seen rapidly sinking in.

His nerves at the breaking point, the young man swung the flashlight wildly around the concrete bunker looking for more signs of mayhem. Iridescent shadows from the lit candle jumped sinisterly across the room as he scanned it, fear nearly suffocating him. Then he saw debris that had been hurriedly gathered together into a pile. It hadn't been there when he'd last visited, just a couple of days before.

He focused the light on the mound of refuse, slowly approaching it. His breathing was ragged and distressed and he felt like his head was going to explode. Popillo stuck his foot out to kick some of the debris away, not sure of what to make of it. He moved a small wooden crate out the way - and looked into the cold, wide eyes of a dead man, his bloodless skin already putrefying in the warm dampness of the bunker. The top of his head was blown off and shattered brain matter hung limply from its cavity. The wound looked rancid.

Unable to tear his eyes away from the horrifying sight, it was several minutes before Andy Popillo's brain fully registered the shock. As he took in the brutal slaying of his friend, he was finally overwhelmed and sagged to his knees, vomited uncontrollably, bile rising from his stomach until there was nothing left to wretch. And then he did what any sane person would do when confronted with such a ghastly discovery.

He began screaming, the kind of blood curdling howl that rises up from the depths of a man's soul when he is witness to an unthinkable act of unspeakable depravity.

And he could not stop.

Twenty-Three

~~~ ~~~

Jacksonville, Florida

'Ya know, Gordon, we've got to turn this sumbitch hurricane over to Washington tonight, but I'll be damned if I know where it is," Grady Norton confessed to Gordon Dunn late Tuesday afternoon. "There ain't a ship within a hundred miles of the bastard and we haven't had a good report since this morning."

"I know, Grady, we've scared 'em all off," Dunn commiserated. "Seems like we done our job a little too good this time."

"You pick up anymore news out of the Bahamas?" Norton asked hopefully.

"No," Dunn replied. "We haven't been able to raise Willis Shipman since this morning. I don't think it's anything to worry about, chances are they
~~~

caught the side skirt of the hurricane and had some wind damage. Probably just phones out. We'll keep trying."

Norton took a long drag from his cigarette thinking over what Dunn had said. "You're probably right, Gordon. Every indication we had from the Bahamas last night was that pressure was rising, wind speed was dropping and the bastard would blow by well north of the islands. Nonetheless, let's keep trying to raise Shipman to be sure."

Although the danger of a catastrophic collision with the Florida coast had significantly diminished by early Tuesday morning, Grady Norton's US Weather Bureau's crew in Jacksonville had been busy all day trying to track the hurricane. Even with severely limited visibility into the storm's behavior, as nearly all shipping activity in the region had been redirected to safer routes, the meteorologists and forecasters tracking the monster storm remained convinced that it would continue on its northerly track and simply blow itself out as the waters turned colder. There was no information to suggest any possibility that the storm had ceased to recurve. The morning radio report issued at nine o'clock in the morning of another fiercely hot day radio in Jacksonville continued to indicate that the hurricane was traveling slowly to the north. Norton had been direct in his announcement, and those listening thought they could hear confidence in his voice.

"Northeast storm warnings are ordered for the North Carolina coast between Wilmington and

Cape Hatteras," Norton said in his deep gravelly voice, a cigarette, as always, in his hand. "At seven o'clock, Eastern Standard Time, a hurricane of great intensity was last located near latitude 28° north, longitude 75° west which is about three hundred miles east of Vero Beach, Florida. It is now moving north northwestward at about seventeen miles per hour. The lowest recorded barometric pressure reported during the night was 28.9."

By three that afternoon, Norton and Dunn assumed that the hurricane was about three hundred fifty miles east of Daytona Beach, and was slowly moving north-northeast. At the same time, they were concerned about the rain band surrounding the eyeball of the hurricane that could bring gale force winds and downpours along the eastern seaboard. Norton issued another broadcast. "The storm will continue to turn north-northeast and move rapidly during the next thirty-six hours," he said. "The center will pass some distance east of Cape Hatteras late tonight or Wednesday morning."

The lights burned late again into the hot, humid night in Jacksonville as Norton and his men doggedly tried to pinpoint the exact location of the hurricane. Still, even with the drastically limited visibility that eliminated any certainty, neither Norton nor Dunn was worried. All indications were that the storm was slowly dying and ultimately would amount to nothing more than a Cape Verde bluster.

"Anything from the Bahamas, Gordon?" Norton asked his friend. He looked up at the clock. It was nearly eight in the evening. If things held, at nine p.m. he would issue another broadcast indicating that the hurricane was continuing to track on a north-northeast heading and would continue to due so over the next twenty-four hours. He would also issue storm warnings extending along the eastern seaboard from north of Wilmington, North Carolina to Atlantic City, New Jersey. At three o'clock in the morning, tracking of the storm would officially pass to Washington, D.C. and young Charlie Pierce.

"No, dammit. We can't raise him, or anyone else for that matter," Dunn responded. "I've had one of the guys on it full time since after lunch. We can't get through by telephone or radio." A young man in his mid-twenties approached the pair, his face wet with perspiration.

"Mr. Dunn," he said, "here's the request for assistance you asked for; we'll need to send it through Washington and then on the Secretary of Defense. Mr. Norton needs to sign it first."

Dunn took the single sheet of paper from him and gave it a quick read.

"The Secretary of Defense?" Norton asked, puzzled. "Why, what are you boys up to?"

"It's a request to have the US Coast Guard in Miami hightail it out to Nassau and find out what the hell is happening on the islands. I'm afraid I don't have a better idea." Norton signed the document and gave it back to the young man. "Send that directly to Charlie Mitchell, he's the senior forecaster in Washington. Tell him we need this as soon as possible, okay?"

The junior meteorologist took the signed document from Norton's hand. "Yes, sir, I'm on it," he said. Norton watched him hurry back to his desk and pick up the phone.

"Ya know, Gordon, we've got some damn fine people here. They're tireless, dedicated…" he said.

Dunn took a drag from his cigarette before responding.

"You're right about that, Grady. But they're frustrated, too," he said.

"Frustrated? By what?" Norton replied, puzzled again.

"Well… and now don't go takin' this personally, Grady…"

"Why the hell would I take it personally?"

"There's a general degree of concern in the room about our failure to nail the location of this thing," Dunn explained. "They're frustrated about being so blind; and to a man, they don't believe we're completely out of the woods yet."

Norton was silent and studied his shoes for a couple of minutes.

"Yah, well shit, they'd be right now, wouldn't they?" he finally replied looking up at Dunn. "Hell, I don't like it any more than they do." He paused, wiping a handkerchief across his forehead. "I mean we goddamn *don't* know for sure where it is."

The tired weatherman looked older than his years as he stared into Dunn's eyes. He spoke slowly, the grave burden of responsibility he carried finally chafing through the rough, tough and confident persona he wore in the office, for the benefit of the men and boys around him.

"And goddamn it, Gordon," he concluded, shaking his head with worry.

"It's a might scary to lose something that's as big as a fucking state and makes enough noise to cure a deaf man."

Twenty-Four

~~~ ൞ ~~~

Aboard the SS Carinthia

One hundred fifty miles north of Florida, the luxury cruise liner *SS Carinthia* had enjoyed warm, clear skies and calm seas for much of its journey after leaving New York City the previous Sunday. Captain A.C. Greig cautiously hugged the Atlantic coastline as he steered the twenty thousand ton vessel under his command, always mindful of the hurricane warnings that his ship's crew were carefully monitoring around the clock. *Carinthia* had never strayed more than one hundred miles off the coast, routing well away from the storm, which at last report from the US Weather Bureau was well south of the ship's position.

Blissfully unaware of the Captain's tireless efforts to ensure the quality of their sailing
~~~

experience, the ship's six hundred passengers had enjoyed the clear warm skies and calm seas the *Carinthia* had found thus far on the voyage. Some of them had paid as much as $112.50 for a thirteen-day sail that would bring the ship to the port cities of Havana, Kingston and Nassau. Greig was determined that the Cunard-White Star Line cruise would not be disrupted by even cloudy weather, let alone a hurricane.

As mountains of cracked crab, chilled lobster and caviar were washed down with a fabulous selection of choice wines and champagnes at luncheon and dinner aboard the vessel, there was not so much as a word of worry about the storm. Even passenger Charles Revson had forgotten about it, choosing to place the safety of his family in the good Captain's well-experienced hands. There were few others in the world that could command such trust and respect from the millionaire businessman.

The fine sailing weather had relaxed even the hard charging Revson, a legend in his own time on Wall Street. As Chairman and Chief Executive Officer of the rapidly expanding Revlon Corporation, he had little patience for even those company subordinates who supported his every action and decision without question and had respect for him bordering on the reverential. Anyone not in that tight inner circle could expect the Chairman to behave with near boorish manners, without apology. Even his beloved wife, Ancky, and two adored young sons, John and Charles Jr., could be victims of his outbursts.

Not on the ocean though. Ancky Revson had long ago discovered the crack in her husbands steely corporate hide when he first invited her to come along on a business trip to Europe. She marveled at the almost magical transformation that came over him from the moment they stepped aboard one of the grand vessels he loved to sail from Chelsea Piers in New York City. His personality changed from Wall Street tyrant to kind and gentle lover and husband with the most impeccable manners. The couple spent hours together on these voyages, holding hands, sharing candlelit dinners and, amazingly, chatting up conversations that often left Ancky spellbound by her husband. From then on, she had demanded that they sail together at least twice a year. The practice had rekindled their marriage and now Charles Revson looked forward to their romantic getaways as much as she.

Late Tuesday afternoon he accompanied Ancky to a fashion show staged in one of *Carinthia*'s two sea-view lounges. Revson was delighted to learn that the featured designer was none other than his good friend, French couturier Gabrielle Bonheur "Coco" Channel. He immediately insisted to a delighted Ancky that she must purchase some of Channel's new fall line out of respect for the famed European stylist. He was disappointed to learn that Coco herself was not aboard, the fashion show actually being sponsored by one of Channel's most important aristocratic clients, Martha, Countess de Gontaut-Biron.

"Why Mr. Revson, I am so grateful that you have come," the silver- haired Countess admitted upon seeing the couple enter the gaily decorated port side lounge. "Countess," he replied, chivalrously kissing her extended right hand, "Madame Chanel and I have similar philosophies.

"One is that we are both driven to excellence," he continued. "The second is that we understand that our rather unique businesses are both industrial and romantic by nature." The Countess was enthralled. "You see, in the factory, I make cosmetics. In the drugstore, I sell hope. I would argue that in the sewing houses, Madame Channel creates designs. But in the couturier boutiques, she sells dreams," Revson said with an obvious sparkle in his eyes.

"Hope and dreams - my dear, it would seem that Coco and I have discovered the secret to life." The countess squealed with delight.

The millionaire's relaxed mood began to shift when he happened to glance out at the ocean through the large lounge windows. He was quite surprised to see that in less than thirty minutes since he and Ancky had entered the dining room, the clear blue skies had turned an ugly gray. As he peered out at the ocean on the port side, he also noticed that the water had calmed significantly, almost glassy save for a slight breeze pushing ripples across its surface. On the horizon, there appeared to be a sickly yellowish pall emerging well off in the distance. While not a trained seaman, Revson had spent enough time on the Atlantic Ocean to know that they were in for some kind of blow.

On the bridge, Captain Greig also had been surprised to watch the weather conditions change so quickly. He instructed his radioman to contact other ships in the area for updates on the sea conditions, but a short time later the crewman returned to report that there was not another ship within one hundred miles of *Carinthia*. Greig had been confident that he had ably steered his ship away from the hurricane he knew to be in the vicinity. It should be far to the southeast of the vessel's current position. Suddenly, he wasn't so certain. In fact, as Greig and his six hundred passengers were about to find out, *Carinthia* was sailing right into the open jaws of the massive storm with winds in excess of one hundred fifty miles per hour.

Near sunset, the sky had turned a hideous shade of yellow that was the talk of the ship. The seas had gone completely flat and there was an eerie calm in the air. Greig's stomach churned as he considered what was coming next, but he wasn't about to waste time fretting about it.

"First Officer," he hollered to his second in command, a young British lad not much more than twenty-five years old. "See to it the boats are uncovered at once," he said, referring to the eighteen lifeboats aboard, then paused for a moment, contemplating his next order for fear of creating panic. He finally erred on the side of caution. "Also, instruct the ships stewards to lay out lifejackets for all passengers immediately."

First Officer Jake McAndrews moved smartly at the Captain's orders. A moment later, Greig ordered that the ship's orchestra conductor be brought to the bridge. The musician, who had just joined *Carinthia*'s crew and did not know the Captain, wasted no time in responding to the summons.

"At your service, Captain, I am Piero Calanti from Genoa," he said in a clipped Italian accent while saluting Greig. He was a short, heavy set man with rapidly thinning, jet black hair. He more than made up for his sparse hairline with a thick salt-and-pepper mustache which was theatrically waxed at each end.

"Thank you for coming Mr. Calanti, welcome to my Bridge." The Captain took up the conductor's sleeve and pulled him aside. "Mr. Calanti, I'm afraid we are in for quite a storm; and I wonder if I can count on you to help us."

"Why of course, Captain, anything. It is not everyday a musician is asked such a thing. I am humbled," the little man said genuinely.

"As the seas pick up and the winds began to howl, I would like you play as loud as you can, and choose music that will encourage the passengers to dance," Greig said. "I am hoping you can help me distract them from the storm for as long as possible."

The conductor smiled. "*Forte e voloce*!" he said. "Loud and fast, Captain, as you request. It will be done."

The sudden activity by the ship's crew went largely unnoticed by the passengers, most of whom were already enjoying dinner, the social highlight of each day on the water. Below decks, stewards broke out lifejackets for each passenger aboard and heavy canvas tarps were removed from the lifeboats at each station. First Officer McAndrews ordered the kitchen to boil extra coffee for the crew. They would need it for the long night ahead.

Greig was right. The seas began to build up shortly and the winds to howl as the orchestra played louder and faster. Soon however, the pitching of the ship was more than any of the dining room patrons could safely cope with and stewards hurried them all to the shelter of their luxury accommodations. Still the orchestra played on until the undulations of the rocking ship were too much even for the brave musicians.

Shortly after nine p.m., Greig watched helplessly but defiantly as *Carinthia* plowed head on into the massive hurricane. There was simply no way to escape. In minutes, visibility from the bridge was cut to zero as sheer walls of rain water dropped from the sky. Winds that would knock a man off his feet hammered at plate glass windows on the promenade decks and the bridge. The weather quickly became more dangerous than anything Greig had ever encountered in more than thirty years at sea.

Worse, the seas turned into a nightmare of terrifying waves the size of mountains that broke upon the vessel with epic force, driving its twenty thousand tons of steel deep down into an ocean trough only to rise up again on the other side a hundred feet higher. Then *Carinthia* would fall again and repeat the horrifying cycle over and over again.

Greig silently wondered which would be the wave that would finally suck his ship so far beneath the surface that it could not possibly rise up again and bitterly vowed to man his station on the Bridge to the end. Inside he was seething at the misinformation broadcast by the US Weather Bureau station in Jacksonville that had led him to believe his ship and its innocent cargo were safe from the hurricane. He felt betrayed by their ineptness, but was crushed by the emptiness of realizing that he had failed in his own responsibilities of command.

However, the pragmatic side of Greig was not of a mind to give up the fight while he had an ounce of strength left. He ordered every stoker on the ship into the engine room and gave instructions to keep the boilers working at full capacity. If the ship lost power, control of the ship would be lost nearly immediately and *Carinthia* would capsize. Only so long as its mighty steam powered engines continued to maintain propulsion did the ship have a fighting chance. With some measure of control, Greig could wage the battle from the wheelhouse, keeping her headed into the ferocious waves. Sweat poured from his brow as he managed the huge ship's wheel himself. In the sweltering and claustrophobic engine rooms, he knew the men shoveling coal non-stop into *Carinthia*'s huge boilers had it far worse. They had to fight both the draining physical labor and the nagging fear of being trapped in the bowels of the iron ship with no chance of escape should she founder.

At midnight, the First Officer entered the Bridge, his protective oilskins draining water onto the wooden deck. He had been working with the ship's crew, all of whom were tethered to safety lines to prevent them from being washed overboard, battening down every door, hatch and porthole on the vessel. They were like drowned rats after only an hour of work, the rain coming down so hard that it was sometimes impossible to catch a breath of air.

McAndrews called out to Greig. "Should we order the passengers to the boats?" The young First Officer was terrified but desperately wanted to perform the duties assigned him. He'd be damned that anyone should ever consider him a coward, no matter what the circumstances.

Greig was about to snarl at the Officer, then thought twice about it, even as he wrested the ship's wheel. "Mr. McAndrews, please come closer so I can hear you," he said. The First Officer immediately obeyed, struggling to keep his feet as he approached his Captain.

When he was sure the other officers on the Bridge could not hear him, he spoke quietly to his inexperienced First Officer, respectful of the man's intention to do his job.

"Mr. McAndrews, in a word, sir, are you daft?" The young man's head snapped back as if he had been struck. "If we attempt to load the boats, they will all be dead in minutes.

"Aye, sir." he responded without questioning his superior. "Then should I at least send out an SOS, sir?"

"No, son -- any ship within reach of us, and I believe there are none -- will be in the same pickle that we are," Greig said.

He looked the younger officer square in the eye, trying to quell the panic he saw in the man's eyes. "We're all fighting for our lives Mr. McAndrews. Now make yourself useful and go and check on the pumps." McAndrews did not respond immediately, shocked by the Captain's calming voice in a nearly out of control situation. He snapped to.

"Aye sir, at once," he responded, his voice quivering but with purpose in his stride as he hurriedly set off to the bottom of the ship. Greig already knew what he would find - a hold taking on water faster than the pumps could manage.

All over *Carinthia,* whatever was not bolted down was upended by the constant gyrating of her hull. The unmistakable crash of falling chandeliers and breaking dishes, the tinkle of shattering crystal and the roar of tables and chairs toppling across the floor filled the main dining room. Huddled in their cabins, passengers held on to their loved ones and desperately fought to keep from being hurled about.

For the very young and the elderly, the trial was that much more severe, and the cries of pain from a gashed head or broken bone rang out below decks. It was a symphony of the natural noises a steel vessel wails when it is dying. *Carinthia* was bent, torn and near breakup, sounds amplified by the creaking and moaning of wooden decks being pounded again and again by waves bent on shattering them.

From the Bridge, Greig, still fighting the wheel of his ship, heard these sounds and knew that *Carinthia* could not take much more before she would founder. He saw her decks awash with the white foam of seawater and watched in awe as waves broke as high as the Bridge. His beautiful ship was being systematically beaten to death, he knew; and for an instant, he wondered how the end would come. The Aussie silently prayed that his wife and children would be cared for.

Still, the white steamship fought on, as did her Captain and crew. In the boiler rooms, hard muscled stokers shoveled for all they were worth. At times the vessel's lights would flicker and go out, only to spring on again a second later. Black from coal dust and rapidly dehydrating from heat greater than one hundred twenty degrees Fahrenheit, the two dozen men attacked the furnaces with every thing they had, and more. The "black gang" swore that if *Carinthia* was doomed, it would not be from cold fires.

The torturous night passed on. Around three o'clock in the morning, Captain Greig, still at the wheel, felt a sudden loosening of the steering gear and feared the worst. Then, as he looked over the horizon, he saw it: clear sky. As suddenly as the storm had drawn *Carinthia* into its powerful grasp, it relinquished its hold on the tired ship. The seas calmed and the winds died at a miraculous pace. She had made it.

Greig immediately informed the boiler room to stand down, and the grateful men dropped to their knees in relief, so tired they were unable to take celebration from their victory. Stewards raced throughout the ship, tending to frightened passengers and the many injured. Slowly, people began to emerge on deck again, some crying, some praying, but all breathing deeply from the crystal clear air that followed the hurricane, as refreshing as the smell of cherry blossoms in spring. They reveled in the surprising warmth that followed the storm and patiently waited for the sun to rise. Only then could most of them truly believe they had survived an ordeal that few ever lived to talk about.

First Officer McAndrews approached the Captain, still at the helm, whose red streaked eyes remained focused on the horizon.

"Captain," he said, choking up. "I have never been so honored to serve with a ship's master. That was the most incredible display of seamanship -- and dare I say it, bravery -- I have ever encountered on the seas or may ever hope to."

Finally relinquishing control to a Quartermaster after more than seven hours at the helm, the Captain slowly pried his fingers from their locked positions at ten and three as the clock goes on the ships wheel. Only then did Greig turn to his junior officer. A broad grin came to his tired face.

"I dare say, young man, I'd like to save this conversation for when we make port in Havana and can share three fingers of the finest whiskey we can find at the first bar we see," Greig said. "But in the meantime, never mistake 'bravery' for 'shit scared', son. Believe me when I say I have never experienced such a night in all my years of living off the oceans. Real courage is simply refusing to give up. I saw a fair share of that in you last night, as well. One day you'll make a fine Captain yourself, lad."

McAndrews, flustered by the unexpected compliment, could only manage a soft, "Thank you, sir," in response. Then he thought better of it.

"To hell with three fingers, sir," he said, a boyish grin coming to his face. "Let's each take a whole bloody bottle and sit on the beach with it."

"Aye, First Officer," Greig replied. "But I warn you - facing the sunrise on the following day will take as much courage as last night." Both men laughed aloud, the night's tension on the Bridge finally broken.

Then Grieg turned deadly serious.

"But first, Mr. McAndrews, please have the radioman ring up our friends at the US Weather Bureau station in Jacksonville, at once."

"Of course, Captain, to relay information on the storm? I'd like to check the barometer readings first, sir," McAndrews responded, all business again.

"Yes, Mr. McAndrews, to relay information about the storm," he replied calmly, "but also to express my regrets."

"Regrets, sir?"

Yes," Grieg snapped, his eyes filled with fury. "Please inform the station chief that if I did not have the responsibility to further "entertain" *Carinthia*'s guests on this voyage, I would be obliged to change course and visit him at the port nearest Jacksonville."

"To what purpose sir?" the First Officer blurted, completely puzzled.

Just then, Charles Revson burst onto the bridge. The look in his eyes told the Captain all he needed to know about his old friend's state of mind. Revson's family was still gathered in their quarters, sick and terrified. Greig's fists balled in anger.

"I want to personally 'thank' the bloody incompetent bastard who placed the monster that nearly killed us last night more than one hundred miles from our course."

The silence on the Bridge was deafening.

Twenty-Five

~~~ ঌ ~~~

Fort Mansfield

Flood lights had been hastily erected inside the ruins of Fort Mansfield just before the Connecticut detectives arrived. Fed by a small gasoline powered generator, the continuous throaty hum of the engine broke the normal rush of the surf breaking just a few hundred feet away. Westerly Police Chief Gil Cianci led the two men to the entrance of the ruins, where one of his patrolmen took them inside.

"Be careful," the patrolman warned them. "Even with the floodlights, you'll find it pretty weird in here. Imagine old Tiger Griswold was living out here the whole time. Who wudda known it..."

"Then we're certain it's Griswold, Chief?" Irv Nicklas asked. He was tired as hell and very
~~~

cranky. His partner, Sam Cawley wasn't feeling much better and he was hacking from chain smoking most of the day. This prick they were looking for was really getting under his skin.

"Afraid so, boys," replied Cianci, not exactly happy about what was happening in his town. "From what the investigating officer told me on the phone, poor Tiger's pretty tore up; but we were able to make a positive I.D. We're running his prints through the F.B.I. just to be doubly certain. A real shame, he was a nice guy. Poor bastard was horribly disfigured in the goddamn war. Just drifted from place to place, wanted to be left alone."

"You think our man done this?" Cawley asked. Sam didn't have much time for grieving someone he didn't know. The job had hardened him.

"Dunno for sure," Cianci replied. "Let's see what we got."

The three men entered Griswold's chamber. Cianci shook his head wondering how it was that no one had any inkling that Tiger had been living there, and for quite some time, it appeared. No one, he thought, but that nice college kid. He spotted Andy Popillo huddled in a corner with a blanket around his shoulders. His eyes were puffy and red, like he'd been crying. Not many folks had the stomach to see someone butchered.

"You okay, Andy?" the Chief asked him, putting one of his beefy arms around the kid.

"Yah, I'm alright, Chief. Just can't believe it, that's all," Andy said quietly, still unnerved two hours after he'd found the body. It had taken him quite awhile to stop shaking from the shock of finding Tiger's mutilated remains and the terror of not knowing if the killer was still lurking inside the Fort. He had prayed to his father to help him fight the panic that nearly overwhelmed him, and then raced the Lapkin's old truck to the Yacht Club to call the police. The young man fought the urge to retch as he led a half-dozen, shotgun-wielding police officers back to the scene within the hour.

Irv Nicklas had already inspected the body; and after a photographer finished taking pictures of the murder scene, he signaled the Chief that they could remove Tiger's remains. Andy Popillo sobbed as two men carried the lifeless corpse, covered by a sheet that was heavily stained with blood, outside to a waiting ambulance.

Sam Cawley, all business, was poring over the huge foot prints that were all over the dirt floor of the underground chamber.

There was no hiding it, Charles Dewey had been there. From the sadistic way Tiger had been killed to the way in which they discovered his crumpled body, which left no doubt that the man's body had been thrown across the room, all evidence pointed to the gruesome giant. The whole gore-splattered, bloody mess reeked of Dewey.

"No doubt about it, Chief, the guy we're looking for did this. He'll do it again unless we find the son of a bitch and put him down hard," Cawley said. He turned to the Westerly Police Chief, squatting to examine the giant footprints engraved in the dust of the stone hideaway's floor. "You got any ideas?" he asked Cianci, a slight but hardly unnoticeable scent of sarcasm in his voice.

The Chief slowly rose to his feet, dusting the dirt off his hands as he stood. Do I have any ideas, he thought to himself…the condescending prick. Cianci bit his tongue, not wanting to risk a confrontation in front of his own men.

"Well for one thing," he finally responded, "we're gonna keep a lid on this fucking mess until we nail the bastard, understood? I want nothing reported to the press, and tell any reporter who telephones that we'll have to return his call. Make sure that Popillo is informed as well. He is to speak to no one about what happened here tonight."

Cawley rolled his eyes as if what he had just heard was stupid. Cianci ignored it. "I think the best way of flushing this guy out is to make him believe we're not on to him yet, let him think we're confused." Cawley rolled his eyes again. The Chief caught it.

"You got a problem with something I just said, Sam?"

"Well, I guess I do," Cawley responded condescendingly. "Not letting the people of this community know that there's some gigantic, weird motherfucker who likes the taste of blood running through their backyards doesn't seem like smart thinking to me… Chief."

The color of Cianci's face changed as he fought down his immediate instinct to wrap his oversize hands around the Connecticut detective's throat and squeeze until his eyes burst. He took half a step forward to do just that before he caught himself.

"Sam, shut the fuck up and let the Chief finish," Nicklas interrupted. Cianci took a deep breath trying to get his anger in control, then fished around for a cigarette which he lit before continuing.

"Well I'm sorry you feel that way, Detective Cawley," Cianci said, regaining his control. "However I hardly think completely terrorizing every living soul in Westerly and out here on the Point will have any bearing on our ability to flush this bastard out. I would expect that anyone with a gun stashed in the house won't hesitate to start shooting at things that go 'boo' in the night -- which will only make things a lot worse.

"What then, Chief?" Nicklas said, at least trying to be respectful to the man. Cianci looked hard at Cawley waiting for some wise ass comment before he continued. Surprisingly, he behaved.

"Immediately we're gonna set up a sort of roadblock, two cars, no lights, just very quiet. Two men in each car. One car will follow any vehicle that enters Fort Road all the way to its destination as far as Sandy Point and then inspect it. Every car leaving from any part of the Point will be quietly – and I mean 'quietly' – challenged before they enter Watch Hill." He motioned to one of his patrolmen, who nodded and immediately left the room. Nicklas noted that Cianci's guys did what they were told without hesitation, but they didn't appear to be intimidated by their supervisor in any way. He wondered if he underestimated the guy.

"Unfortunately, it's too late and too goddamned dark to have much chance of finding this frigging ape now, and I don't want to put my guys at risk," he continued. "So, what we're going to do for the rest of the night is send two-man teams to walk the beaches on both the Ocean and Bay sides and see if we don't find him trying to hide in the dunes. "Harry, call Dispatch and have him call in every man who's off duty for any reason." Nicklas saw even his jaded partner raise his eyes at the speed at which the chief's orders were followed.

"At first light we're gonna sweep the whole of Napatree Point, go door to door of every house in the entire neighborhood until we unearth this bastard. If we don't find him, then we're going to use clam rakes on the whole goddamned fucking beach if we have to." He was trying to hide his anger about eventually being forced into scaring the hell out of the whole town. Shit, the whole state, he thought. "We won't be able to hide the situation if we don't flush out our boy before morning. It will scare the friggin' bejezus out of everybody, but it can't be helped."

Unexpectedly, he continued, looking first at Nicklas and then taking aim at Cawley. "Before we wrap this up, I'm going to give you boys a chance to add your own thoughts." Cawley rolled his eyes again, but Cianci didn't bite.

"Because after you do, the two of you are to shut your fucking mouths, is that clear? I've had enough of your condescending bullshit and quite frankly, haven't seen much substance since you big city detectives graced our town with your presence. So here's your chance, boys – spit it out now or shut your fucking traps."

Irv Nicklas winced, but didn't blame the man. They hadn't shown the guy much respect. Sam Cawley acted like he was going to cough up a cat and his face turned beet red. Nicklas responded for both of them.

"You're on the money, Chief," he said sheepishly. "You're the boss, no questions asked." Cianci nodded, emotionless. "We'll get this motherfucker if it's the last thing we do," he said.

There was silence in the cold concrete tomb as Cianci let the tension ease off.

"Okay, let's go get him," the Chief said. He turned to a tall, slightly overweight uniformed cop and spoke to him clearly and succinctly. It was Jimmy Calderella, a twenty-year man who'd made lieutenant just a year ago.

"Lieutenant Calderella," he said, his voice strong but composed. "One last thing. Please see to it that every man in the department is aware of the following order under my authority." Every eye that hadn't been on the Chief now was.

"If our man turns up, shoot to kill the son of a bitch," he said, stone-faced. "And use as many bullets as you can. "

Wednesday September 21, 1938

Twenty-Six

~~~ ❧ ~~~

Jacksonville, Florida

While the rain slowly abated and Charles Dewey hunted in vain for dry shelter along the Napatree Point beach, the office lights were burning bright in the national headquarters of the United States Weather Bureau in the Capital city. Responsibility for tracking the monster storm had passed to it from the Hurricane Center in Jacksonville. It was nearly three a.m.

That was not to say that Grady Norton, Gordon Dunn and their two dozen staffers had closed up shop in Florida. It was just the process. By policy, when a major event had bypassed one of the Bureau's stations, the next in line was the natural recipient to locate, track, monitor and issue advisories about the potential storm.
~~~

For Grady Norton, following his sign-off advisory to the residents of the state of Florida, finally putting them to ease that the state had indeed dodged a very large bullet, such times generally were accompanied by a great sense of relief. He and his men had done their jobs, a big chunk of the world was safe and the sleep would be good tonight.

At exactly three a.m. on the 21st, Norton took the shortwave microphone and in the comforting voice that had eased Floridians through this and countless other potential weather catastrophes, informed his listeners that the Weather Bureau now believed that the hurricane was located about two hundred seventy-five miles off Cape Hatteras and was moving rapidly but predictably on a north-northeast track, but still well off the coast.

"Be advised that dangerous hurricane-force winds and high tides on the coastlines can and should be expected and residents are urged to take appropriate precautions and make emergency preparations," Norton advised. "This storm is moving at approximately forty miles per hour, as we had forecasted earlier. Given its track and speed, storm warnings remain in effect as far north as Atlantic City, New Jersey." He paused for a moment, choking up a bit. This one had been a nightmare to track, and emotionally, he and his colleagues were entirely spent.

"Finally, this is Grady Norton of the United States Weather Bureau in Jacksonville, signing off," he spoke into the microphone, his collar open, sleeves rolled up and a cigarette dangling from his bottom lip. He was bone tired, and the oppressive heat of the last ten days had also taken its toll. "For further updates on this still dangerous storm, please tune to the continuous Weather Bureau updates that will commence immediately from Washington, D. C."

He paused again before adding the refrain for which he was legend, the words that once and for all put his anxious listeners at peace.

"Good night and God bless." He released his grip on the trigger of the microphone and gently placed it back on his desk.

Immediately, Gordon Dunn and all of the exhausted staff in the small quarters of the Jacksonville office rose to their feet and broke into loud applause and cheers. Grady Norton had done a hell of a job, as usual, but each man in the room knew that he personally had also contributed in some way. Their performance together had personified the solidarity of purpose that any man who worked for Norton had to embrace completely and absolutely. To become one of his hand-picked hellcats, a man had to beat a storm to death with instincts and analysis before admitting defeat. Gordon Dunn swore that sometimes they killed a storm just by haranguing it to death.

Unfortunately, this wasn't one of those times.

As the lights finally began flickering off in the Jacksonville office shortly before four in the morning, the mood of the men departing for home and much needed rest was now relaxed and confident. In the celebration of the moment, it hadn't occurred to any of them, including Grady Norton, that in actuality they indeed had "lost" the storm and were only assuming they knew its location. Granted, a lot of experience and wisdom went into that assumption; but nonetheless, the exact location of the monster hurricane was, at best, an educated guess.

Unfortunately, the men of the United States Weather Bureau in Jacksonville had based their conclusions on erroneous deductions born of severely curtailed data, a handicap that could only guide them to conclusions that were off the beam. At best, their final determination was the equivalent of a theory based on instinct and experience. Even as the Jacksonville gang closed up shop and gave their innate, academic and intuitive skills -- the very stimuli that drove Norton's hellcats relentlessly – not a man among them had the slightest inkling that they had come to the wrong conclusion. Yet the ultimately inescapable truth was that the best brains in the weather business had got it all wrong.

Dead wrong.

Twenty-Seven

~~~ ~~~

Sandy Point Beach

Mercifully, the rain that had been falling nearly non-stop for the last three days along the ocean coastline between Atlantic City, New Jersey and Bar Harbor, Maine, stopped abruptly just after two a.m. on Wednesday morning. As quickly as the rain stopped, the skies cleared to reveal a glorious array of stars, some just dust marks of light, others so bright they seemed to jump out of the sky. The moon gave off a foggy haze; but the sea air sparkled with clarity, unusually void of its salty pungency. A sweet scent seemed to fill the shoreline of Napatree Point, and indeed all of the beaches along the Rhode Island coast.

For those natives fortunate to have grown up on the Westerly peninsula, the sweetness of the air was
~~~

known as *"Le bouquet apres la pluie"* (the fragrance following the rain). It was a romantic French fable that grew in credibility as each generation fell more in love with the lore. In truth, the "bouquet" was real and often invigorating, enough to awaken one from a deep sleep. At night, with the windows of the great beach houses opened at least partially so as to capture the cool and refreshing ocean air blowing in from the Atlantic side -- calm winds that had traveled thousands of miles from Africa to the sandy shores of the New England coastline – the sudden after rain fragrance was enticing. The old timers, especially, were beckoned enough by the scent to climb out from under their down comforters, put on their robes and slippers and find seats on the great porches facing the sea.

Comfortably ensconced in their wicker summer chairs and rockers, perhaps with a steaming cup of freshly brewed coffee, there they would have a perfect view of the natural spectacle that inevitably followed. Whole families on Napatree Point and Sandy Point watched together as the sun broke through the watery horizon. What emerged was a muted pallet of color that grew broader and stronger in brilliance with each second of the emerging daybreak. The beauty lay not only in the breathtaking halo of tints and shades, but also in the sudden sensation of warmth. It was like a Monet coming to life. *"Le bouquet apres la pluie"* was anticipated after every heavy nighttime summer rainfall on the peninsula, and each was an unforgettable experience.

However breathtaking the new dawn was, there was a man who felt fear from the emerging light of day and took not a moment's peace from nature's show. Charles Dewey had spent the night huddled deep under leaf and branch droppings in search of some relief from the freezing cold rain just a few yards from the warm mansions. He hadn't had a real meal or shower in days, but that was the least of his problems. He was smart enough to know that he was probably being hunted by police in at least six states for multiple counts of first degree murder.

He knew that they were probably referring to him as a "monster" -- a man whose intimidating appearance caused others to cower from him, utterly frightened by his giant, darkly grotesque features. But despite their fear of him, his very appearance made people angry and remarkably cruel to him without cause. He was a man who had been abandoned, abused and locked away nearly his whole life, who had forgotten - or perhaps even worse - had never felt the sensation of what it was like to love or be loved. Consequently, he was a man filled only with hatred and failure who had an overwhelming desire for vengeance and violence which his wretched physique did nothing to cloak.

He was huge and horrifyingly ugly, afraid of no one and nothing, save for one exception: he was reduced to cowardice by the fear of loneliness. No matter his grotesque appearance and violent emotional development, Charles Dewey knew instinctively that he had never deserved to be alone, to be deprived of human relationships. Yet he had never known anything but deprivation.

The convict had been shattered to find that not even life in prison relieved him of this fear. For the very rules of conduct commanded isolation as a method of rehabilitation and even as a mechanism to return him to a useful place in society. Although he *existed* among others, he was prohibited from truly *living* with them. Prison brought an even more hideous form of isolation - it was a place in which there was no hiding from those who would sit in judgment of him.

In the days leading up to his escape from the Wethersfield prison, Dewey had silently vowed that he would not allow himself to be trapped like a wild beast ever again. After running for nearly a week now, the analogies between man and beast hung heavily in his thoughts, and there were moments when he could not be sure of which he was.

These were the venomous thoughts that filled the head of the hungry, exhausted and confused Charles Dewey, now sitting on wet sands in the receding tide. Soon the ocean would begin its creeping progression inland again, slowly retaking the sand bars that the tidal retreat had revealed. Sometime after noon, he figured, the sand bars would flood again, and maybe the day would bring some warmth along with it. He was stilled chilled to the bone, but he knew that the coming sunshine would only make him a bigger target - and increase his dangerously engorged anger and anxiety.

Charles Dewey's few opportunities to become a contributor to society - no matter the status - had by now passed completely, a matter that he surprisingly grappled with in those rare times when he was cognitive of what others saw in him. He had moments of overwhelming self pity, but he was also intelligent enough to know that the vengeance he felt for those who might have helped him had sentenced him to a Frankenstein-like existence. It no longer mattered. Deprived of physical and emotional care his entire life, Charles Dewey was an animal that existed in the body of a man.

Now, he had reached the point of desperation that enables a man - indeed, a violently unstable man - to not only consider the most heinous thoughts and actions, but also to act upon them without pity or remorse. This was the state of mind of the man who was huddled alone on the beach - the small strip of sand that separated the ocean from Fort Road, and his only path to escape.

The glare of a flashlight in the darkness, its narrow probe jiggling around in one hand of a nervous policeman, a fully loaded Smith & Wesson .38 caliber revolver in his other, unexpectedly appeared on the beach about two hundred yards from where Dewey was sitting. He panicked momentarily having no plan of escape, and then recklessly made a run for it. The convict ran across the brush line between the beach and Fort Road, then stopped, realizing he was silhouetted by large street lights. He looked quickly for more flashlights or the telltale beams of a moving car. Seeing none, he sprinted across the road to the first mansion he saw on the Little Narragansett Bay side of Sandy Point Beach, running past its finely trimmed lawn and flower garden beds deep into the darkness of the backyard that ended at a floating wooden dock for tying up small family boats. He waded into the water, its cold temperature nearly taking his breath away and hid down below the Bay edge of the dock and waited. If any one of the lawmen came closer, Dewey thought that he could dive below it and hide beneath its weathered gray decking. He was shivering again in the cold water and fantasized about taking a long pull from a bottle of whiskey.

It was another one of those sudden urges that came over the convict without a moment's thought of the consequences.

Twenty-Eight

~~~ ~~~

U.S. Weather Bureau Headquarters, Washington, D. C.

As the torch was passed to Charlie Pierce in the Washington, D.C. Bureau headquarters, the mood was celebratory. Pierce, filling in for two other more seasoned forecasters, was particularly pleased for Grady Norton. He greatly admired Norton, especially for his instincts, and had been enthralled with his legend while studying meteorology in school. For Pierce, it was certainly no slight to be passed the job of cleaning up the few loose ends that the Jacksonville Chief had left behind.

The responsibility for tracking and warning now fell on the shoulders of the junior forecaster in Washington. He was more than enough up to the
~~~

task, but a shortage of manpower made his job that much harder to manage.

At seven thirty a.m., following the instructions of the senior forecasters on duty, Pierce made his first report on the progress of the storm which he and his colleagues agreed was still headed for deeper and colder water. This proposed northeast track would do nothing more than ruffle a few seagull feathers off the eastern seaboard. The Bureau's report, which was distributed to regional newspapers and local radio stations, placed the storm one hundred forty miles east-northeast of Cape Hatteras at 35° 20' N, 73°W. In fact, the report actually downgraded the storm to a tropical disturbance at the insistence of the more senior Washington forecasters. However, the early-morning forecast for the northeast Atlantic Coast did report that a "broad trough of low pressure extends from New England to the tropical disturbance" in a northerly direction.

Pierce issued the warnings as directed by his superiors, but still had an uneasy feeling in the pit of his stomach about this storm. Actually, the junior forecaster was the only member on duty that morning that was not a believer that all Cape Verde hurricanes died a natural death out over the ocean. But he had little to argue with. Cape Hatteras was reporting that the storm's barometric pressure was easing back up toward 29.7 inches with wind speed estimated at between thirty-five and forty miles per hour blowing from the northwest. What was to worry? Less than thirty minutes later he would find out when his nagging worries went from imagined to real.

At a few minutes after eight that morning, Pierce, who was poring over his charts yet again, received a call directly from Grady Norton. The Jacksonville Chief had returned to work after only a couple of useless hours of trying to sleep, his brain going over and over the data his team had gathered over the last forty-eight hours. He was sure they had touched all the bases, but still, something didn't sit right.

"Charlie, this here's Grady Norton, mornin' to ya boy," he said quickly. "I think we may have a problem with this big old hurricane we've been wrastlin' this week."

Pierce closed his eyes, not knowing what to expect.

"I'm sending you a report we just got from the *SS Carinthia,* one of the fancy cruise ships that floats out of Manhattan and into the Bahamas for a couple of weeks at a time," Norton continued, the stress putting an edge into his voice. "It seems that the poor bastards aboard rode through a helluva storm. In fact, they sailed right into the middle of the hurricane - even though they followed the forecasts and warnings we've been feeding sailors in them waters."

Pierce was still silent on the other end of the phone, trying to assimilate the information Norton was feeding him. "Shit, Charlie, we had this storm pegged more than a hundred miles from *Carinthia* and sixty miles farther east. I all but told the goddamned navy they could throw away their fucking life jackets."

Norton hesitated before going on. "Fact is, son, we don't really know where this thing is."

Pierce remained silent, mostly out of respect for Norton and his obvious embarrassment at such a monumental mistake.

"And get this Charlie," he continued. "We've been flappin' our gums down here about the pressure trying to level off again. I'm afraid we were wrong there too." He paused. "When the storm caught that big boat late yesterday afternoon, in less than one hour and a half, she was recording barometric pressure of 27.65 inches."

Pierce couldn't help himself. "What?" Why that's impossible," he said, disbelieving. "The lowest pressure we've ever recorded was in that monster that blasted the Florida Keys a few years back, something like 26.85 inches. And Christ, that storm was even more powerful than the Galveston disaster back in 1900. It can't be, Grady, it's impossible."

Norton wouldn't budge. "The one thing I've learned in this business - the hard way unfortunately -- is that anything can happen when it comes to the weather," he responded a bit abruptly. Pierce felt the gentle sting. "But in fairness, son, I wouldn't have believed it either at your age. So as I'm talkin' to you on this telephone, I'm also reading another handful of reports that came in from small boats that somehow survived last night following our advice, and they all pretty much tell the same story."

"I'm sorry, Grady, I didn't mean to..." Pierce began to apologize but Norton's next unexpected expletive got in the way.

"What the fuck..." the senior forecaster mumbled into the telephone. "I was wrong again, Charlie. One of these reports was filed later than the others, about an hour ago. I never thought I'd live to see the day..." The tired man's voice trailed off.

"The last boat to report measured 26.9 inches and one hundred forty-five mile per hour winds," Norton said.

Pierce felt the first twinge of panic. He'd never faced anything remotely as powerful as this hurricane. "What about the Bahamas, Grady? Have we had any reports yet from Nassau or any of the other islands?" This time it was Norton's turn to be silent.

"Seems I just did, Charlie," who caught a sudden commotion in the background. "The Coast Guard cutter we sent over yesterday couldn't make radio contact until they were halfway back to the mainland. That's 'cuz all communications on the islands have apparently been wiped out."

"That doesn't sound promising. Grady," Pierce responded, still struggling to make sense of the whole thing. "The Coast Guard guys get any impression of damage over all?"

"What I'm reading here says the waters are so full of debris around the main islands, that they couldn't get the cutter in close enough to inspect." There was a catch in Norton's throat as he finished.

Pierce felt tremendous empathy for the U.S. Weather Bureau's living legend. The younger forecaster couldn't imagine anyone in the service who didn't share his respect and admiration for him.

"Mr. Norton... Grady...you couldn't have worked this any harder," Pierce interjected, trying to buoy the man, especially now, when he would be needed the most. "We're just not going to beat Mother Nature all the time. Hell, we'll be lucky if we get ahead of the game fifty percent of the time."

"Thanks for the support, Charlie, but there's more." Norton suddenly sounded like an old man, Pierce thought. "The Coast Guard report indicates they were able to get close to Marsh Harbour on Great Abaco, the most northern of the Bahamian's. Population of at least five or six thousand people, I'd guess." Norton suddenly stopped and for a moment Pierce thought he has lost their landline connection. Then Norton spoke again.

"The Coast Guard reports that the whole of Great Abaco has been devastated. Completely washed away. They spent time seeking survivors but found no one. In fact, they didn't even find any remains." Then there was silence.

Pierce hung on, expecting Grady Norton to continue, but there was nothing. He could hear some sort of turmoil in the background with people yelling but couldn't make out more than a few phrases like "loosen his tie" and the word "ambulance". Pierce hung on, resisting the thought to hang up and call back. The line was lifeless for a good fifteen minutes with nothing to be heard but what seemed to be turmoil on the other end until finally, Gordon Dunn picked up.

"Charlie, you still there?" he asked.

"Still here, no problem," Pierce responded instantly. "What happened? Is Grady alright?"

"That last bit of news Grady shared with you about the Bahamas knocked him out of the game for a while, Charlie. He just suddenly dropped the phone and grabbed at his chest. We think he might have had a heart attack. Trying to get him to a hospital as we speak."

"Shit, Gordon… it's not his fault. The Good Lord might have had something to do with all this, you know."

"Yah, you try telling that old Alabama buzzard he can't part the waters…" Dunn said, then added, "at least not everyday. I'll keep you posted on his condition. In the meantime, we've got to convince the boys with the bigger desks at your place to take a hard look at this new information immediately. There's not a minute to waste if we have any chance of getting out effective new advisories and warnings."

"I hear ya, Gordon," Pierce said confidently, but already knowing that it would fall to his shoulders to convince his superiors they had to consider a change of plans. "Get me all the data you can, and I'll start working my charts again and putting together a plan of attack. I'll get back to you as soon as I can."

"Charlie?" Dunn said quietly before hanging up.

"Hope you know that we worked this son of a bitch as hard as any storm I've ever been involved with. I'm as shocked as Grady. There ain't no other way of explaining it: we goddamn lost a whole hurricane."

Twenty-Nine

~~~ ☙ ~~~

Sandy Point

Despite the pandemonium that was breaking out in Washington as the Weather Bureau frantically sought to pinpoint the exact location of the hurricane that was still indeed a killer, Wednesday morning September 21, 1938 dawned as one of the most spectacular days of the entire summer. All across Southern New England that year, the gray clouds and torrential downpours that had so oddly defined the usually warm, dry and sunny climate were for the moment, a memory. The surprisingly warm surf was roaring all along the coast with long, tall breakers and rolling waves that surfers dreamt about. Exquisite layers of cirrus clouds stretched across a canvas of sky that was the most brilliant blue tone seen even before the
~~~

summer solstice. Way off on the Atlantic horizon, an odd, mustard-like shade of yellow could be made out stretching across the line where the sky met deeper green waters. The scene was a painter's delight.

In Westerly, the air was crystal clear and sweet, missing the slight aftertaste of salt that had been in the air all summer because of the nearly constant rain Geoffrey Lapkin almost felt guilty sending his three youngest children to school on this day, just because spending it on the beach would simply have been the most spectacular way to officially end the summer. He finally ruled against the thought, unable to concede to the unwritten but widely quoted Lapkin academic philosophy that education was the highest priority of the household, and absence from school was reserved for only those dreadful situations where the decision was unavoidable.

Geoff laughed inwardly as he gave the idea the once over again. He concluded that there was no hope of winning the battle. He would probably have a better chance of success in teaching a whale to talk than he would in mounting a rationale that would convince Emily to let the children take the day off from school because the sun was out. Secretly though, he had an admittedly selfish motivation that resulted in him informing his boss that he wouldn't be in for a couple of days so he could take James back to school. He also had a more reasonable strategy to deal with Emily's concerns and was confident she'd be on board the moment he laid it out for her.

A neatly stuffed, oversized steamer trunk in the corner of James's bedroom actually was the explanation for Geoff's entirely out-of-character absence from the office. In the trunk were the particular requirements of a New England prep school, and an especially prestigious one at that. There were a dozen or more white, oxford cotton shirts with button down collars; one summer weight and one winter weight navy blue blazer; a half dozen school neckties, all properly embroidered in a club pattern of the blue and gold school crest; several pairs of crisply pressed, charcoal colored woolen dress pants, some corduroys and casual shirts and sweaters, sport clothes, a heavy winter pea coat, underwear, polished leather dress shoes, athletic shoes and on and on.

Geoff and Emily would drive their oldest son to the Choate School on Thursday. The boy found leaving home particularly difficult. Silently, Emily took it harder. Geoff expected the drive to Connecticut would be a quiet one, but that the drive back to Napatree Point would be very difficult on Emily. From his own prep school experience, the elder Lapkin knew that by the time they arrived home to Westerly by the following night, James would already be comfortable in his new dormitory room and probably enjoying the season's first touch football game on the campus commons. Geoff also knew that Emily would want to move back to their house in Westerly as soon as possible, probably by the weekend. It seemed to help with James's absence.

The unexpected break in the weather gave father and son a last few hours together. Geoffrey reserved the grandest of the Yacht Club's single mast, day sailers for the entire afternoon. After exploring Little Narragansett Bay together, father and son planned to anchor off Sandy Point in front of the summer home, row Emily and the children over to the boat and then sail to Stonington, Connecticut to *Skipper's Dock Restaurant*, a Lapkin family favorite. He could afford to take his family to just about any restaurant they desired, but the Lapkin men delighted in picking their own lobsters out of *Skipper*'s display tanks, most of which had been dragged from a shallow water pot no more than a few hours before.

The boys had a fondness for *Skipper's* fresh lobsters after a particular dinner they shared there one night about a year ago. Both Emily and Katie were deathly afraid of the weird looking sea creatures though, so they set some ground rules. Neither of them would be responsible for choosing their lobsters from the tank for fear of establishing a relationship with the creepy looking crustaceans. Emily and Kate elected Brian to take command of the duty and he was raring to go.

Of course, the most mischievous of the brood just had to find a way to make his mother and sister pay for being "sissies". So, after carefully selecting their lobsters along with his own, he promptly began to articulate the personal characteristics of each of the two special invertebrates he had selected for his mother and sister. The *coup de grâce* was his graphic description, despite their pleading with him to stop, of how the unsuspecting creatures squealed, instantly turned bright red and thrashed about as they endured the agony of being boiled alive.

Shocked, Katie said she was going outside to throw up; and Emily, whose normally rosy pallor had taken on the appearance of chalk, excused herself for a visit to the ladies' powder room. Brian's fun was short lived. Geoff could no longer contain himself.

"You know Brian, sometimes you just go a little too far," his father finally said, trying to keep his anger in check.

"So rather than put the rest of the evening's success in your surprisingly juvenile hands, leave your mother and sister to me. With one exception. When I finish 'your' explanation, you are to immediately apologize to both of them. I would also strongly urge you to consider something with a ring of 'sincerity' as I believe another lobster joke may get your mother to begin thinking of sending you to a boarding school in South Carolina where you can prepare for a career in shoveling pig slop. Now, lad, would you have any questions regarding the aforementioned strategic plan of recovery?"

This time there was no smile on Brian's face. "No, dad."

Emily and Kate were picking their way back to their table even as Brian responded. Neither looked very pleased. Geoff actually saw a touch of disappointment in Emily's eyes. Katie, on the other hand, looked like she was ready to drag her older brother down to the beach and stone him.

Geoff wasted no time. "My darlings, we have had an interesting conversation in the last few moments about how real men never hurt another person intentionally. Perhaps the embarrassment that *all* the Lapkin men share at this moment will serve as a good reminder of the love we share for each other, but how fragile it can sometimes be.

"On the other hand, real men also try to make sincere amends for their mistakes. I am proud of Brian's decision to take it upon himself to speak directly to the head chef, who he has asked to prepare two especially unimposing lobster meals. Each will feature poached lobster - meaning the sometimes intimidating shell has already been removed - with fettuccini, snow pea shoots and ricotta, a recipe recommended by Chef Skipper himself. You may not be aware that Skipper has commanded the kitchens of several restaurants in Paris. Brian and I promise the recipe will make you salivate over lobster, langoustines, or any of the crustacean family in the future."

Emily stared at her husband for a moment, admiring not only his articulate way of helping his son get out of hot water with her and Katie, but by the way he had turned it into a lesson on respect. Before she could say anything, Brian stood up from his seat, walked around to his mother and hugged her. He said nothing for a moment, and then stammered, "I love you mommy, and I didn't mean to hurt your feelings." She kissed him on the cheek and held him tight for a moment. Katie was all smiles. Without a word, Brian plucked a flower out of the small bouquet of mums on the table, and gently placed it in his sister's hair. Geoff laughed to himself. The boy actually has some élan, albeit a tad clumsy. Geoff blew a kiss to his wife who was wiping tears from her eyes.

Geoffrey Lapkin was not unaware of the sometimes downright pain families, otherwise full of love, could encounter. Being the best husband and father he could wasn't always simple for him; but when it came to his love for his family, absolutely nothing could challenge it in terms of priorities.

Over the years, that love would ultimately shape the kind of man he had become. While he enjoyed the fruits of his labor, it was not the house at Sandy Point or any other of the trimmings of success that defined him. Hardly. None of those "things" could approach the value that he placed on the love of his wife and children. Geoff Lapkin was truly fortunate to have learned beyond any doubt what true wealth really was. Earlier today, it had struck him that commanding a small sailboat together with his oldest son, the wind at their backs and no lack of things to talk and laugh about, made him simply the richest man in the world.

God help the poor fool who ever mistreated or took advantage of any of the people he loved.

He had risen early that morning, awoken by the *"Le bouquet apres la pluie"*, then made the short drive into town to pick up a copy of the Providence Journal and the New York Times All he could get in Westerly were the latest editions of the paper, but they were still awash in news of the impending war that Hitler was so eager to start. The world nervously watched as British Prime Minister Neville Chamberlain visited the Fuehrer in Berlin negotiating to prevent war between Germany and Czechoslovakia - a confrontation which would inevitably drag Great Britain and all of Europe into an other world war. Like most American men of his age, Geoff knew that war was inevitable, and detested the thirst for blood so obviously driving the German leadership.

At the same time, he knew that if the U.S. was drawn into the fracas, his company would make millions in military contracts manufacturing elastic webbing for gas masks and other gear. Lapkin took some comfort from the knowledge that no matter what, even if America was drawn into the war and he was called up to serve, at least his family would be taken care of financially. As well, Emily had plenty of family close by to help her through the loss of her husband, if it came to that. He worried more about his oldest son. James was only fourteen now; but if things got bad enough and the confrontation dragged on, he could be called up as early as seventeen.

It was a subject that Emily had never broached with him, or would be able to, Geoff knew. For now, it was something neither of the loving parents could do anything about. Nearly always the optimist, he was fond of at least temporarily putting the family's long term concerns in their proper place.

"Look around, guys," he would often say to them at dinner together. "We're all happy, healthy and safe. Life is grand, let's enjoy it together. After all, it's not as if the big bad wolf is outside waiting to blow our house down.

"Or has someone seen a wolf around here that they're not telling me about?" he would grin.

Thirty

~~~ ~~~

The Lapkin Mansion

Emily was just finishing packing school lunches for Katie, Geoff Jr. and Brian when the door bell rang. It was Andy Popillo at the screen door ready to take on loading the pickup with the first loads of clothes and other possessions for delivery back to the family's home in Westerly. It really wasn't a huge adjustment for the younger children, but Emily liked to close up the cottage at Napatree Point as soon as possible after James left for school so life could quickly return to some form of normalcy.

It was Wednesday morning, and with Andy's work shuttering up the Yacht Club mostly completed, he figured he'd have five days left to get the Lapkins home to Westerly and the house at
~~~

Sandy Point completely closed before driving home to Cranston. He planned to spend a couple of weeks with his mom and brothers in Cranston, then head back to school at Brown. Popillo was jittery though, still recovering from the shock of finding his murdered friend. He tried to hide his emotions.

"Morning, Mrs. Lapkin," Popillo called out to the gracious woman who had been so kind to him all summer. She always had a smile for Andy and the way she spoke to him never changed - no matter who might be within earshot. There wasn't a false bone in the lady's body, he thought; and it dawned on him that she just might have been the classiest woman he had ever known. She was also a great mom to four super kids. He was actually happy that she hadn't become aware of the Tiger Griswold murder, only because he would hate to see her be sad.

"So how come some guys get everything?" he wondered aloud as he began filling the stake bed of the truck with the first boxes. Not that he had any complaints with Mr. Lapkin, who always treated him with respect, paid him well and was always clear in his instructions of the job he expected from the young college student. The only problem was that the young man was totally infatuated with his boss's wife.

It wasn't that Geoff didn't recognize the boy's interest in Emily. Hell he thought, who wouldn't be infatuated with her. What was important to Geoff was that Andy respected her, understanding that to act on his emotions in any way would create a terrible awkwardness in their relationship. He had a hunch the boy would instinctively handle the situation just as it should be.

In fact, Andy Popillo didn't know it, but Geoff was seriously impressed by the young man and thought he might have stumbled over one of those diamonds in the rough the business world was always on the lookout for. Consequently, he had already made some inquiries to Brown University about the young man's academic direction and performance. What he heard back from Brown was good enough to get him thinking of picking up the balance of the tab that his scholarship didn't cover for his last two years of university, and then to invite him to move in with the family during the summer months. The bottom line was that Andy would get a real advantage in learning all there was about the George C. Moore Company, which would put him first in line for one of the two or three jobs Moore tried to recruit for each June after graduation. The competition for the jobs was getting more and more challenging each year. He hadn't broached the thought with Andy yet, but planned to before the boy left for Cranston.

"Morning, Andy," Geoff said, walking off the back stairs and down to the beach where the truck was parked. He had a couple of steaming mugs of hot coffee for them, and the two dropped the tailgate to discuss the day's plan.

"Just want to say thanks for all the work you gave me this summer, Mr. Lapkin," Popillo said casually without looking up from his coffee. He was hoping his boss hadn't heard something about Tiger Griswold either, and having sworn to the Chief last night that he would be silent, did not mention it to him.

"Well, Andy, I figured you and me made a fair trade," he said whimsically. "You got everything done that I asked and did it well. I needed some help around here and you did a helluva job. Seems like that's how it ought to work, wouldn't ya say son?"

"Yah," Popillo laughed, and you paid me well, Mr. Lapkin. "Things don't always work out so fairly. Sure didn't for my dad," he said. Lapkin let it drop.

"You and I need to talk about some things before I settle up with you next week when you head for home," Geoff said. "Got an idea or two I'd like pass off on you."

Popillo turned quickly to look at Lapkin's face, not quite sure what to make of his comment - or where it was headed. Surely he hadn't done anything to make him angry or jealous or anything like that... maybe he was on to Tiger's death?

Geoff caught Andy's effort to hide his concern and laughed. "Relax, Andy. It's not like I caught you checking out my wife or anything," he teased him, knowing that he'd probably just scared the hell out of the boy. "Just want to talk about your future plans, that's all. Nothing to worry about."

Popillo nervously reached for a cigarette and lit it before replying, a bit more confidence in his voice.

"Why sure, Mr. Lapkin, I'd really like that." He moved to change the conversation somewhat. "But the way things are going, I've got a feeling I'm going to be spending some time digging foxholes in Europe after graduation.

"Shit, Andy… give me one of those cigarettes." It was one thing to worry about it himself, another entirely to hear the words related to death and dying coming from the lips of a young man who'd barely tasted life.

"Depressing, ain't it?" Geoff responded, then realized how smoothly Andy had taken control of the conversation from him. Sharp kid, he thought.

They shared a laugh and headed back to the house.

"Say, Andy, one other thing," Geoff reminded himself. "Caught an editorial in the *New York Times* in this morning's paper. It was entitled 'Hurricane' or something like that and congratulated the U.S. Weather Bureau for the great work those guys do in forecasting hurricanes and major storms. The editorial claimed that every year an average of three hurricanes threatens the tropical North Atlantic between June and November," Geoff said.

"You know, it's the damndest thing, but I've lived my whole life in and around Westerly and in all those years, I can't remember getting hit by any storm even resembling something as powerful as a hurricane."

"I mention it because on the same page of the paper, the Times also ran a short story about a hurricane sweeping up the North Carolina coast. It didn't mention any possibility of belting us, but you never know. My grandfather use to tell me that hurricanes were more fickle than women…"

Popillo laughed. "And he lived to talk about it? Lucky man, you're grandfather."

"Yah, that he was, Andy. Anyways, just keep an eye on the sky today for me, will ya?" he said. "Those cirrus clouds sure are something to see, but they often also mean that there's a heavy duty change in the weather coming our way."

"Happy to, Mr. Lapkin. If it starts acting up this afternoon, I'll take the truck and go pick up the kids at school, okay?"

"I couldn't ask for more, Andy, much obliged."

"Funny," he added, "the mansion has never been tested by a major storm. I wonder if we'd have any leaks."

Thirty-One

~~~ ~~~

Sandy Point Dunes

At least he was finally warm, Charles Dewey thought as he crouched in the tall, ragged switch grass that stood tall among the sand dunes of Sandy Point. His clothes were still wet, his legs were scratched and painful from the hairy spinifex plants that he had run through last night in the darkness, and he was hungry. No matter, he was still a free man, somehow having survived another twenty-four hours of freedom despite every cop in New England looking for his head.

He knew they were closing in on him, the flashlights that lit up the beach last night and the constant crisscross of police patrol cars along the length of the peninsula told him all he needed to know. He could probably run another day, hiding
~~~

like he had last night, but exhaustion would eventually catch up with him and he'd do something stupid. The convict came to an obvious conclusion: he needed another escape plan from what was fast becoming his new prison.

An old pick up truck he'd spied driving back and forth to the very end of the peninsula several times over the last twenty-four hours suddenly appeared on the road below him. He ducked lower in the tall switch grass but watched to see where the truck would turn in. Sure enough, the truck pulled into the very last house on the point, the huge one that the boys he had met down by the docks on Sunday had pointed out from across the Bay. The little girl said that's where she lived as well.

He knelt back down in the grass and thought about how nice they'd all been to him, even being a stranger. He smiled at the thought. That's why he liked kids. For the most part they were either too much in awe or too afraid to be mean to him. Yeah, he thought, he'd always liked kids. So, Charles Dewey decided, as it made perfect sense to him, to join the family in the great mansion on the point as their house guest.

With or without an invitation.

Thirty-Two

~~~ ~~~

Washington, D.C.

"Nice piece in the *New York Times* this morning, hey Charlie?" a voice rang out behind Charlie Pierce as he huddled over his newest analysis and charts of the hurricane that would not die. It was Chief Forecaster Charles Mitchell, a man as passionate about to his work at the U.S. Weather Bureau as any the organization had ever seen.

He was not a man to be taken lightly, possessing a very sharp tongue that he was not afraid to use to upbraid subordinates in open discussions. He was also brilliant at his work, and was renowned within the service for his 1924 published paper, "West Indies Hurricanes and other Tropical Cyclones". In it, for the first time, Mitchell traced many hurricanes and behavioral patterns to
~~~

weather events initiating near the Cape Verde Islands.

"Yes sir, it was," Pierce responded, not having the foggiest notion of what Mitchell was talking about. The young forecaster had hardly had time to read a newspaper but didn't want to waste time talking about it. This was exactly the opportunity he needed to raise a large red flag over what he was now convinced was a major disaster in the making.

"Yes, yes, nothing quite like a slap on the back from one of the nation's greatest newspapers, hey Charlie?"

Pierce pounced. "Sir, there are several new developments as regards the Atlantic hurricane we've been tracking between Jacksonville and here for the last couple of weeks, which I urgently must speak to you about. I've revisited the analysis of my charts on the storm just now and…"

"Whoa, Charlie, slow down," Mitchell admonished Pierce. "That storm is nothing to worry about. It's a classic Cape Verde blow and by this time tomorrow it will just be another one of those hurricanes that scared the dickens out of us but just went away. Why you almost sound like you've been talking to Grady Norton, whose similar paranoia caused him to call me far too early this morning."

"In fact I have talked to Grady, Mr. Mitchell, and I…"

"Nonsense, Charlie," the Chief Forecaster said, holding up his hand to signal the end of the discussion. "It's nearly 9 a.m. I need to see the report you're preparing before it goes out, okay?" He turned his back and walked away.

Pierce quickly considered calling Norton for help in getting Mitchell to reconsider, but the Chief Forecaster's tone hardly indicated much respect for him. He sat down and began to write the report, the clock ticking down on him. With ten minutes to spare, he handed Mitchell his report for approval to distribute. Pierce hoped that he had found a way to upgrade the storm to hurricane status again, but without challenging Mitchell's steadfast disagreement.

"This is Charles Pierce, meteorologist of the U.S. Weather Bureau in Washington D.C. with a weather update for Wednesday, September 21st at 9:00 a.m.," the report began in the calm, formal manner that was the Bureau's consistent style.

"Northeast hurricane warnings are ordered north of Atlantic City and south of Block Island. Southeast storm warnings are ordered from Block Island to Eastport, Maine. The hurricane is apparently about seventy-five miles east of Cape Hatteras and is moving at a more rapid pace than previously reported in a north-northeastward course..." Mitchell abruptly stopped reading, and Pierce watched as his superior carefully drew a red pencil line through the two references to the word "hurricane", inserting in both places the words, "tropical storm." Then he watched as Mitchell also edited out the references to the location and speed, essentially indicating that the storm was dissipating and moving away from the coast.

Pierce was stunned, and immediately began to argue. Mitchell simply said, "Enough, Charlie, get it out immediately. Then please arrange for a meeting of our senior forecasters on duty for noon today. You can explain to us all what your 'urgent' theories are."

Pierce hung his head, not in embarrassment, but to hide his fury. "Yes, sir," he replied, and turned to leave.

"Charlie, a minute please," Mitchell called after him. Pierce turned to face him.

"Be careful with this son," he warned, "You could do yourself and your young reputation a lot of damage by exaggerating this situation. The men in our meeting will have decades of experience to back up their conclusions. Just think about how many 'months' you have on your side to argue the case. Okay?"

This time, Pierce said absolutely nothing in response and walked out of Mitchell's office in complete disgust. As he walked back to his desk, he thought about backing off. If he doesn't care, why should I? Then he remembered his conversation with Grady Norton earlier that morning. The arrogant Mitchell was no Grady Norton, Pierce thought silently, getting angrier by the second. "Hell, I'd swing with Grady anytime before I'd bet on that asshole," he mumbled to himself. "Of course Norton's right. Because I am too, goddamn it!

Price balled his two hands into fists as he walked back to his desk, no longer trying to hide his fury. "Okay you infallible pricks," he thought to himself. "Let's just see how valuable all your experience is when you decide to leave common sense out of the equation."

He sat down at his desk and began pulling together the mounting data, which would, if he was right, prove to his more experienced colleagues that the entire New England coastline was in for a direct hit from a severely dangerous hurricane - one that was packing winds in excess of well over one hundred miles per hour and bringing with it an incalculable storm surge that could come in the guise of countless tsunami-like waves -- in less than five hours.

"Wish me luck, Grady," he said out loud for no one's benefit other than his own. "This one's for you."

Thirty-Three

~~~ ঌ ~~~

Elm Street Elementary School, Westerly

Old Pat Collins was enjoying a last cigarette while warming up the engine of his dilapidated yellow school bus in the parking lot of the Elm Street Elementary School, just as he did every weekday morning before picking up students spread out all over Napatree Point and into the Watch Hill Harbor. He didn't like to smoke in front of the kids, so from the time he picked them up until he dropped them off, cigarettes were off limits. The air on the bus was bad enough with diesel exhaust fumes, burning oil, rubber tires kicking up dust and road dirt, and the "fragrance" of forty perspiring children that only got worse as the bus
~~~

filled and the kids got more energetic the closer they got to school.

It was actually worse on rainy days with the windows closed. Collins had to admit though, that after completing his route -- which began with him picking up his little friend Katie Lapkin out on Sandy Point and ending nearly an hour later in the school yard -- it was the day's second cigarette that was the most satisfying.

He was safely in the schoolyard and had just lit up his Pall Mall when an old friend of his, Dino Tartullo, approached the bus and called out to Collins. A second-generation Italian bricklayer from a family that had lived along the Brenta River in the charming city of Bassano del Grappa in the Veneto region, Dino Tartullo was now a full-fledged American citizen. He owned three large fishing boats with his two sons, both in their early twenties, each of whom had deservedly earned reputations as slick haired gigolos along the Watch Hill Harbor docks.

Dino was okay in Collins book, a hard working guy with a warm smile and a strong handshake. He wasn't quite so sure about his boys, who didn't quite fit the mold of Rhode Islanders, many of whom hailed from Italy. Quite a few had settled in Westerly and Watch Hill.

"Buon Giorno mio amico, Patrick!" Dino said and hugged his Irish friend of more than twenty years."

"Top of the mornin' to you, Dino," Collins laughed at the greeting. He spied a large box that the Italian was carrying and had a hunch it had something to do with the warm greeting.

"Why Dino, is this a gift for me?" he asked playfully.

"Wella, 's not so much a gift, but I would like you to take it from me."

"Huh?" Collins asked in genuine confusion. The box must have been a foot square in size and heavily wrapped in the kind of brown paper they used to wrap cleaned fish. Collins took the proffered carton from Dino and found it was heavier than he expected and had an address for the Abercrombie & Fitch Company in Maine. It obviously had to be dropped off at the post office in Westerly.

"Okay, Dino, I'm intrigued," he said to his friend who had a hopeful look in his dark brown eyes. "What the hell is this that I think you're asking me to drop off at the Post Office later today? And, by the way, why would you be sending anything to Portsmouth, Maine?"

"Ah, sì, é confusa," Dino apologized for not having explained better.

"You see, Patrick, since being a boy, the weather has always given me reason for many thoughts," he began. "I save my lira many times to buy a barometer," he continued. "You know what this is?"

"I've lived my whole life on the ocean coastline. Yeah, I've heard about them," Collins said sarcastically, which was just one of the ways the two men enjoyed each other.

"Well, I send my money to "Abercrambee n' Fisha" or whatever, because I see it in the book they send to me. So I order it, and three weeks later it comes to me! *Figlio di puttana, così frusteante!"*

"Yeah, life's hard sometimes, Dino," Collins said with a straight face.

"So, I open quick and I see it is just what I want. Then I notice, 'summanabitch, *figlio di puttana, così frusteante*!"

"I get the part about them being sons of bitches, but tell me what the problem is?" Collins asked.

"It doesn't work!" The Italian was about to burst a blood vessel. "I open, I look, it only tells me one word. Si, one word."

"What do you mean, Dino? You have to measure the pressure per inch."

"What, you thing I'ma stupido? I know. But all it says is "Hurricane". Every time I look at it, it tell me I am a stupido figlio di puttana - a stupid son of a bitch who getta cheat. All it says is 'Hurricane'. Bastardos, where is this 'hurricane' for two days, eh?"

"I guess you got a point there, Dino," Collins said. "I take it you want me to send it back to them after my homeward route this afternoon? Did you include a letter inside explaining the problem?"

"Si, si amico mio," Dino shook his friend's hand. As the game went on between the Irishman and the Italian, now Dino would owe a favor to Pat Collins. It usually came down to one buying the other a bottle of wine or a few dark ales.

"Strange day already," Collins thought to himself as he set out to gas up the bus again. He'd only been working since about 7:30 a.m., but already he had noticed that the Westerly Police were very busy all over town and the outlying areas including Napatree Point. There was also that beautiful sky to watch, which seemed like a gift after the rain stopped and considering it was the end of summer. He wasn't really worried about it, especially after the weather had been so fickle all summer; but those cirrus clouds were growing, no doubt, and that strange yellow light over the horizon was a bit unnerving, although he really couldn't say why. Along with Dino's haunted barometer, it had been a very odd kind of morning. But he was relatively sure there was nothing to worry about. If there was some kind of storm action headed their way, it would be all over the radio by now and he'd be out buying spare batteries and making sure the gas tank was filled on the school bus.

Hell, he thought, the weather was too darn beautiful to spend the day worrying. But just for the hell of it, he reminded himself to catch the noon U.S. Weather Bureau report on the radio to see what was cooking.

Those guys would know for sure. It said so right there in the *New York Times* this morning.

Thirty-Four

~~~ ঌ ~~~

The Lapkin Mansion

Dewey waited quite a bit longer in the tall switch grass early that morning, hungry and in need of sleep, but desperate to check the bus schedules. Sure enough, a yellow bus arrived about 7:30 a.m., driving all the way to the end of Sandy Point to the last mansion on Fort Road. He paid attention when two boys got on. Sure enough, they were the nice kids he'd met already. About thirty minutes later another bus appeared and the little girl - the one who had held his hand - boarded, skipping her way happily to the door.

As Dewey watched the bus pulled away, a great looking curvy blond came running out of the front door and waved good-bye. The bus driver hit his horn in response as he drove the bus down Fort
~~~

Road, headed back to Watch Hill and then into Westerly. That meant that three out of the four kids were gone, but for sure mom was in the house with at least the hired college kid. He hadn't seen any evidence that the father was anywhere around, but his Cadillac convertible was sitting in the driveway. So he figured that in all likelihood, there were at least four people in the mansion: the parents, their oldest boy and the young guy who drove the pickup.

Still he wasn't about to rush his next step. He couldn't see any others, but wanted to be as certain as possible as to how many people he was going to taking on. If just one of them got away, he was screwed for sure. Just then he saw what looked to be a matronly type, a larger, older woman in a uniform stepping outside to hang some fresh laundry out on a rope line at the water's edge. Sure enough, that made it five.

Out of the blue, he saw a patrol car pull up in front of one of the mansions on the Atlantic side of the road, and two uniforms got out. One had a shotgun. Less than a minute later, another police car pulled up on the other side of the street, and two more patrolmen stepped out. He watched as the first two cops slowly approached the front door, while the other two worked their way around each side of the exterior and into the backyard. The cop with the shotgun had it aimed belly level on the front door of the house when his partner drew his own revolver out of its holster, and rang the doorbell. The whole thing looked pretty well organized, and it was only a matter of time before the guys who almost nailed him on the beach last night caught up to him. They could corner him in an instant if he let down his guard. The loaded shotgun in his hand and three fully loaded pistols jammed into his filthy coveralls said that wasn't going to happen without a bloody fight.

Some time went by before someone, obviously afraid, cautiously appeared at the front door, shocked to find armed police wanting to come in and visit. One of the guys in the backyard came jogging back to the front and stood guard as the two patrolmen had a brief conversation with the homeowner. Dewey bet the cops were telling him just enough to get them inside as quickly as possible. A minute later the three entered the house together.

He had to make a move now, or never. The escapee gathered up the backpack of ammunition, binoculars and the long stretch of rope he'd stolen way back outside Stonington, then crept slowly through the naturally growing switch grass, often as tall as six- or seven-feet high, down to the backyard of the Lapkin Mansion. He hugged the ground checking for cops and the maid who had been outside hanging laundry. She was expendable, he thought, probably not bright enough to follow instructions but capable of doing something very dumb.

He stepped carefully away from the last bit of cover he had, ran the few feet to the northeast corner of the house and stopped. He was so big and his boots were so heavy that the gigantic man couldn't help but make noise, so sometimes he had to wait for the victim to come to him rather than rely on the edge of surprise. Sure enough, as he hugged the backside of a stone chimney on the side of the mansion, he heard the sound of footsteps scrunching toward him in the sand. They were light and short, sandals perhaps, but a woman's steps for sure. He was right.

Just as Shelly turned the corner, she said softly, "Is there someone there? Is that you, Tiger?" Dewey emerged and grabbed the woman, twirling her around with the speed of a ballerina and clamped one of his giant, hair-matted hands over her mouth effectively stifling any possible chance of a scream. Shelly's eye's widened in terror as recognition set in that she was being attacked by someone or something of monstrous proportions. Dewey wasted no time playing around with the woman, although he would have enjoyed that had he the opportunity. With the serrated hunting knife in his other hand he reached up and plunged the ten-inch blade into her heart. He held her up for a few minutes, letting her bleed out some, and then simply dropped the woman's lifeless corpse to the sand. He had an urge to kick her in the head like a hunter celebrating a trophy kill, but uncharacteristically stopped, and thought about it first. The mad man's logic told him it might make too much noise.

One down, four to go he thought, but then desperately reminded himself that he couldn't kill them all even if the urge was overwhelming. Without hostages, he had no leverage and would just become target practice for those who were hunting him like an animal. He had to stay in control.

Dewey stood his ground a few moments longer, just listening. Hearing nothing, he crept along the back of the house after stepping over Shelly's dead body, careful to keep below the six-foot high porch deck that surrounded the house. A short distance away he could hear two people talking, definitely men. From the sound of it they were loading up the pickup with boxes or something; and a deeper voice, one he took to be the blonde's husband, seemed to be in a rush.

"Just a couple more Andy, then I have to get out to the factory for a few hours," Geoff said.

Popillo smiled at him. "Why don't you get going, sir, I can handle the rest from here."

"Thanks, Andy. I'll just slip inside then to kiss Emily good-bye and be off. See you tonight." He turned toward the house.

Dewey reacted in a split second. They were completely off guard and he thought he could handle both of the men without breaking a sweat. This was make or break time. The enormous, ape-like creature instantly launched himself from behind the house with a chilling growl that instantly froze Geoff where he stood. Andy couldn't react fast enough to even turn his head to see what was happening. Without a word, Dewey used the butt end of the shotgun and clubbed the young man across the back of his skull, dropping him instantly to the sand. Geoff was so shocked that he stood there watching the scene unfold as if it was a movie and he was outside the script. It took long seconds before it registered that what he was seeing was real. Then, without hesitation, he hurled himself at the terrifyingly ugly man.

Dewey let out a deep laugh at the ludicrousness of what was happening even before Lapkin bounced off the monster's chest like a rubber ball hitting a concrete wall. The convict reached down and pulled up one of Lapkin's hands to inspect it, then laughed out loud again. Here were the hands of a man who had never known a life of backbreaking, shoulder punishing, arm stretching labor for days and weeks and months on end, without the prospect of relief. Here was one of the men who kept all the wealth and good to himself while depriving people like him of any way to ever become a complete human being, let alone someone who could become a contributor to society.

His grip tightened on Lapkin's arms, and an intense desire to rip them off the man surged through him with a fury that might have enabled him to do it. A screen door that squeaked opened, then slammed shut with a bang distracted him. The noise jolted him back to what few shreds of sanity he was still operating on. It was just enough to make him drop Geoff's arms. Lapkin lay motionless at his feet, as did the younger man a few feet away. Dewey thought the one he had clubbed with the gun was dead for sure and didn't bother with the motionless body.

Leaving them unconscious, Dewey began to climb the steps up to the porch to take care of the kid and his mother. He'd have to be careful with these two – he needed them alive. But that didn't mean he couldn't have some fun with the blond bitch, did it? He reached for the handle of the screen door, mulling over what to do with the kid when he heard the unmistakable sound of the break-open action of a double barrel shotgun. He stopped and listened as the gun was loaded and the safety set for one of the barrels. Just as fast, he heard the gun lock back together, fully cocked, meaning whoever held it knew how to use it. Dewey stopped dead in his tracks. From the kitchen, he could hear a boy comforting a woman. It must be the boy and the blonde, he thought, and backed away from the door.

"Get back you bastard," James Lapkin yelled as he pushed through the screen door and onto the porch. "I shoulda known what you were the minute I saw you down on the dock: a piece of shit." Emily, behind him, trembled at the voice she heard coming from her oldest son. She didn't know he was capable of such rage.

"Back up some more," James yelled at the hideous man who had probably just killed his father and his friend Andy. He'd already made up his mind to blow this guy's head off his guerilla-like shoulders if he had to.

"Now throw away those guns in your pockets, you hear me? There, over by the back tire on the pickup, throw them there," he repeated. Dewey complied, tossing two handguns where he was instructed. "Now lie face down, hands behind your back, understand me, you fucking animal!" He was silent for a second, then called inside to his mother, still hiding in the kitchen. "Sorry, mom, I didn't mean to swear."

"It's okay," she said, almost whispering. "Is your dad okay? Andy?"

"I don't know mom; can you come out here and check?

"I'm so afraid, James, please tell me if your dad is okay, please, please," Emily said, begging. She was rapidly going into shock.

"Never mind mom," the remarkably composed fourteen-year-old boy said. "I want you to pick up the phone and call the police, okay? I've got this....what ever he is... covered. Just call, mom,"

"I already tried, James, the phone isn't working. Oh, God help us," Emily began to cry."

"It's okay mom, he will," James hollered back in his most reassuring, but wavering voice. "But it's like dad says, sometimes you have to remind him you need help before he gets involved. So here's what we'll do. Get up and run out the front door. Go to the first person you can find and tell them to get the police. Do it, now mom."

"Okay," Emily said weekly, simply terrified by what she had seen when the grotesque man had hit Andy with the gun and hurt Geoff. "Here I go... be careful James, please honey, I need you so much right now…"

"Just go mom; I'd just as soon put two shells in this asshole's face before I'd turn around on him. Just get help, mom. Go!" A few seconds later he heard the front screen door slam. With his mother safe, he decided to maneuver over to where his father and Andy were to see if they were alive.

"Don't make me remind you, motherfucker, that if you move, you die; and I swear that one of these shells is going into your fucked-up face. The second one is gonna rip your sick balls right out from under your ass. Come to think of it, I have to remember not to get confused. Your ass and your face actually look alike."

Dewey didn't respond, but was seething inside as he listened to the little boy talk like a man. Then he couldn't help himself. "Must feel a whole lot better doing all that swearin' now that your mother can't hear you. Guess you learned how to cuss like that down at the docks." Dewey grinned at him. "But I got news for you. Cussin' don't make you a man. Why, you're still a sissy. You ain't got the guts to pull the trigger on that gun. Killin' takes some learnin', boy. You'll never get the hang of it." He laughed with ridicule at the teenager and mocked him again." Why, you're just a sissy ass, pretty little momma's boy."

With fury still coursing through his veins, the boy somehow managed to keep himself together, refusing to be baited by the murderer. He cautiously made his way to his father, who was still motionless on the sand, but found him to be breathing. "C'mon, dad, please wake up," James said to him loudly. The boy sensed that his father was struggling to regain consciousness. Andy's condition was not as clear. His breathing was ragged and he was motionless.

James turned back to the intruder. "Where's Shelly?" James asked, remembering she had been out doing laundry."

"Aw, I've got her all prettied up behind the house there; turned her into a real hot number, I did," Dewey baited the boy again. "Why don't you just peak around the corner and have a look – if you've got the balls, sissy-boy."

James was nearly tempted to run over to the beast laying face down on the porch and stick both barrels of the shotgun right up against his backside. "Get up," he said, "take me to her."

"Well now, I might have been funnin' ya a bit son. If I remember, she – what did you call her, Shelly?" – might need a few minutes in the powder room before her next gentleman caller. See for yourself." He stepped aside, revealing Shelly's bloodless face. James screamed at the sight and lowered the shotgun just long enough for Dewey to manage to pull out the third pistol he'd been hiding in his overalls. He reached out with one of his enormous legs and kicked the shotgun out of the boy's hands. James went down on his knees, vomiting.

"See, I told ya that you was a sissy-boy. Why that there is a work of art. I might even sign it.

We'll have to talk about that later. Right now, you and I have some unfinished business, son." James looked up at the monster, perhaps the most evil presence he had ever been exposed to. Now James was afraid.

"You had the gun, so you had all the power. That made you a man, right? The gun let you say anything your sissy little mouth wanted to, am I right?" Dewey was trying to provoke him, but James was suddenly just a fourteen-year-old boy again.

"Then, in the blink of an eye, I had the gun so I had the power and that made me the man. But there's another difference between us James," Dewey continued, a snarl coming to his lips as he finished each sentence. "You see, I don't very much like talking. Me, I'd rather be killin'. But I ain't going to kill you James, at least not right away while I need you to get me outta here. I'm just gonna hurt you like hell."

Dewey raised the gun and shot the teenager in the left shoulder without giving it another second's thought. James screamed as the bullet tore through the muscles at the side of his neck, and snapped his collarbone as it passed through. The pain was almost unbearable.

"See there, I told you," Dewey sneered down at him. "You ain't nothing but a sissy-boy."

This time he didn't care about making noise. The time was over for that with the blonde running around looking for cops. So just for the sake of hurting his adversary a little more, the six-foot-eight monster stomped down hard on James's shoulder, using all his weight. Then he spit on him. The boy mercifully lapsed into unconsciousness.

He looked around the Bay side of the Lapkin Mansion, littered with bodies. Not a bad hour's work Dewey thought to himself. Then, methodically, he hoisted up James and roughly brought him inside to the family room, throwing him to the floor. He did the same with Geoff Lapkin and Andy Popillo who were still out cold. The sadist in him wanted to pull Shelly's ruined body around to the front porch to send a message to the police whenever they got there, which he assumed would be soon. The thought of scrounging up some hard liquor in the kitchen pantry was more appealing to him though, and within minutes he was swallowing mouthfuls of twenty-five year scotch like it was lemonade.

"Man, it don't get much better than this, hey James?" He walked over to the severely injured boy and poured liquor all over his face. "We really popped your cherry today. First you swore in front of your mother and now you're drinkin' like a man. Why, I'm almost proud of you, sissy-boy." Then he left the house to retrieve the backpack of supplies he had left at the edge of the dunes and carried it back inside.

Quickly, he tied up the three men with lengths of three-quarter inch hemp rope so he wouldn't have to worry about them when the fun began and or if they regained consciousness. He kept the bodies close together and out of sight of any window, so the bastards would think twice before storming the place for fear of shooting the wrong guy. Then he collected all the guns he'd brought and added James's shotgun to the pile. He fully loaded each one. Dewey had every intention of escaping Napatree Point with the help of the police, but he also planned on leaving a few behind for them to bury.

The thought brought a wicked smile to his face. James, lying quietly on the floor, lapsing in and out of consciousness from the blood loss, happened to look up at Dewey at that exact moment. The sight made him draw in his breath sharply, like he had done at a Saturday matinee a few years back when he first saw Boris Karloff as the monster, "Frankenstein". His friends had ridiculed him for weeks after.

What he saw in Dewey was the same incarnation of pure evil, only now in real life. It wasn't the freakish size of the monster that had terrified him at all. Rather, it was the horrifying aberrations of the face he had to wear.

Frankenstein's grotesquely thick, heavy brow, like a bony ledge that shielded his deeply recessed, soulless black eyes, kept them and the lower portion of his face in perpetual shadow. Worse, his abnormally small eyeballs appeared to have been bored into his profoundly misshaped skull, to a depth half again that of a normal man. But it was the startling, glassy redness of his corneas that were the most compelling evidence of the evil within him. Looking at Dewey was like staring into the face of Frankenstein all over again. James shut his eyes to the face, and was on the verge of losing consciousness again from loss of blood. Somewhere out in the ocean - or was it in the clouds -- he thought he heard the sound of sirens growing louder. The noise in his ears was confusing; but all the exhausted boy prayed for was that sleep would come.

Because then, he knew, in the ultimate of ironies, his nightmare would end.

Thirty-Five

~~~ ~~~

Washington, D.C

It was nearly time to make his case and Charlie Pierce had just about exhausted the supply of recent information from the few boats at sea along the Atlantic Seaboard that he'd manage to scrape together during the morning. The meeting was to be held at noon in Chief Forecaster Charles Mitchell's office, with roughly a dozen other senior forecasters and meteorologists. The senior men were all anticipating Pierce's arguments about the status of the hurricane, and some were even crass enough to openly take bets on the consequences of his arrogance in challenging Mitchell. Right now it was even money on banishment to the filing room or just plain getting himself fired.
~~~

Pierce had already heard the ridicule from the men who averaged at least fifteen years more experience than he had, some of them as much as twenty-five. Charlie Pierce had a total of three years in the forecasting business. He was going to give it his best shot against a stacked deck, but the young man was glad he wasn't a gambler. But by God, after revisiting his charts and analysis, including the latest data from the few ships at sea and the scathing report from *Carinthia,* which indicated in no uncertain terms that the storm was still a hurricane and not some "tropical event" as the Bureau had down-played in their reports since yesterday afternoon, Pierce was more sure than ever that he still had a very angry hurricane out there.

Carinthia's Captain, A. C. Greig had made it very clear in his report to the Jacksonville office that the magnitude of the error in the information contributed by the Jacksonville Weather Bureau was the equivalent to comparing a misty spring shower in Paris to eight continual hours of tsunamis taller than the Eiffel Tower crashing down upon the city.

"I have long been an admirer of the U.S. Weather Bureau, my dear Mr. Norton," the tough minded Australian captain began, "and especially the Jacksonville, Florida operation made famous for your leadership. So I am certain that you will understand my profound disappointment in discovering that my perspective on the competency and heroic spirit of your administration has been so misguided. In fact, sir, it is the general conclusion of the still terrified passengers of the *USS Carinthia* (numbering more than six hundred) who lived a night in perpetual fear of foundering while huddled together with their loved ones, that you are an idiot of the most profound level."

While the *Carinthia*'s report may very well have been supportive of Pierce's convictions concerning the erroneous conclusions of the Jacksonville Bureau, the young meteorologist would not consider including it in his data base. He simply could not blame the entire miscalculation on Norton who perhaps was guilty of errors in analysis and had made the venial sin of assumption based on experience. This particular hurricane, however, had behaved oddly since its mysterious conception in the Sahara.

At noon sharp, all of the senior forecasters and meteorologists were beckoned to Charlie Mitchell's oversized office. There they settled in assigned seats around a long, rectangular table, which clearly had a pecking order. Pierce had taken a guess as to his stature and immediately taken a seat along a wall. The meeting began promptly when the Chief Forecaster cleared his throat loudly.

"I see everyone is here except for our colleagues on vacation, but we have young Mr. Pierce to thank for supporting their work," Mitchell said in his typical formal style. He did not suffer humor or fools well, and he expected any meeting of which he was acquired to attend to be tightly run and very succinct.

"The issue before us, as I'm sure you know, is Mr. Pierce's continued concern about the activity that gave us all a scare earlier in the week. To the best of my knowledge, and true to the nature of its inception, the storm has turned northward where I expect it to blow itself out in the colder Atlantic waters. This has all the markings of the Cape Verde-style hurricane, which as you know, I have studied significantly. Thus far, the storm has done exactly what I would have suspected and has recurved northward."

Charlie Pierce wasted no time in taking Mitchell on. There was none to waste. Even given the opportunity to let the entire east coast know of the approaching dangerous weather, there wouldn't be a lot they could do to warn the effected areas.

"Mr. Mitchell, I believe that your analysis, which I know is based on extensive experience in Cape Verde blows, is, in at least this case, in error. Further, I believe that the advisory we issued at 9 a.m. this morning was seriously flawed and misleading." He looked up from his notes to find everyone in the room staring at him like he was a lunatic, and Charlie Mitchell was doodling on the back of a graph pad, very much trying to look bored.

Unruffled, Pierce continued. "New data which emerged last night includes a detailed report from the British ship *Carinithia,* which had the exceedingly unfortunate experience of sailing directly into the storm despite that it was navigating a course we had recommended and which should have taken the ship over hundred miles out of harms way. As it turns out, *Carinthia,* with six hundred passengers aboard, endured the worst seas that its well regarded captain said he has ever endured in forty years of crossings, including routine roundings of the treacherous Cape Horn." He paused for a moment letting the point sink in and hoping for a question, but the room was silent.

Pierce continued. "One of the most convincing arguments I found is that based on the information provided by the *Carinthia,* this storm is in reality not a 'tropical disturbance' at all. It simply is not scientifically possible."

"Oh, come now, Mr. Pierce," Mitchell finally interrupted, very irritated with the junior man's confidence and the very temerity with which he challenged him in his roll as the Chief Forecaster with so many more years of experience. If Pierce were his own son, he would have slapped him down for just such a degree of grandstanding with no visible accreditation. "This storm and many other Cape Verde-style storms before it have behaved in the same fashion we see now."

Pierce hung his head momentarily, giving some in the room the thought that the younger man had said all he was going to and would back off now to try to sustain his job. Imagine the Chief Forecaster's shock when Pierce fired right back.

"That is hardly the case, Mr. Mitchell. Need I remind you that the most powerful hurricane in United States history smashed into the Florida Keys on Labor Day of 1935, causing the death of more than four hundred people who were provided warnings to move to higher ground too late, an error for which the Bureau was held accountable. Mitchell looked up again from his scribbling, as if suddenly interested in the conversation. How dare this little son of a bitch challenge me publicly, he thought.

"If I am not mistaken, Mr. Mitchell, the Florida Keys hurricane of 1935 was a classic Cape Verde-type hurricane that did not recurve to the North Atlantic. The decision to downplay the 1935 storm and attempt to evacuate as many people as possible in the short time available hurt the integrity of the U.S. Weather Bureau.

"An interesting theory, Mr. Pierce. But where, of course, is your evidence?"

"There are several indicators upon which I've based my conclusions," Pierce responded immediately. "The first is the barometric pressure readings which were reported by the *Carinthia.* When she was first able to reach us, *Carinthia* indicated that less one and a half hours after encountering the storm, the air pressure had dropped to a remarkably low 28.75 inches." Pierce didn't bother to look up from his notes, but knew there were suddenly people in the room who would be startled by that number.

"Additionally, although we are desperately awaiting more information from the United States Coast Guard and several US Navy ships that are now on site, we believe some portions of the Bahamas have suffered grave damage. Most of the ports and harbor facilities of the main islands are buried under debris which extends in some cases to more than a mile offshore." Someone in the room let out a loud whistle. "The Coast Guard was able to make it inside Marsh Harbour on Great Abaco Island, the most northern of the Bahamian's. Its population is at least five or six thousand people, I'd guess."

"How bad was the damage, Mr. Pierce?" one of the older men in the room asked calmly.

"I am told that a small landing party inspected the island and found it barren." With that statement, the room went completely silent. "The entire island was wiped clean of physical remains, including bodies or any physical structural entities. It is all gone." Most of them shook their heads or narrowed their eyes in disbelief. To a man, they were hearing more than they wanted to know.

"By which you mean to say that the Jacksonville office did not accurately assess the timing of the supposed recurve away from Miami?" Mitchell asked.

"Something like that, sir," Pierce responded. "The actual truth, however, is that we misjudged the speed of the storm's recurvature and progression as it headed north. When the storm actually did recurve, its forward speed slowed to as little as twenty miles per hour and was forecast to increase slowly to up to about forty miles per hour or so today before dying a natural death by tonight or tomorrow morning.

"But my more immediate concern, Mr. Mitchell, is the manner in which we notify several million people along the coastline from Atlantic City to

Lewiston that first, the hurricane is much closer to the coast then any of us suspected; and as we speak, is about one hundred miles away from the Virginia coast. Second, we must sound an alert that the storm we announced as no longer a threat and dissipating as early as the morning has regained its extraordinary characteristics as one of the most powerful hurricanes in American history, with sustained winds as high as one hundred forty miles per hour, which is..." He paused looking through a stack of charts. "Yes, yes, I have it here... which is heading directly toward them at a speed in excess of seventy miles per hour."

"What? What are you telling me?" Mitchell jumped up from his seat in anger for what he thought was an intentionally exaggerated claim of danger. "So far, all I've heard is evidence that is at least twenty-four hours old and perhaps - just perhaps - not related to the storm we've been watching for the past week at all. Please, Charlie, get a grip."

Pierce looked around the room for any sign of support. There was none. Mitchell had long ago established an environment of intimidation. But Charlie wasn't about to give up yet.

Pierce stood and faced the now enraged Mitchell, who was expecting someone, Christ, anyone, to spit out what the obvious statement for the situation should be and get on with life. It seemed Charlie Pierce was still in the way.

The young man refused to rest his case. "Before you all dismiss the evidence I've brought to your attention, could I ask Mr. Mitchell to enlighten us with the possible consequences of the 'Bermuda High' effect in this situation? It was a direct challenge to Mitchell. The room was silent. Mitchell loathed being 'tested' by his subordinates, in any situation, but particularly by someone of Pierce's caliber. He was also smart enough to see an opening to finally put the argument to rest.

"As I am certain you remember from your earliest classes on the subtropical high of the North Atlantic Ocean, the 'Bermuda High' is a principal weather action that holds in place a high pressure, high humidity area over the eastern United States, particularly in summer. It has been positioned particularly high in recent weeks," Mitchell concluded.

Pierce would not let him off the hook. "And you are aware, Mr. Mitchell, that the frontal system coming from the west effectively combines to create a tunnel of sorts that can push this hurricane system right up the entire eastern Atlantic seaboard?"

Finally, one of Mitchell's subordinates interrupted, as much to put an end to the argument as to try and save Pierce, whom he genuinely liked, from slitting his wrists any deeper.

"Ah…I'm sorry Charlie, I really am," interjected Welker Stennington, a transplanted Brit who had found the U.S. dedication to building an effective weather service more attractive than operating a light house on the Irish sea. "I admire you taking on old geezers like us, but I can't buy this bloody Bermuda High bullshit."

Once Stennington opened the floodgates, each man in the room went on record as saying he believed the storm would follow the prevailing thinking on Cape Verde-style hurricanes and their predictability of dying a slow natural death over colder waters. Pierce was beat and he knew it. When the meeting ended, he was alone in the room.

At two o'clock that afternoon, the few people in the Northeast coastal area who cared, now that the urgency of the hurricane watch had so diminished, turned into the regularly scheduled United States Weather Bureau report and listened to the posting – which did not even mention the word "hurricane". If there was any news, it was succinct.

"Northerly winds along the New Jersey, Maryland and southern Delaware coast will likely increase to whole gale force this afternoon," the report read, "and back to northwest and then diminish tonight." There was not so much as a small craft warning for the New England states farther east. The advisory was sent out for normal distribution to weather posts, newspapers offices and radio stations across the Northeast. The reaction was no surprise to Charlie Pierce. When people get bored, they take a nap. Most of his customers were fast asleep as he stared anxiously at the office clock near his desk.

He might have had his confidence a little shaken and his reputation soiled, but he was far from beaten. What bothered him was not the embarrassment of failure no matter which position he had taken. What was making him sick to his stomach was the knowledge that several million people were about to face a nightmare of unfathomable destruction.

And there wasn't a damned thing he could do about it.

Thirty-Six

~~~ ஒ ~~~

Sandy Point

The gravel and clamshell surfaced Fort Road happened to end in the driveway of the Lapkin summer mansion on Sandy Point. Just before 1 p.m., when Emily Lapkin had run from the house shrieking for help, luck would have it that a Watch Hill police car was parked in front of a neighbor's home just several hundred yards down the road. The patrol car was empty so she ran to the house and barged in the front door screaming to get the attention of the patrolmen.

Immediately, two armed police officers intercepted her in the house and demanded identification. She had none, and between her anxious state and being out of breath she could barely spit out the situation at her home. "I think he
~~~

may have killed my husband," she stammered out, barely in control. "My son has a gun and he's holding him now, but I'm so afraid this monster will hurt him too. Did you hear me? He's like a real monster." She was shivering from shock and was having trouble breathing.

Emily's story sent a shiver down Officer Ed Ranklin's spine. He had a wife and three children at home in a small cottage in Misquamicut. "We gotta get some help out here, Billy. I'll go to the car and radio in," patrolman Ranklin said to his supervisor, Lieutenant Billy Sullivan. "Okay, go, Ed" said Sullivan." I'll head over towards the Lapkin's; maybe I'll get a shot at the bastard. Better call for a couple of meat wagons. I've got a feeling about this. Guess we got our man."

Within ten minutes Fort Road was crawling with police cruisers, ambulances and even State Police who were being dispatched to the scene. They were all parked about two hundred yards from the Lapkin mansion. Sullivan, the officer in charge, called his men together after having talked with Emily as calmly as possible.

"Okay, guys, listen up," he said in the middle of a tight grouping of eighteen policemen. They immediately stopped talking among themselves, all sharing great respect for the young lieutenant, who at just twenty-eight was the youngest man in the history of the Westerly Police Department to make the grade. If he hadn't been wearing his uniform, he could easily haven been taken for a Marine or a pro quarterback. He didn't have an ounce of fat on his six-foot, one-inch frame and was tough enough to take on anybody with the wrong attitude – if he had to. The man was a natural leader, with intelligence and a strategic feel for police work that had already pushed him a cut above his peers.

"I've just spent some time with Mrs. Lapkin over there," he said, pointing to Emily who was still sobbing and being comforted by a neighbor. "From what she was able to tell me, the freak we've been looking for is holed up in her place. Her fourteen-year-old son had the motherfucker lying on his face with a shotgun pointed at his head when she left. Whatever the kid's situation is now, the boy was a real hero. Let's hope it didn't get him killed. But I'm betting that by now the gorilla's got the upper hand or we would have seen the kid."

He looked around at his guys. Every eye was glued to the young Lieutenant's face, tight with the tension of the situation. Sullivan looked at his watch. It read two o'clock.

"She also says there are two injured males inside, her husband Geoff Lapkin and that college kid, Andy Popillo, the boy who's been working at the club this summer. Don't know how bad either one of them are hurt or even alive. There's a housekeeper inside too or somewhere on the property, but Mrs. Lapkin has no idea where she's located or what her condition is either." Sullivan paused for a moment, getting his thoughts in order.

"Ed," he said to Ranklin, "do we have those two shooters out here yet?" referring to the two trained snipers assigned by the department for just such situations. Ranklin shook his head. "No. They're on their way, Lieutenant. Ten minutes, maybe."

"Well, while we're waiting, take two guys and go scout out some locations for possible long range shots at this guy. There's a lot of glass in that place, we might just get lucky. Get somebody on the binoculars, too, see if we can locate the son of a bitch inside. Everybody hang loose, keep your safeties on, we're probably in for a little wait."

He paused again. "By the way, the Chief has a vested interest in this motherfucker and is coming in to take command," he said with a deadly serious look on his face. "Or at least to yell shit at us to make him think he's in charge." He grinned slightly. There was no nervousness in the laughter that followed as each man in the department had as much respect for Chief Gil Cianci as Billy Sullivan himself.

"At ease, boys," he said to allow them to light up if they wished. Cigarette smoke filled the air quickly. "Man, anybody know what's up with this friggin' weather?" he asked aloud, looking up. The morning's stunning cirrus clouds had burned off and the sky had taken on a flat, sickly yellow color that seemed to be slowly turning into a deeper shade. There was no wind, and it was moderately warm but not humid. It was just weird.

"I hope we don't have to deal with weather when we take this ratfuck out of there," he said to no one in particular.

Thirty-Seven

~~~ ~~~

Long Island, New York

Sometime after two o'clock, on the brightest New York City afternoon of the summer, Farnham H. Henchworth III, managing partner of the prestigious law offices of Dunham, Ferris, Henchworth, Lewis & Day, settled into the great leather chair from which he ruled the world. The view was from his sumptuous office located eleven hundred feet over the streets of Manhattan, on the 93rd floor of the Empire State Building.

The view across the city was exceptionally clear, and with wide views of Long Island and the Connecticut horizon, he mentally snapped a postcard picture scene that represented his kingdom. Nothing could have made the moment any more satisfying, except for the abrupt thought
~~~

that he had nothing to do. The phone rang at his desk, rescuing him from the tedious challenge of boredom. It's your wife, Mr. Henchworth. Shall I put her through, sir?" Rose Chamley asked promptly, with a voice that always seemed to be singing.

He sighed. Talk about tedious. "Of course," he told his secretary.

"Darling, I do hope I'm not interrupting something desperately important," asked Kay Henchworth. It was the classically haughty socialite greeting worthy of the very rich attorney who just so happened to be her husband. It wasn't really a question because she would go on, unapologetically, no matter the answer. Nonetheless, Henchworth played the game.

"Actually, Kay, I'm right in the middle of something and still hoping to leave a bit early to make it to the beach house before midnight," he half lied. He stood up at his desk, impatient with Kay's interruption, busy or not. Out of the corner of his eye he saw what appeared to be a strange, yellowish hue high on the horizon, northeast of Manhattan. Behind it were ominous looking black clouds which seemed to be bearing down on Long Island Sound. If he was right and the weather was turning bad, driving to his beloved Southampton house would be a nightmare in late afternoon traffic. The long weekend he and Kay had been planning would not get off to an easy start, but he was determined to reach Southampton tonight one way or another. He had an 8 a.m. tee time at Sebonack Golf Club which he would make even if he had to walk the length of Long Island to do so.

"Oh, of course, darling, I'll let you run," Kay replied, oblivious as usual to her husband's innate impatience. "I just wanted to remind you to pick me up at the train station tomorrow afternoon, promise?"

"I dare say my love, not even a hurricane could make me miss that train," he said as romantically as possible.

At the same moment nearly sixty miles away from the Empire State Building, a Long Island fisherman well off the Atlantic coast was also suddenly aware of the weather shift. In a matter of minutes, as he was tending to his last nets before beginning the slow return to Simmons Point in Peconic Bay to offload his hold of bluefish, a yellow sky had descended on his small trawler, the likes of which he had never seen in more than thirty years at sea. Beneath it, on the distant horizon, he saw what appeared to be a massive fog bank - extending as far as he could see to the east and west, rolling towards him at extraordinary speed.

As the fog bank came closer, the sky turned from yellow to green and finally to a darkness that resembled night. The mild headwind that he had been enjoying for most of the day began to pick up at an alarming pace; and the fisherman, alarmed, picked up the pace of hauling in his nets. He needed to head for shore - quickly.

But it was too late.

With a horrifying recognition that came with the darkening horizon, he was astonished to realize that the fog bank coming toward him was not fog at all. In fact, it was a mountain of roiling, screaming sea water that he instinctively guessed to be at least seventy feet high coming at him with astonishing momentum. As it raced towards him, he heard what sounded like the distant rumble of a locomotive rapidly grow to a deafening roar, like a tidal wave reaching the crescendo of its unimaginable power, drawn from the endless source of energy beneath it.

When the wave finally washed over the boat, the fisherman's senses were completely overwhelmed. He could not see or breathe for the water, and died from the deadly blow of the gargantuan wave even before he could drown from it. His boat did not sink, but instead disintegrated as it was tossed by the surge as effortlessly as a dried leaf was blown off a tree limb by a strong gust of wind.

The fisherman died not knowing that the incalculable storm surge was speeding towards the entire New England coast at more than seventy miles per hour, and that the wave that killed him was the product of a vacuum generated by vastly reduced barometric pressure and winds of at least two hundred miles per hour blowing across the open ocean. Or that the thirteen million people in the path of the devil's wind and water would be as equally surprised by it.

For his part, Farnham H. Henchworth, III would not realize until much later that afternoon that it was his good fortune not to have left his mahogany-paneled office as early in the day as he had planned.

Thirty-Eight

~~~ ~~~

Elm Street Elementary School

Precisely as the clock in her classroom at the Elm Street Elementary School reached 3 p.m., a shrill alarm bell sounded signaling the end of another school day. With a sigh of fatigue audible only to Carol Crandall, the second-grade teacher dismissed her class. "Have a wonderful afternoon, and I'll see you again tomorrow," she said to the small children, including Katie Lapkin, who smiled at Mrs. Crandall's goodbye.

Both Brian and Geoff Jr. had left school just after their lunch on a field trip with nearly sixty other classmates to the Boston Children's Museum, an exciting adventure that wouldn't get the Lapkin brothers home until much later that evening. Katie had waved to them on a large rented bus as they
~~~

pulled away, so jealous that she couldn't go to Boston as well. She'd have her own chance next year as a third grader.

With the children filing out of the room, Crandall suddenly remembered. "Oh, class, would one of you remind Mr. Collins that I'll need a ride home on the bus today? My car is being repaired." She hurriedly packed up her school bag so as not to keep Pat Collins waiting and followed the children outside several minutes later.

"Why hello, Mrs. Crandall," Collins greeted the teacher as she stepped aboard his yellow chariot. "It's a pleasure to have you join us. Will you be the first stop today or the last?" he enquired politely but in jest, fully planning on making the short detour to her cottage on the Misquamicut edge of Westerly his first priority.

"Well thank you for that kind offer, Mr. Collins," she said with a business tone to her response that did little to hide their close friendship of many years. "Actually, I would prefer to be the last. It seems like a nice afternoon for a ride with my favorite people," she said, never missing an opportunity to grow closer to her pupils.

In fact, it was a rather nice afternoon. The sun was still beaming even this late into the afternoon, there was a refreshing breeze blowing through the open bus windows, and the trip out to Napatree Point, which offered the most exquisite views of Little Narragansett Bay would be a delicious way to end her day.

Collins looked up into the rear view mirror to catch her face, raising a brow at her answer. She winked in return as the driver put the dilapidated old bus into gear and pulled away from the school.

The mood on board was relaxed and happy as the twenty-five children, all seven- or eight-years old, were delivered to their homes one by one as Collins followed the same orderly path he took five days a week beginning in Westerly and ending at Sandy Point. No more than ten minutes after leaving the school, he was startled to notice the skies changing from the west, with a darkness brewing behind it. Rain would probably be close behind. He hoped it would hold off until he dropped Katie off at the end of Napatree Point so he could avoid driving the bus to the end of Sandy Point.

Completely unaware of what was transpiring at the Lapkin mansion just a few miles ahead, Collins continued to drop off his passengers. By now the sky had changed dramatically and Carol Crandall felt the first twinges of concern.

Something about being out on the exposed Napatree Point peninsula during a storm gave her an uneasy feeling.

Thirty-Nine

~~~ ~~~

The New England Coast

By the time the storm surge swept onto the Connecticut coastline just before three in the afternoon, the trail of death and destruction it had left behind was wide and complete. New York City, just fifty-five miles from the hurricane's farthest edge, escaped with torrential rain and flooding that shocked the whole of Manhattan and left ten dead. More than a hundred great old Elm trees were knocked over in Central Park, and Manhattan was closed from 59th Street on due to flooding. The devastation over Long Island, however, was beyond imagination. The monstrously huge storm surge had washed over the entire eastern half of the Island, taking with it most of whatever stood in its way.
~~~

Hundreds died as the killer surge struck, with many of the dead local homeowners and sightseers who had come to the beaches to watch the yellow sky and the building surf that precipitated the surge. By the time they realized their mistake, it was too late. There was nowhere to run.

The shingles that tore off the roofs of mansions and beach houses along the wealthy Hamptons flew across Long Island Sound onto the Connecticut shoreline, followed soon by whole trees, telephone poles, cars and whole buildings. The mountain of debris rained down onto the small towns of Madison, Clinton, Westbrook, Old Saybrook and the great houses of Fenwick. Piles of wreckage more than fifty feet high blocked Route 1 and local roads along the entire Connecticut shoreline as nearly every beachfront home was first shredded by the staggering winds then swept clean off its foundation by the enormous storm surge.

Still the incredible wave continued to race unchecked across the southern coastline of New England, pushed by the unimaginable fury of the storm for which not a single warning or precaution had been heard or taken. Hundreds more died in battered Connecticut, people completely blindsided by the violence. More than one drowned in their homes, confounded by the complete lack of warning which had not allowed them even minutes to escape.

In Washington, reports of the storm's impact on New York and Connecticut began dribbling into Charlie Pierce. The monster had hit almost directly where he had predicted and just thirty minutes later, but with a speed even greater than he had imagined. The hurricane had swept over Long Island so fast that there was no time to warn Connecticut it was coming.

The Washington Weather Bureau staff were stupefied by the reports and raced to put out hurricane warnings for Rhode Island, but it was far too late for anything to be done to protect the "Ocean State" from the murderous killer taking aim at it. For all intents, Rhode Island had no more warning than its devastated neighbors, and only minutes more than Massachusetts. In Jacksonville, Gordon Dunn stared out the window in front of Grady Norton's unoccupied desk, turning over in his mind again and again how so many people working so hard to track a storm the size of a state -- could have completely failed at their task, and allowed millions of people along one of the most wealthy and populous stretches of land in the world – to be utterly and completely ambushed.

Norton and Dunn had reason to be frustrated. In the Weather Bureau's extensive history of tracking hurricanes, this storm had broken all the rules.

To begin with, after miraculously "recurving" just hours before the storm was predicted to slam into southern Florida, the storm had then course corrected again. The event astonished forecasters who had banked on the storm taking a slightly southerly direction. It would be days before they recognized this turning point or the disaster that swept the Bahamas. At this time, Norton and Dunn had assumed the storm, which they had always believed to be a classic Cape Verde hurricane, had already taken a decidedly northern turn. Unfortunately, the limited information they had available to decipher the storm's behavior led them to assumptions - almost all of which were wrong.

Then, as first identified by Charlie Pierce, the unusual height of the Bermuda High, combined with a frontal system to the west, bent the normally east flowing jet stream's winds to the south before pushing them northwards along the eastern Atlantic Coast. Consequently, instead of blowing out to sea as expected, just as the hurricane reached the area of Cape Hatteras, the forward direction of the storm swung to the left. The effect was to create a pathway for the hurricane to travel, unimpeded, right up the seaboard.

As well, the Jacksonville and Washington, D.C. offices vastly underestimated the forward speed of the hurricane. While warnings were continually posted regarding the speed of the storm, again the information was based on assumptions. As the storm continued to turn north, the forecasters agreed that colder waters would slow the maelstrom down to the twenty- to thirty-miles per hour range that was typical of a Cape Verde-style hurricane. In actuality, blinded by a now almost acute lack of information as nearly all normal shipping activities came to a halt, the hurricane had actually picked up speed again and was barreling up to the Long Island coast at an unheard of speed of more than seventy miles per hour. No hurricane on record had ever moved so fast.

Finally, the extraordinary speed of the hurricane also prevented forecasters from getting an accurate fix on its exact location, in fact causing them to severely underestimate its location and forward progress and providing the storm with perhaps it's most powerful weapon: surprise. All these ingredients combined to allow the killer hurricane to soar up the eastern seaboard at the speed of an airplane.

While survivors on Long Island and in Connecticut began to realize the magnitude of the event that had just befallen them and that death and destruction was everywhere, in the tiny state of Rhode Island the only indications that something was wrong were the approaching yellow and black skies and the first few drops of rain. Only a few people had picked up any news of the calamity, spread by shortwave radio. There was no official warning from the United States Weather Bureau or anyone else about the monster that was sprinting towards them. The full force of the hurricane struck even as small craft warnings were being raised for the coastal waters off Rhode Island and Massachusetts.

Simultaneously, on the half-mile spit of sand known as Sandy Point in the community of Napatree Point in the small town of Westerly, the hostages held by a freak of a man were already struggling with a surprise that had invaded and corrupted their lives forever.

They were soon to learn that neither of the evils would show any mercy.

Forty

~~~ ~~~

The Battle for Sandy Point

Patrolman Ed Ranklin verified that the two snipers were in position, then reported to Chief Cianci. The Chief was talking over the plan to free the Lapkin hostages with Connecticut detectives Irv Nicklas and Sam Cawley when Ranklin arrived with Lieutenant Sullivan at his side.

"We think we can draw him out Chief, get him into a conversation or something, then let one of the long barrel guys bag his ass," Ranklin said, somewhat eagerly. "DiGregorio and Peterson are both in position. I've seen these guys shoot. They could rip the balls off a cockroach at two hundred yards, I swear."

Ranklin's report was a little too excited for the three senior officers gathered behind a patrol car
~~~

several hundred yards above the Lapkin mansion at the end of Sandy Point. Virtually every cop in town had shown up at the scene, Nicklas observed, including the guys who had been manning the roadblock at the entrance to Napatree Point at the Watch Hill docks.

"Whoa, slow down, Ed," the portly Chief cautioned his well-intentioned officer. "First of all, have we verified who this fucking maniac has inside - who the hostages are?"

Sullivan took the ball without being asked. "Yeah, Geoff Lapkin, his oldest son, James, who's fourteen, and that young Italian college kid, 'Andy' something or other," Sullivan said. "Mrs. Lapkin thinks the bastard already took out the maid, don't have her name yet, and busted up her husband and the college kid pretty good. Emily… I mean, Mrs. Lapkin, said she escaped because James came after the ape with a shotgun and had the situation in control, supposedly."

"Yeah," Sam Cawley interrupted. "I don't suppose any of the rest of you are surprised that we haven't seen the kid since that gunshot we heard, huh?" Cawley was always irritable and a devoted cynic. "I'm betting the kid is down. I hope he's alive, but that big ugly boy is fully in charge, count on it."

"Shit," Cianci murmured in response. It was hard to argue Cawley's logic, even if he did have the charm of a cement block.

"Yeah," Nicklas agreed. "There's only one way to find out. We gotta go flush that motherfucker out of there. I'm supposing those hostages are wounded and need help or we're going to bury some more people. This guy won't hesitate to let them all die to save his own worthless ass." The detective was repulsed by the trail of murder that escaped convict Charles Dewey had left behind him in his run through Connecticut and Rhode Island. Secretly, he would have given anything to be the guy to pull the trigger with the cross hairs lined up in the middle of Dewey's forehead.

"Okay, Sullivan, who's your guy?" Cianci asked, wanting the name of the officer the Lieutenant proposed to draw the murderer out into the open. There wasn't a second's hesitation.

"You're looking at him, Chief," Sullivan said, his tone flat and calm, not giving away the slightest hint of either braggadocio or fear. Cianci had expected nothing less. The Lieutenant turned to his patrolman. "Ranklin, you just make sure the riflemen are ready, got it?"

Although Sullivan was his superior when out of uniform, Ranklin and the young lieutenant were inseparable. The junior man was clearly not in agreement about the decision to send Sullivan in.

"Sir, I..."Ranklin began. Sullivan immediately cut him off.

"Just answer the question, patrolman."

"Yes, sir, we'll be ready," Ranklin snapped back, obviously still pissed off. "What's the plan, Lieutenant?"

"Simple," Sullivan said quickly. "No one but the big bastard gets shot, right?"

Ranklin calmed down. "Right, sir," he said, a grin coming to his face.

"Chief, I'm going to approach the house very slowly from this point. You can expect he's made us out here by now and is making his own plans," Sullivan said calmly. "I will call him out by name after identifying myself and attempt to engage him in a trade for the hostages. You know, a car, boat, whatever the hell he wants. Of course, all of us know that's not going to happen."

Cawley shifted uneasily. He had been standing quietly for a change, leaning against the back fender of the patrol car.

"What's to stop him from dropping you right on the spot, Sullivan?" Cawley asked, in the sarcastic tone he was so fond of. "We know he's got weapons and we certainly know he's not afraid to use them."

Nicklas piled in behind his partner. "Sam's right…"he hesitated to make too big a deal out of agreeing with his obnoxious partner.

"It happens," Cawley said.

"You're going to be a sitting duck, Sullivan," Irv Nicklas continued, his respect for the young officer having grown over the last twenty-four hours. "In fact, I'd bet this fucking asshole will try to drop you just to make us think twice about sending anyone else. You need to find a way to give your snipers an immediate shot and dump this pile of garbage at the curb. 'Mi capisci?' "

Sullivan smiled and would have responded if his Italian Chief wasn't there. No one said anything for thirty seconds until Ranklin broke the silence. "I think we should forget the barter crap and just go for the shot." Nods from the rest of the group brought agreement to the issue.

"Okay, we'll just go for the shot then," Sullivan said without thought that he would be in the firing line either way. "As soon as I get him outside and am confident there's no one else in the way, I'll drop to my knees. Have DiGregorio and Peterson take their best shots."

"But know that one else is to fire, do you understand?" Cianci added. "If all these guys up here in blue start lighting it up, we'll turn the house into Swiss cheese and probably take the hostages out ourselves."

"Yes, sir," Sullivan said. "Ranklin, spread the word. I'm going to talk to the long guns and then take a stroll."

"You hurry back, son," Sam Cawley said, as close to a vote of confidence that he was able to give another man. Sullivan nodded to the detective and walked away. Suddenly, it started to pour. The group had lost track of the weather.

"Hell, this ought to make it easier," Cawley said. No one responded.

A little more than a half mile away, Pat Collins was very unhappy that the heavy rain had come just as he was about to drop Katie Lapkin off from the school bus. He hated driving to the end of Sandy Point and turning the long bus around in such a tight area. Downshifting, he sighed but waved at Carol Crandall in the rearview mirror.

She looked absolutely terrified by the sudden weather.

"Relax, Mrs. Crandall," the old man said. "I'll have you home and snug as a bug in no time after we drop Katie off." By now the rain was hammering away at the metal school bus, each drop making the sound of a marble bouncing on it.

For his part, Pat Collins was driving out of feel, the rain now making it impossible to see anything through his windshield. Off to the side of the road ahead he spotted what look like a lot parked cars. *Somebody must be having a party*, he thought. He drove by without giving the scene another look, completely missing the uniformed police officer that was attempting to get his attention.

He headed slightly downhill toward the Lapkin's place and slowed the bus to a stop. "Wait a minute, now Katie," he yelled. "Maybe the rain will slow down," Collins said.

Strange, Collins thought. Emily Lapkin always met her daughter at the door when she heard the school bus pull up outside. The front door was wide open, but there didn't seem to be anyone around. He decided to wait for a minute or two before letting the child off alone. From his vantage point, he could not see that Emily had bolted from the protection of the police at the first sign of the school bus and was running for her life back into danger.

In the meantime, Pat Collins, Katie Lapkin and Carol Crandall sat silently in the school bus, listening to the rain pounding down and together heard a siren-like sound coming from the ocean. The bus driver rolled down his window just a bit to peer outside. He squinted, trying to make sense of what he saw.

"What a queer day, ladies," he said innocently. "It was such a beautiful day. Why that looks like a fog bank coming at us now."

Forty-One

~~~ ঌ ~~~

A World Torn Asunder

The first Rhode Islanders to see the great sea surge approach were actually visiting in Stonington, the small village on the Connecticut border. They were the lucky ones, perched safely on high stone cliffs that overlooked the ocean.

It seemed one minute they were enjoying the glorious sun that had warmed the coastline throughout the morning, the next worrying about the approaching sickly yellow sky. The torrential rains and winds that followed were not the last of the shocks they would experience from the bluffs that afternoon. Nor were the dozen or so tidal waves, each greater than thirty feet high that followed the initial surge taking with them
~~~

whatever had not already been crushed, mangled or swept away.

What these witnesses would remember forever was the horror of watching the helpless below them caught completely unaware that death had arrived. It had come without warning, without giving them so much as a moment to consider the finality, and it was instantaneous.

Little boys and girls in their bathing suits, building sand castles near the surf, died where they played. Lovers strolling at the edge of the surf succumbed without so much as a final kiss. Artists with their still wet canvasses, men enjoying a cigar on the beach and old women walking in their wide-brimmed summer hats all were helplessly and violently drawn into the vortex of the surge.

In minutes, what had been tranquil inlets, ports and marshes all along the Rhode Island coast became churning, deadly tidal maelstroms. Whole houses, buildings and barns were washed away. Hundred-year-old trees were shattered or uprooted like dandelions plucked from a lawn. Thousands of cars, busses, trolleys and even locomotives were washed into harbors or sucked out to sea. Many became tombs for the helpless trapped inside.

The hurricane continued up the New England Coast, its terrifying pace unchecked even by landfall. Church steeples toppled and bridges were washed out by the gigantic surge and the following waves. Railroad tracks were ripped from their beds and paved highways washed out. Often the only warning of the approaching storm was the preceding loss of telephone and electric service as poles were snapped like matchsticks in the storm's path. Curiously, the seagulls and sandpipers, cats and dogs went silent.

No prayer, sacrifice, rosary or blessing could stop it. Life or death hung on where one might have been standing or sitting, playing or reading, eating or talking. The odds of living or dying were as good as the flip of a coin.

In the few moments it took for the hurricane to find Watch Hill, its massive sea surge, a wave still as much as fifty feet high despite making landfall, had swept clean the entire coastline between Stonington and Watch Hill. The few people who survived the total exposure to the most powerful storm to hit New England in more than one hundred years, described it all the same.

The first indication was a slight vibration in the ears. Gradually, the noise became a chord of distant voices and then finally rose to a spine-chilling siren that signaled the arrival of the wall of water. When the wave actually hit the coastline of Watch Hill, its impact was so powerful that it registered on earthquake sensing seismographs at Fordham University in New York. At Watch Hill, the sea surge smashed into the helpless fishing boats moored to their docks and slammed into the village of small cottages with unimaginable fury, wiping most of them away instantaneously.

In the breathtaking few minutes in which the surge and a dozen following tidal waves of more than thirty feet battered all of Little Narragansett

Bay, the few people who survived the initial massive blow could do no better than to find something to hang onto or to get to higher ground. Both were tragically elusive and many along the Watch Hill Coast, who miraculously survived the surge, met their end while swimming for their lives before the next tidal wave hit. Debris also took its toll on the few initial survivors - uprooted trees and telephone polls became crushing battering rams, and literally tons of wreckage from destroyed cottages filled the waters and moved at lethal speeds that simply ran over the helpless in the water.

There was the slightest of breaths before the hurricane surge found Sandy Point and then swept over Napatree Point in the next blink of an eye. There were thirty-nine summer homes on the whole of the peninsula when the storm struck including the Lapkin mansion. Some were swept off their piers and vanished into the waters in an instant. Others came apart more slowly, disintegrating one piece at a time giving some families the chance to climb higher for a few minutes more of safety. But it was a fleeting refuge from an inevitable force that would ultimately return the peninsula to the sandy spit that had been created by the geologic process of long shore drift that had begun eons before.

On Sandy Point, the torrential rains hid the oncoming surge. A man could barely see a foot in front of him, it was teeming so hard. Only one did - and he could hardly comprehend the wall of water coming directly at him in the Lapkin mansion. Surprisingly, he felt no fear and took no action to try to save himself. He had seen the devil in his dreams and in his actions for all of his life. In an instant, Charles Dewey recognized the monstrous storm for all his narcissistic mind could make of it: certain death for him and those who would not stop pursuing him, or the possibility of escape into an anonymous world of chaos where no one would care who he was. At least for a while. Either way, the devil was finally offering freedom to the monster that had been born to his fate for no reason he could understand.

In the seconds before the surge hit Sandy Point, Dewey studied the dozens of police cars parked up the road, containing dozens more cops. He knew that the minute he walked out the front door, one of them would put a bullet through his brain as certainly as he would if given the opportunity.

Casting his eyes down into the school bus, its occupants unaware of the impending disaster, he knew the vehicle would provide him no opportunity for escape. It would be swept away as surely as those training their guns on his head at this very moment would be. He turned to glance out at the Bay again, the wave cresting higher and higher as it approached the house. Then, almost instantly, he turned back to the bus, just thirty feet from where he stood. Something had caught his eye, something that filled his tortured mind with anguish - an emotion he may never have felt before.

In the bus, sitting behind the driver was the little girl. It was the same small child who had walked with him, asked him for his name and told him hers, the child who had shown no fear of his monster-like appearance or how he towered over her when she reached for his hand.

It was the same beautiful child who had touched him in so many ways he could not understand, but who had, for a few fleeting seconds, drained the anger that had imprisoned him his entire life from his thoughts and being.

It was Katie.

Forty-Two

~~~ ✥ ~~~

Of Winds and Rage

Chief Cianci knew it was over instantly. He heard the siren-like roar almost before he could see the wave, blinded by the torrential rains. He didn't have to see it; he knew what it was even before it hit.

Cianci had lived in Watch Hill his entire life and had grown up on the stories his father and his grandfather had told him about tidal waves and their screams and devastation. He suddenly saw the great wave, as high as a five-story building, rear up to sweep over the Lapkin place, the first house on Sandy Point. He immediately knew that he and most of his guys wouldn't stand a chance totally exposed with nowhere to go.
~~~

Lieutenant Billy Sullivan instantly heard the deafening whine of the surge, but had no idea what to make of it. As he walked toward the Lapkin front door to attempt to draw Charles Dewey out of the house, and hopefully to save the poor bastards in the school bus who had unwittingly driven right into the line of fire, his mind screamed for answers. He stopped no more than twenty-five feet from the front door of the mansion, just about adjacent to the school bus. Out of the corner of his eye, a huge dark shadow darted from the Lapkin doorway. Sullivan turned back quickly to see the ape-like man, a shotgun in one hand and a revolver in the other, standing at the edge of the porch. Dewey lined up the shotgun on Sullivan before the police officer could even move. The young man waited for the blast of buckshot that would send him to his next life. It didn't come.

Dewey tossed the guns away just as the great wave broke on top of the house, blowing out each window on the first floor and some on the second. The unbelievable strength of the wave hurled him from the top of the porch directly at the open doors of the school bus. He grabbed on to a metal railing, holding on for all he was worth even as the bus filled with water. Katie screamed as Pat Collins was thrown through a window after smashing his head on the windshield post. He was dead before the sea swept away his body.

To his right, Dewey watched a house of comparable size to the Lapkins' disappear before his eyes - the entire house was just swept away and there were people on the third floor screaming out the window begging for help. Before his eyes, the house somersaulted across the water, driven by furious wind which was now also upon them. He screamed to Kate.

"Little girl, c'mon, grab my shoulders, I will get you into the house. Hurry..."

By this time Kate was near shock from watching the death of Collins and seeing her next door neighbor's house completely swept away. "I just want my mother and father...Charles," she begged.

Despite the overwhelming situation, Dewey's heart shuddered when he heard the little girl actually say his name... she had not forgotten him. "We'll go get them together Kate, your father is inside..." He was interrupted by a woman's voice behind him, frantically calling to the girl.

"Emily," she cried out, "hang onto the man, he's big enough to drag you back to the house. We're all going to move to the third floor to Shelly's room, okay? The mother was so desperate she had forgotten that the only man who could possibly save her daughter was the same man who quite possibly had already killed her husband and son. "Please, Katie..."

Kate calmed herself just enough to remember Mrs. Crandall sitting behind her. "Mrs. Crandall has to come too. Mom!"

The giant man pulled himself on board the bus, which was already beginning to lose its grip with the road and would be just another submerged victim of the storm surge in the next few seconds.

To the right of the Lapkin place, the entire roof abruptly blew off a house and sailed into the sky, climbing tens of feet before crashing into the remains of another summer home a quarter mile away on Napatree Point. The site sent Kate jumping into the arms of Dewey.

Carol Crandall, by now so terrified that she could not move from her seat, sat dumbly as Dewey tried to pull her up. "No, no, leave me alone, please, I'll wait for the next bus…" she said deliriously.

"Honey, if there's one time in your life you ought to trust a piece of shit like me, it's now," he said in a calm voice that even surprised him. "Now get up and get on!" he yelled at her with a voice that would scare away a shark in open water. He pulled her to his feet and wrapped one of his giant arms around her waist. With his other arm, he pulled Katie close to his chest and moved to the front of the bus. Just as he went to step down he realized the water was moving so fast he couldn't tell how powerful the current was. Before he could consider the consequences, he heard Emily scream from inside. Another surge, a tidal wave of more than thirty feet had broken across the house again. It had nearly swept her out the door while she had been dragging her still unconscious husband up to the temporary safety of the second floor. She had already moved James, still bleeding profusely from the gunshot wound, and Andy Popillo who was coming around.

The wave caught Dewey weighed down by Katie and her teacher, and staggered him. He fought to keep his balance and tightened his grip on the little girl. Crandall was kicking and screaming in terror and Dewey yelled at her to stop struggling. Finally he lost his grip on the woman just as a wave pushed them all beneath the water. As Dewey battled back to the surface, a section of the Lapkin's dock that had broken free slammed into Crandall and ripped into her head. Before he could reach out to snag her again, she was gone, her arms flailing just above the surface for a few yards until she disappeared completely under the water.

Dewey knew he had no time to waste. Wrapping both of his massive arms around the little girl, he kicked away from the bus just as it washed down into the Bay. The immensely powerful current pushed him back trying to force him into a similar fate. Around him he could hear the screams of some of the policemen who only moments before were aiming to blow his head off. They had no chance of survival. Many of their colleagues had been drowned in their patrol cars. Cianci had been killed nearly immediately, and Sam Cawley had been crushed by a garage that had been picked up by the wave and slammed back down on top of him. Irv Nicklas was nowhere to be seen. Billy Sullivan had been blown into the parked school bus headfirst and appeared to be dead.

If not for the enormous strength of the convict, Katie Lapkin would also have been swept out into the Bay with no hope for survival. Dewey turned over in the water, Katie still clutching his chest, and with amazingly powerful strokes, side kicked his way to the front porch and the open door with the little girl. He managed to grab onto a porch railing and held on with all his strength, the water surrounding him churning into a vortex that was sucking in all manner of debris.

As he found strength and began hauling himself up into the house, another tidal wave struck the house broadside, collapsing the entire left side of the mansion. The wreckage crashed into the surf. Dewey heard Emily screaming upstairs. "Help me, please, help me someone," she shrieked while desperately trying to move her husband and James up to the third floor of the house, the only portion that still looked remotely stabile. Thankfully, Andy Popillo had finally regained consciousness and was able to give her some help. The first thing he did was tear off a length of one of Shelly's aprons and fashion a bandage around James' bleeding wounds. On the other side of the house he could hear Brian and Geoff Jr.'s bedroom being torn from the mansion and with a horrifying shriek, the entire corner of the building tore off and flew away. While it was only late afternoon, the sky was so dark and the air so full of salt and mist, it seemed as though it was past midnight. Andy could not make out where the remnant of the house actually landed.

With Geoff and James Lapkin pulled to shelter inside Shelly's room on the third floor, Popillo raced down the rapidly collapsing staircase to the first floor, where Dewey was just dragging Kate and himself into the living room. The water was already chest high on the six-foot, eight-inch convict. Andy waded to Kate, ignoring the ugly bastard that had nearly caved in his head, grabbed her from his arms and raced back up the stairs to join the rest of the Lapkin family.

Dewey, thinking he had survived the worst of the storm, found his way to the kitchen and was looking for hard liquor. He had no other way to celebrate the only decent thing he'd ever done in his life, and that thought alone took the joy out of his single moment of triumph. He finally found a bottle of scotch in a cabinet and drained half the contents in a single swallow. Momentarily satisfied, he turned around and slumped against the icebox, one of the few pieces of furniture that had not been swept right out of the house when the surge hit.

Irv Nicklas was inside and had been waiting for a sign of Dewey. The detective had somehow dragged himself to the house after the surge hoping to help Billy Sullivan. When the first following tidal wave hit, he fought the current by hanging on to a drainpipe, then pulled himself inside and hid in a servant's pantry off the kitchen.

He had witnessed Dewey's remarkable feat of getting the little girl and the woman safely out of the bus, amazed by the man's size and strength. But even as he watched the murderer become a hero, he could not rid his mind of the images of his old friend Melvin Hill on the floor of his liquor store, his body shredded by the shotgun blast at close range. Or, the two college boys who had died begging for mercy at the edge of the surf in Stonington after hours of terror at the hands of the monster. Finally, Tiger Griswold's battered face came before his eyes, a man who had come to terms with his fate, only to have his lonely life ended at the hands of a maniac.

It was now or never, he figured and the detective stepped out of the pantry in which he was hiding. He somehow had not lost his gun in the crashing waves and gripped it as tightly as if his hand was a vise. Nicklas had every intention of using the gun. He couldn't give a shit if the asshole had rescued the Pope, he was a cold-blooded killer with evil in his veins - and he had to die. Now.

Dewey heard his voice before he saw Nicklas.

"Stand up you miserable sack of shit," Nicklas said calmly to the convict who had just taken another long pull from the bottle. "I want to see you, you understand? You simply can't be as ugly as they say."

Dewey laughed aloud, then turned to look the detective in the face. He pushed his mop of greasy black hair back off his face, unmasking the terrifying eyes set back into his skull and the ape's thick, angry brow across his forehead. He was no more afraid of a cop with a gun than any other man alive; and to prove his point, he casually drank again from the bottle, nearly draining it.

As Nicklas took in the huge man in front of him, he was stunned. The pictures and descriptions he'd had to prepare for this moment weren't enough. Charles Dewey was simply the most hideous human being the Middletown detective had ever seen.

He blurted out the first thing that came to his mind. "Jesus Christ man, what the fuck did your mother look like?" he said as cruelly as he could muster.

Dewey listened carefully, Nicklas' words dragging him full circle from hero back to the murderous killer he was.

The corner of the convict's mouth turned up and he sneered at the cop. "Don't know," Dewey replied calmly, tired of running, tired of living. He thought for a moment about rushing the detective, a sure way to commit suicide. He held back instead, preferring to bait the cop for a while as he sorted out his thoughts. He had just risked his sorry life for the benefit of the girl instead of using the opportunity to escape. He was confused by his feelings for the child and completely unsure of his next move.

"My mother? I don't remember the bitch," he replied in the kind of monotone that usually ends badly, "but some kin told me I tore her up pretty bad when she spit me out. I probably scared the shit out of her too -- they said she screamed, then gave me away on the spot after taking one look at her baby. I guess you could say we never bonded."

Nicklas imagined the horror of the moment.

"Sorry I ain't all weepy eyed, asshole, but I'm all out of tears from cleaning up your bloody mess since Wethersfield," the veteran detective said sarcastically. He had an overwhelming urge to shoot his prisoner right between the eyes. But that would be too quick, Nicklas thought. Killing Dewey here would be an act of mercy compared to months on Death Row and the electric chair. No, the detective decided, he wouldn't pull the trigger on this asshole no matter how tempting it would be, but he would sure as hell be in the gallery when they pulled the switch.

The house shuddered again as another huge wave hit and engulfed the two men. The entire first floor was now under water. As Nicklas fought to get back to the surface, what felt like a pipe wrench grabbed him by his lower left leg. It was Dewey with a vise-like grip and his one- handed hold. He slowly pulled Nicklas back to the bottom of the kitchen floor and held him down with his weight. The detective had dropped his gun and had no defense as he felt a gigantic forearm wrap around his neck and tighten. The detective tore at Dewey's clutch with his hands trying desperately to release the pressure against his windpipe. He frantically thrashed and kicked with every ounce of energy he had left, but it was useless. Nicklas' eyes began to bulge from the pressure of Dewey's grip, and then went blank and lifeless as the convict released him. The detective reactively breathed in water and was dead within seconds, drowned and with his throat crushed.

Dewey kicked Nicklas' dead weight off him and with his own last seconds of air kicked to the surface, just below the kitchen ceiling. He took in great, heaving gasps of oxygen and rested to regain his strength. The water was continuing to rise so he knew he had to make a move. Filling his lungs with air, he dipped back below the surface and swam in the darkening underwater towards where he remembered the staircase to be. It was his last chance.

Finally, just as his lungs were almost completely emptied, he felt, rather than saw a riser and step followed by another and another. It was the main staircase to the upper floors. He kicked off the floor again racing to get to the top of the water, pulling himself up one step at a time. Just as he began to black out, his head broke through to the surface of the second floor, only to meet the waiting face of Andy Popillo.

"Why won't you die, you goddamned freak?" Andy screamed at Dewey as he rested momentarily on the second floor landing. "Haven't you had your fill of blood yet? You're not going to hurt these people, do you hear me?" Then, with the adrenalin fed strength brought by his fury, the young man lifted a heavy oak end table off the floor and threw it down on top of the resting murderer. It hit Dewey full on the head, splintering, and opened a sizeable gash over his left eye.

Nothing happened for a full minute. There was no motion under the oak rubble, and there was not another sound to be heard above the rain and wind still beating down on the house. Then, abruptly, the wooden splinters were tossed aside and Dewey rose from the water, blood streaming from his head, but otherwise unhurt. Popillo was dumbfounded.

Dewey was pissed and came after the boy with newfound energy.

"You can't run from me, college boy, I'm gonna crush your fucking skull, you son of a bitch," Dewey screamed, with only vengeance on his mind. Popillo backed away from the huge man, defenseless and with water now up to his knees on the second floor. He entered Geoff Lapkin's library with one eye on Dewey and one scouring the room for a weapon. There, he had it, he thought, reaching for a wrought iron poker hanging from a rack of tools in front of an oversized field stone fireplace. Popillo grabbed it and waited for Dewey to follow him into the library. Just as the murderer walked through the doorway, the young man swung at the giant's head, landing a heavy blow to the side of his face. Dewey staggered for a moment then fell to his knees. His head was just above water. Popillo struck him in the head again from behind and the giant man fell face forward into the still rising water.

Popillo struggled to reach the staircase again, half walking and half swimming. The surge was half way up the third floor staircase when he finally burst through and was able to run to Shelly's room, where Emily was watching over her husband, Katie and James. Geoff had regained consciousness, although still woozy on his feet; but James, who had lost a tremendous amount of blood, was still out cold. Katie was holding her oldest brother's head in her lap. The little girl was trembling with fear, and perhaps for the first time since she was an infant, was silent. She was certain they were all going to die.

When Popillo reached the group, there was a strong sigh of relief from Emily who hugged him as one of her own, ironically unaware of the young man's feelings for her. At that exact moment, another massive tidal wave slammed into the house and separated it from the dozens of piers on which it was built over the sand. Water raged through the third floor windows that had been smashed when the first tidal wave swamped the Point. Emily and Popillo were knocked to the floor. Without warning, most of the roof covering the house ripped off and sailed away into the air, leaving the five survivors completely exposed.

"Hang on to any thing you can find," Geoff Lapkin yelled, barely audible above the howling wind, "the radiators, door knobs, anything you can grasp for a few more minutes. This has got to stop soon."

Emily, who had fallen closest to an open window, pulled herself up enough to peer out towards Napatree Point. Through the dense torrential rains, she could see that only the wreckage of a few homes had survived. Most were completely gone. Geoff screamed at her to get away from the window, but she was completely mesmerized by the churning waters, crumbling houses, and trees and other debris flying through the air into the roiling Little Narragansett Bay. It was too far away to see clearly, but she couldn't pick out a single building on the Watch Hill shore.

As she went to heed Geoff's instructions, the large house on the left, two removed from their own, took the full brunt of another wave. As Emily watched, the house was torn off its footings and rolled over into the maelstrom in the Bay. She couldn't bear to watch any more and crawled to where Katie was holding James. Taking a piece of the rope she had cut off Geoff and Andy after Dewey had bound them, she wrapped it around the three of them and a leg of a nearby cast iron radiator. Then she prayed.

Another wave, then another slammed into the house, the final one completely freeing the great mansion from its grip on the beach. Fortunately it stayed together, probably because without the roof the wind could not build pressure inside. Emily could feel the house begin to float into the Bay, feeling it settle down into the water somewhat. Geoff and Popillo released their grips on another radiator and stared out the windows, looking for anyone to help get them out of the house. There was nothing but debris everywhere and not a living thing in sight.

With their backs turned, neither of them noticed the huge presence that unexpectedly emerged in the doorway of the slain Shelly's former bedroom. Somehow, with strength that an ordinary man could only imagine, Charles Dewey had not only managed to survive the savage beating by Popillo, but the wrath of the storm itself.

The giant said nothing, barely glancing at the two men in the room and strode directly to Emily and Katie. The little girl was frightened of the blood streaming freely from two gashes on his face, but strangely not of the man.

"Charles," she said, with an almost welcoming tone, which struck Dewey like a hammer. Even after the hideous things he had done to her family, Katie Lapkin smiled at him, a singular, simple act that struck the murderer deep in his heart.

As he approached, yet another wave struck what was left of the house. Emily screamed and held Katie tighter as she felt the remains of Shelly's room rip itself off the second story framing and with it two complete walls. The odd shaped piece of wreckage became a sort of raft. It appeared to be in no danger of capsizing, but the two still upright walls behaved as sails. The odd v-shaped walls could not stand up to winds still well in excess of one hundred miles hour and began to tilt the raft on its side. They were helpless as they drifted out into the Bay on the unstable piece of wooden floor. Another wave would surely send them all to the bottom.

The last wave had driven Dewey to his knees, but he scrambled to his feet as soon as he could make footing. He may have looked like a primate; but after studying the two upright walls, he was intelligent enough to surmise the problem and attack it.

Without the aid of a single tool but his two enormous, callous-hardened hands, he took aim at the wall nearest him and began punching the plaster surface covering the wood studs behind it.

When he had punched a hole large enough to get a grasp on the two-by-four inch lumber, he turned around, wrapped his hands around the board and pulled ferociously. He grunted as he bent over from the pressure of pulling on the stud and refused to let up. Nothing happened for several minutes; but then, slowly, a creaking sound began that finally became a resounding crack. There was the sound of splintering and ripping when Dewey snapped the top half of the section loose, held only in place by some plaster.

The eight-foot wall had six studs spaced every sixteen inches apart and Dewey did the same thing to each of them. When the final stud was snapped, he pushed the remnants of the top half of the wall back until it broke off and fell overboard. He let loose with a resounding roar of satisfaction that could be heard even above the howling winds. Then he pushed and kicked the lower half until it separated from the floor and fell over into the water. Immediately, the wind's effect on the swirling raft lessened. He turned his attention to the second wall, which was anchored only to the floor, and with his huge body pushing in the center, and Popillo and Geoff Lapkin at either end, the trio made short work of eliminating the raft's last sail.

By now the waves had stopped, but the wind was still whipping up the water in Little Narragansett Bay into a rapidly moving sea of twelve- to fifteen-foot waves that were blowing south-southeast. The raft – the only visible remains of the most spectacular summer home on Sandy

Point -- had itself been reduced to nothing more then an eight-foot square oak floor built over framing lumber. It was continually pummeled by the storm, but was stable. Sections of water pipe that had been snapped off below the third floor still remained, jutting through the floor where Dewey had torn the walls down. The appendages at least gave the small band of survivors something solid to hold onto as they rose and fell with the angry sea. Emily and Katie had continued to care for James, who had somewhat regained consciousness after the two had been able to stem the bleeding. He was weak, but he was alive.

Dewey sat in silence, watching Katie as she continued caring for her brother. He found her kindness and emotions simply confusing. He had never seen such behavior before. Once, she caught him staring at her. It frightened him for her to look at him so directly. He turned away. When he looked back she whispered, "Thank you for fixing the raft." He could not respond.

It was after eight p.m. when the seas began to abate, and Geoff thought they must have drifted at least ten miles from Sandy Point. The wind was still full and blowing toward the south, so he expected they would eventually end up somewhere on the Watch Hill coast after having been blown across the Bay. There was not a light anywhere on the coast to give him an inkling of their whereabouts. He wondered what was left of Westerly and his factory, Watch Hill, Napatree Point, and his beloved Sandy Point. He fought to keep his mind on the immediate problem – to keep them alive until they touched the shore again.

The raft was relatively stabile now and safe from danger of capsizing, but they had constant concern over debris in the water. Dead bodies that could have come from anywhere on the coast floated by. Hundreds of boats were floating all over Little Narragansett Bay, most overturned, some upright but barely making the surface. The worst of the dangers were the uprooted trees that floated everywhere in the Bay. Almost all had been stripped clean of leaves, but large branches had been snapped like kindling and the sharp, jagged remains of the growth emerging from the tree trunk could be exceptionally dangerous. They had to stay awake at all times on the lookout for floating trees which they would dodge, push away, jump over or lie prone to escape. In the darkness, the game became deadly.

Sometime after midnight, shortly after the numbing rain had stopped, Charles Dewey actually lost sight of what he was: an exceedingly violent human being who only knew one way of eliminating problems, wants or disappointments. He killed anything that got in his way, and he did so in such manner that strongly suggested he enjoyed killing. Absurdly, the temporary proximity to the Lapkins on the raft made him feel as if he could become one of them by simply willing it to be.

"Hey, Katie," he called out in the darkness late into the night, the air cold and the silence making the night even longer. They were all cold, hungry and miserable and first light was still at least five hours away. Geoff and Emily, and especially Andy Popillo, jumped at the sound of his voice. Dewey hadn't spoken a word in hours.

"Yes, Charles," Katie answered, still too anxious and keyed up to even attempt to fall asleep in her father's lap. She was cold, too.

"Why don't you come over next to me and I'll try to keep you warm," he said, perhaps the only time in his wretched existence that he had ever offered a kindness to another. His voice was so deep and guttural that no one else on board the raft took it that way.

"You stay the hell away from her, you understand? Just leave her alone," Andy Popillo snapped back. "She doesn't need your help."

Dewey felt a small explosion go off in the back of his head. It was as if the hammer of a gun had been cocked. He glared back at the boy.

"Listen you little worm, stick your nose back in your college books where it belongs and butt out," the murderer said quietly, seemingly in control. "You really don't want to make me angry or I'll gouge your eyes out with the silver spoon you were born with." Katie whimpered at the angry words.

"The both of you shut up," Geoff said. "Andy, lets not rile up our guest here. He's already shown us his style of hospitality. And as for you," he turned to face Dewey, "if you so much as touch my daughter, I will personally rip your balls off and feed them to the hammerhead sharks in these waters. They'd like you -- thanks to the trail of blood you leave everywhere. Do I make myself clear, pal?"

Dewey was quiet for a minute, considering the senior Lapkin's words. Then he laughed aloud. He knew he could make chum out of the guy and the college kid without so much as breaking a sweat. His anger unabated, he decided that Popillo would have to go, just to prove his point. The monster stood up to his entire six-foot-eight length. There was dried blood from the gashes he had sustained in the house all over his face. Facing down the two men, Charles Dewey wore the face of Satan himself.

Andy Popillo jumped to his feet as Dewey stood up, the giant's fists balled and a look in his eyes that would scare the crap out of a dozen drunken fishermen in a bar. He wasn't afraid of Dewey, but he knew he was hopelessly overpowered. But Andy would die trying to protect the Lapkins, if that's what it took, because he was just like his father: a fighter who never backed down, no matter the odds.

Geoff Lapkin jumped to his feet as well when he saw Dewey begin walking towards Andy. He wasn't a hothead like his younger friend; but he wouldn't back down either, especially if his family was at risk. He jumped in front of the two men.

"Listen, Charles, or whatever the hell your name is. You'll have to get through me before you can touch this boy," he growled in a voice that Emily had heard only once before on the night he ran to her defense at the Yacht Club so many years before. It frightened her and scared Katie so badly that she screamed out: "No daddy, please don't. Charles stop, please don't fight, please," she whimpered.

The little girl's terror made the giant man stop in his tracks. He didn't want to hurt her in any way. "Sure honey, no one's going to fight. As soon as this barge lands somewhere I'll be getting off. Okay?"

Katie shook her head in relief and managed a smile at the giant man. Emily breathed again, puzzled by why her daughter had such a hold over this vicious man. The woman was so afraid of his looks alone that she would cross the street rather than walk by him.

Dewey stepped back as if to return to where he had been sitting. Then he stopped; Lapkin and Popillo watched as his eyes narrowed to thin slits, looking right in their direction. A minute went by, but he said nothing. The night was silent now and all that could be heard was the rustling of some leaves behind them.

Then, with a sudden leap forward, accelerating faster than any of them thought possible for such an enormous man, Dewey suddenly sprang toward Lapkin and Popillo, his arms extended as if to gather them both in his mammoth arms and crush the two men. Instinctively, Geoff lowered his body and let loose a punch into the giant's solar plexus. He felt like he had broken his arm as the punch did nothing to slow Dewey. Popillo leapt to the side, missing Dewey's outstretched arms by inches. Both men went sprawling to the deck of the raft, inches from going overboard. Then out of the blackness of the night, they saw it. A huge uprooted elm tree, some fifty- to sixty-feet long, appeared out of the night. Astonished, they watched as a jagged stump of a branch, with spears as sharp as knives jutting from the viciously twisted and torn outgrowth of the tree, drove directly across the wooden raft with the speed of the running tide exactly where Geoff Lapkin had been standing seconds before.

Dewey, unable to stop as he had run to knock Lapkin and Popillo out of harms way, ran directly into the sharp end of the branch, chest high. Emily and Katie both screamed into the night as they saw the branch pierce his chest, and with a crunching, shredding sound filling the silence of the night air, watched as the tree limb exploded out of his back.

The forward motion of the tree and Dewey's running start impaled his body deeper and deeper into the branch. In his last breathing seconds, as his huge feet still touched the wooden raft, he threw his weight to the right and pushed left with his legs to force the wooden platform away from the huge tree trunk that was about to crush the makeshift raft. It worked.

As the raft finally slid from beneath his feet and Charles Dewey was carried away into the night still grotesquely pinned to the tree stump, he turned his head toward the horrified little girl who had given him a fleeting taste of affection, however small, however simple.

Even in the final agony of his death, he found the strength to whisper two words to her:

"My friend..."

Epilogue

~~~ ~~~

September 22, 1938

Near dawn, the raft carrying Geoff, Emily, Katie and James Lapkin and the brave Andy Popillo ran aground on the salt marsh shore of Barn Island at the tip of Stonington, Connecticut. The storm had pushed them safely across the entire Little Narragansett Bay. Of those who had been blown into the Bay on the wooden floor of Shelly's small room, only the madman, Charles Dewey, was killed. His body was never recovered. Brian and Geoff Jr., having left school just after noon on a field trip to the Boston Children's Museum, escaped the ordeal and were reunited with their parents and siblings two days later.

Few families who had been exposed to the hurricane's full fury as directly as the Lapkins'
~~~

survived intact. Nearly six hundred New Englanders died in the catastrophe, among them entire families. Thousands more died in the Bahamas. On Napatree Point and its Sandy Point extension, thirty-nine summer mansions, most already closed up for the winter, were destroyed by the storm. Of the forty-two people who lived on the peninsula in the summer months, fifteen perished. Of the nearly four hundred who were killed in the state of Rhode Island, more than one hundred alone perished in Westerly and Watch Hill. Eight children died together on a school bus in Mackerel Cove in Jamestown. In all, the hurricane of 1938 destroyed more than nine thousand homes and businesses across seven states.

The United States Weather Bureau was vilified in the next morning's newspapers all across the country, not only for its failure to accurately track the deadly storm, but also for its failure to provide adequate warnings even as the storm was making landfall. "Losing" a hurricane was even more than a generation of depression victims could tolerate, even those who had become fatalistic about the future of the country. The Weather Bureau was reorganized to make up for its pronounced shortcomings, but it would be years before it would regain credibility with the American people.

By and large, however, the Great New England Hurricane of 1938 was short-lived news. Within forty-eight hours of the storm, the front pages of the nation's influential newspapers were full of the British Prime Minister's failures to appease Hitler and the Czech government's decision to roll over and play dead rather than fight the re-born German military juggernaut. Less than a year later, Hitler attacked Poland and the world was at war again.

For some however, the wounds and memories of September 21, 1938, remained deep in their hearts and minds. It seemed that no one along the New England coast didn't suffer a loss, whether it be family, friend or financial. Of course, losing a loved one in such a violent manner can never be forgotten or resolved, and nearly all survivors of the disaster carried some terrible memory of the grief with them all the remaining days of their lives. Helen Lathrop, fifteen years old and living in Westerly at the time, recalls the bitter hurt of hearing a fire whistle blow each time another body had been discovered and brought to the Westerly High School gymnasium which served as a temporary morgue.

"Every time they found a body they would blow the fire whistle over and over again," Lathrop recalled years later. "That was to notify people who had lost someone so they could go down to the morgue to try to identify them. They would blow the whistle, and you could see the people, we were near the center of town, you could see the people running down the hill, going to see if it was their mother, wife, child, other family member or friend."

The sordid story of Charles Dewey also became old news quickly. Dewey was tried and convicted in absentia of the three murders in Middletown and Stonington, Connecticut. Andy Popillo pressed to have him identified as the killer of Tiger Griswold and Shelly Loringer, the Lapkin housekeeper, as well. Unfortunately, other than Andy, there were no other witnesses to the murder that occurred in the Fort Mansfield ruins or in the backyard of the Lapkin mansion, as anyone associated with the investigation had been killed in the storm.

It was only years later that Kate Lapkin discovered the real truth behind Charles Dewey. She would spend a lifetime trying to understand the ultimate dichotomy: how such a man could have been born, deprived of any sort of affection, abused physically and psychologically his entire life and then have people question why he turned into a real monster full of hate and anger.

Kate would often think of the day shortly before the hurricane when they had met at Sandy Point and had briefly held hands. Such a simple act would have long been forgotten other than for Kate learning about Dewey's life before they met. Up until the day she died, she tried to rationalize the killer's actions and even how he had hurt members of her own family and murdered her friends, Tiger and Shelly.

She never did find a true understanding of Charles Dewey, but she did learn to forgive him. Kate was the only person on the raft that night that heard the killer whisper to her as he went knowingly to his death. She often wondered what Charles Dewey the "man" might have become in spite of his fearsome appearance, if only Charles Dewey the "boy" had had someone to call "my friend".

Many died at the hands of nature on the afternoon and evening of September 21, 1938. Considering the circumstances - the incredible power of the storm and the complete lack of warning to all in its path - the death toll could have been much higher. The stories and legends of survival that day are endless and riveting. There were many survivors who also had strong feelings about God's role in saving them, or singling out their whole families for salvation from harm.

There were, however, only five survivors who witnessed two simply unpredictable and violent storms merge on the tip of a mile-long peninsula jutting out of Watch Hill Harbor.

For those five, the storms would always be remembered as the night when Satan, who had fought mightily to build his angry tempest in secret in order to ambush the innocent, won only a portion of the battle, finally being defeated by the winds that killed the rage.

##

Author's Note and Acknowledgements

Of Winds and Rage is a work of fiction that combines historical facts concerning the epic 1938 New England Hurricane with both real and imagined events and characters. Of particular note however are Grady Norton, Gordon Dunn and Charlie Pierce of the United States Weather Bureau, each of whom had distinguished careers and were highly influential in the future success and development of the service. Captain A.C. Greig of the *Carinthia* was another real life hero whose seamanship probably saved the lives of the more than 600 passengers she carried.

Charles Dewey was a real-life felon who successfully, if only briefly, escaped from the Wethersfield, Connecticut Prison in 1913 in a shirt packing crate. He was in his second year of a five-to-nine year sentence for highway robbery. Dewey got no farther than the train yard before being apprehended. I lived quite near the prison and can still recall the night in May 1960 when the town's light dimmed when the last man to be executed at the Wethersfield Prison died in the electric chair. He was Joseph "Mad Dog" Taborsky, a real serial killer behind the character of Charles Dewey.

Growing up near the Connecticut shoreline and often visiting Rhode Island's Misquamicut Beach, I was intrigued by the bits of pieces of stories I heard about the "tidal wave" that had wiped out the coast long before I was born. I was a young man before I became aware that Katherine Hepburn was a famous actress - and not just a young girl who scavenged for her family's silverware in the ruins of their "cottage" at Fenwick in Old Saybrook, Connecticut the morning after the hurricane. So I offer particular thanks to several sources for providing me a real education on the facts behind the disaster. They include author R.A. Scotti for his riveting account, "Sudden Sea: The Great Hurricane of 1938"; PBS' American Experiences: The Hurricane of '38; "Wind that Shook the World" by James Dodson by for Yankee Magazine; "Hurricane", by K. E. Parks and Russell Maloney for The New Yorker Magazine, November 1938; and, Scott A. Mandia, Professor, Physical Sciences at SUNY's excellent website, "The Long Island Express".

F. Mark Granato
July 2011

About The Author

F. Mark Granato's thirty year career as a corporate executive in a Fortune 50 company brought with it extensive international experience in the aerospace and commercial engineering and building fields. Now that he has served his time, he is finally fulfilling a lifetime desire to write and especially to explore the "What if?" questions of history. In addition to *Of Winds and Rage,* he has published *Beneath His Wings: The Plot to Murder Lindbergh* and *Titanic: The Final Voyage.* He writes from Wethersfield, Connecticut, with the help of a large German Shepard named "Groban", who occasionally asks probing questions.

Made in the USA
Middletown, DE
05 July 2020

11942727R00221